Honor Raconteur

Alright, who let Henri name it?

Death Over the Garden Wall

There is nothing wrong with my title, dear.

Published by Raconteur House

Published by Raconteur House
Plymouth, MI

DEATH OVER THE GARDEN WALL
The Case Files of Henri Davenforth Case 7

A Raconteur House book/ published by arrangement with the author

Copyright © 2022 by Honor Raconteur
Cover by Katie Griffin
Green Stone Wall by ArtRudy/Depositphotos; *Clockwork spare parts* by donatas1205/Shutterstock; *male man toilet* WC by yougifted/Shutterstock; *vintage bronze seamless background* by Kompaniets Taras/Shutterstock

This book is a work of fiction, so please treat it like a work of fiction. Seriously. References to real people, dead people, good guys, bad guys, stupid politicians, companies, restaurants, cats with attitudes, events, products, dragons, locations, pop culture references, or wacky historical events are intended to provide a sense of authenticity and are used fictitiously. Or because I wanted it in the story. Characters, names, story, location, dialogue, weird humor and strange incidents all come from the author's very fertile imagination and are not to be construed as real. No, I don't believe in killing off main characters. Villains are a totally different story.

All rights reserved.
No part of this book may be reproduced, scanned, or distributed in any printed or electronic form without permission. Please do not participate in or encourage electronic piracy of copyrighted materials in violation of the author's rights.
Purchase only authorized editions.

For information address: www.raconteurhouse.com

LONADI SEA
ZOVA
DAGEN
CHERITHE
NAESE
HAVERFORD
MCONUES
CIPARIS
SAI
TUELI
DOLIVO
FIREATHOUSE
RANIER
SINGH
DESAI
THORSTEN
IONADI
BE HOSI
TEBIE
LISHI
TITELUNER
WIXX
BAO
CABOT
SAARI
SUKO
DRISCOLL
MELGREN
ITE
NINOMAE
NICE
ALBERTINE
ITAUEN
CADDEL
ASHBLUFF
LUZ
MCANUES
CASKCOT
HINART
FIBRETHAN
GALLIO
TAHHAN
TREVINO
UNDERGROVE
ELSHER
AUS
GOVAIN
NOVI
UIOTTO
WEST
SHEFFIELD
VOZENILEK
ZIBIA
VANDENBERG
HART
BYTHESEA
SAGESPARK
BRISTOL
KINGSTON
WOLSTENHOLME
SUSSAMS
YARBROUGH
JORDANE
BRIXTON
DEEMS
PARREIRA
UNCHARTED WESTERN SEAS
THE VOZENI STRAIT
UNCHARTED SANDS
THE KNOWN WORLD

Report 01: New Case, Incoming!

After two back-to-back cases that called for a lot of late nights and early mornings, I was not, needless to say, altogether conscious this morning. Clint had woken me up and insisted on my taking a shower. And being awake. For the life of me, I couldn't understand why.

I stood in the shower, letting the water pound against my head with the hopes it might revive some brain cells. What was today, anyway? The fourth? The fifth? The minor fall? The major lift?

A baffled chorus of "Hallelujah" rang in my head.

Crap. Now I was going to have that song stuck in my head for the rest of the day.

No, but seriously, what was so important about today that I had to be up at this gods-forsaken hour of the morning?

I meandered out of the shower, toweled off, and went into the bedroom. Clint had laid out clothes for me—nice clothes. So this might be an important thing? Crap on a stick, I couldn't think of what it might be. And with both cats out, no one was in the apartment for me to ask.

When all else fails, ask Henri.

I reached for the pad and wrote: *You up? Busy?*

He responded a moment later: *Free for you. Busy for others.*

Stop being so cute.

Cute for you. And rude for others.

He sounded more awake than I did, at least. *Why am I up right now?*

Queen Regina called us late last night wanting to see us

this morning, remember?

I do not function before I've had caffeine. *Did she mention why?*

You remember nothing, I see.

Not a blessed thing.

I'll get you for breakfast in thirty minutes.

Ok.

If he wanted to fill me in then, that was fine by me. I may even be dressed and ready to go by then. Who knew?

I went back to the bathroom because, if I was to be walking on palace grounds, I should probably at least dry my hair. And, you know, do something with it aside from a ponytail. I spent several minutes futzing with hair, putting on a little makeup, and finishing putting clothes on. I was one sock in when I heard my pad beep, and I realized I'd missed a message from Sherard.

First message read, *I hear you're coming to the palace this morning?*

Second message: *Jamie, hellloooooo?*

I responded, *If I have failed to respond to you in a timely manner, please know I am trying very hard to be a person.*

He sent back a drawn laughing emoji. I had taught them well. The emojis were important.

I paused long enough to write, *I'm told that I agreed to be at the palace this morning.*

You were told?

I have no memory of agreeing to this meeting, to be honest.

Ahh. Well, after you're done meeting the queen, swing by and let me stabilize your core. I think you're going out of town for this next case.

I was?

Dear me-of-last-night, if you could fill in me-of-today, that would be awesome sauce. Seriously. How sleep deprived had I been that I had no memory of any of this?

Henri came by with cats in tow, and we all walked to our favorite bakery for a quick breakfast. As we walked, I put my hand in his, and he gave me that warm smile he always did when we held hands. That smile did funny things in my chest, let me tell you.

"Alright, I don't know how much you remember," Henri started.

"Literally nothing. Start from the beginning."

He grimaced. "You were basically dead on your feet. I had to pour you into bed. That last case was exhausting."

"Preach."

"We received a call from Queen Regina at roughly eight o'clock last night?" He eyed me as if expecting a nod of recollection. His brows beetled together a little when he didn't get one. "She requested that we come in first thing this morning because there was a very troublesome case. We're being called in as kingsmen consultants for this one."

"Ah. Okay? Do we have any other details?"

"She only mentioned that it dealt with the death of Countess Giada Barese."

Everything was starting to make more sense. I'd read in the newspaper that Countess Giada Barese's body had washed up on a beach two days ago, causing quite a stir. She'd apparently been missing for about two weeks prior to her body being discovered.

This case smacked of a lot of political stuff going down, and that didn't even cover the angle that she was presumed missing now found dead, and that no one was sure of the cause. "So, are we looking at another high-profile case with reporters pestering me?"

He shot me a droll look. "Why do you ask a question that you already know the answer to?"

"I keep hoping I'm wrong. For all that I hate them, I have far too many reporters in my life." I grimaced, trying to think ahead to mitigate the problems. "Well, in that case, I see why Queen Regina called us. The kingsmen are not trained for this kind of case."

I pondered that as we went into Miss Amelia's Bakery and placed our orders. This case reeked of potential trouble, and it wasn't something I wanted to do with Henri alone. Besides, this would be a good case to train someone. A certain pair of kingsmen came to mind.

"Is this a done deal that you and I are going?" I asked. "We're just meeting with her to get some details and the proper authority to go?"

"That's my understanding. Why?"

"Figured I might as well give Niamh and Foster a heads-up to pack. I'm not losing a good opportunity to train them."

"Fair enough." Henri stirred his tea, looking thoughtful. "Weber, I imagine, will also be handy to request. I don't know if I trust anyone else to look at a body that's been at sea for two weeks and glean anything useful from it."

"Good point. You contact him, I'll poke my ducklings." It wasn't like we had all the time in the world, so I made sure to eat my breakfast between messaging people. Still, the atmosphere was nice here. We sat near the window, the cats lying on the sill and basking in the sun, purring away in contentment. Henri looked content, too, and I had the worst impulse to reach out and muss his curly dark hair.

I blamed his reactions for all the urges I got to touch him. He made fun squeaky noises.

We loaded into a taxi and headed to the palace. I'd barely caught Foster and Niamh up to speed with what I knew before we arrived. Which wasn't much, granted, all I was basically doing was giving them a heads-up. They promised to start getting ready on their end, assuming we'd need to leave tomorrow. Which was likely true.

We followed the routine of signing in at the gate and collecting our visitors' badges, with a palace guardsman escorting us in. Even as we walked, I caught Henri eyeing the palace wards with the same suspicion you would a sneak thief. I didn't know if he'd ever properly trust the wards again, not after having to 'repair' them so many times.

Queen Regina was not in her study, but instead in her private garden. It was more a conservatory, really, glass enclosing all sides with lush plants filling the interior. I'd been inside maybe a handful of times? It smelled amazing with all the exotic plants mixed together.

When we stepped through, a wave of warm air wafted over me, which felt nice compared to the chill of outside. Winter had hit as of last week, dumping a foot of snow on the ground, and no one had been pleased to see it. The cold was why I had two cats lurking in my pockets like overgrown lint.

Phil, I noticed, was ensconced in the scarf around Henri's neck and flat refusing to budge. He had found a warm spot on his person. It was perfection for kitties.

I caught sight of Jules and Regina as I passed through the curtain of plants. A formal greeting died on my lips when I spied Regina with a Felix in her lap. Now, I knew Jules had been playing around with feline color schemes since I showed him the cat encyclopedia on my Kindle. We now had calicos, Russian Blues, orange tabbies, you name it, all running around.

That said.

"That's a freaking tiger!" I blurted.

The cute-as-all-get-out little Felix turned its head, blinking large golden eyes at me. It looked just like a tiger, with deep orange and black stripes on top, white fur tufting out on the bottom, and a tail idly twitching across Regina's thighs. He wasn't the size of one, though, more the size of Clint.

Jules Felix, mad genius that he was, had created a miniature tiger.

Regina beamed at me over the Felix's head. "Isn't he darling? Jules brought him to me last night and introduced us. We've spent the morning playing hide-and-seek in the garden and have had a perfectly lovely time."

I was mesmerized by him, and so were my cats. They poked their heads out of my pockets, getting a good look at this new addition. Jules sat nearby, taking in my reaction with a proud smile, but I wasn't paying much attention to him. I crossed to the tiger, sunk down on my heels, and extended a hand for him to sniff. Intellectually, I knew he was perfectly domesticated, but I couldn't shake the feeling I was approaching a wild animal.

"Hello. I'm Jamie."

"Hello, Jamie," he answered in a light, childlike voice. "I'm Khan. My Regina named me."

He'd already gotten the possessiveness down, I saw. Cats, after all, did not belong to people. People belonged to cats.

"It's a good name," I said, although I was curious where it came from. I looked to the queen questioningly. "Khan?"

"I just finished reading *The Jungle Book* last week," she explained brightly. "That is a proper tiger's name, isn't it?"

Ah. Shere Khan. Got it. In her shoes, I'd probably have done the same. "It suits him well. Come meet your predecessors. This is Clint and that's Tasha."

All three reached out and touched noses to each other, whiskers going crazy as they picked up on things the rest of us humans couldn't.

Henri dropped down and helped Phil untangle himself so he could say hello, too. Khan seemed quite pleased to meet potential playmates, and I had no doubt that's exactly what they'd become.

I settled in a nearby chair and let the cats sort themselves out. "I see you finally got tired of being threatened with beheadings," I teased Jules.

"It's not like I was dragging my feet on purpose," he protested mildly. The royal mage looked unruffled in his three-piece navy suit, fair hair combed back into a low tail, like a Byronic poet in search of a stage. "But the Felixes have very much been in the experimental stage over the past five years. I didn't want to hand my monarch a prototype. And I learned so much from you about what a creature of this design can do that I had to modify things. It wasn't feasible to hand her anything prior to now. Besides, when I learned of the tigers and the size a cat could grow, it occurred to me that the mix could become a splendid bodyguard."

I looked at that innocent expression and started to question things I normally wouldn't. "Jules. I ask because the suspicious side of me is suggesting this, but did you make it so this cat can change sizes at will?"

"Quite so. Just two—the size he has now and the full-sized version. He'll max out at almost eleven stone, roughly."

So almost a hundred and fifty pounds, give or take a twinkie. I looked at the tiger with renewed respect. No wonder Regina had named him after the ferocious tiger of *The Jungle Book*. To the bad guys, that's what he'd be.

"The energy consumption for that change must be exorbitant," Henri commented.

Jules gave him a nod. "So it is. He'll need to rest in the sun for a good hour afterwards to recoup, but it's feasible. Also took me forever to figure out how to even accomplish it, hence the delay. Still, I'm quite satisfied with the results. I dare not say my creation is now perfect—I'm sure there are things I'll learn along the way that I might want to adjust—but they're very stable and a benefit to society, so I'm quite pleased."

Because we were on the topic, I remembered a question Clint had asked me the other night, one I had no answer to. I'd promised to ask the next time I saw Jules, and this seemed the right moment. "Speaking of, Jules, you never did tell me what their lifespan is."

He stared at me like a deer looking straight into headlights. "Oh...dear."

Wryly, I guessed, "You forgot to give them one, didn't you?"

"Oh dear, oh dear." He sat there, staring at the cats with a very perplexed expression.

"Oh, Jules, really," Regina said with a sigh. "You didn't give them an age limit?"

Henri was trying to hide a smile and failing. Badly. "I'm sure time will tell. It's probably just as well. No one likes to live with death staring them in the face."

True, but it'd be nice to know when 'old age' is for them so I can adjust accordingly.

Oh well. Henri was right—time would tell. I'd just have

to keep an eye on them.

Henri cleared his throat and bailed Jules out. "Your Majesty, I believe you have a case for us?"

"Oh. Yes, so I do." She shook herself a little, visibly changing tracks. "Thank you for coming in to meet me here. I wanted to give you the report personally. The one thing we don't want at the moment is rumors flying about. I asked you in because Countess Giada Barese has died and we're not sure of the cause. I need the very best to investigate her death and you're the only one I trust."

Well, this should be interesting.

Report 02: An Extraordinary Offer

You say that, but I saw this coming.

What? How?

Me too.

pffffft, you suggested it

cackles

I'd heard, of course, that the countess had died and that her death was unusual, but that was from the newspapers. Which weren't to be trusted. I'd expected Queen Regina to know more details since the body had been recovered and examined now. I pressed this point with, "But surely after the autopsy, the reason has become clearer?"

"No, I'm afraid not. The cause of death was undetermined by the medical examiner. Her body spent two weeks at sea, washing up in Sheffield, and I'm afraid the state of her..." Regina looked away, expression disturbed. "Suffice it to say, the coroner on scene couldn't make any firm determinations. I want you to perform another autopsy. I am not satisfied with the report I received." Her lips compressed for a moment. "I feel that perhaps this person was not... qualified to handle the matter. You have someone you trust to do the examination?"

"Weber," I confirmed immediately. "I've worked with him many times, and he's quite good. Whenever we have a question about a body, it's him I bring in."

"Excellent. Then, let me lay out the facts to you as I know them." She turned, picking up a report from the small table nearby and handing it to Jamie. "This is the official report, which you may keep to read. I might be able to share some insight as well. I knew Countess Barese personally." Regina paused and her expression grew clouded for a moment. "I knew her better in her teenage years. Her maiden name was Lastra."

My ears perked. I knew that name, more through association than anything else. The Lastra family was one that had not fared well at the end of the war, losing much of their property and wealth. Or so my parents had mentioned; I was too young to remember a war that ended before my birth, of course. The family had been in steady decline since then. They'd auctioned off huge parts of their libraries and I'd gained several unique volumes from them as a result.

"The family has always had a rocky relationship with money, is the best way to put it, I suppose. They've either gained incredible wealth or lost it, often within the same generation. When Giada was born, the family was suffering from a lack of money, and that continued up until the past...oh, I'd say ten years or so. As a teenager, Giada was stunningly beautiful. She chose to become a model, partially for the income it brought in, but mostly because she enjoyed the attention." Regina shook her head with a smile, expression tinged with sadness. "Ever vain, that one, but charming and fun. I enjoyed her company; many did. She was self-indulgent but never to the point of pettiness or cruelty. She married rather early—barely twenty—to Oliver de Mancini."

Knowing Jamie wouldn't recognize the name, I leaned in and murmured, "He's a billionaire, specializes in steel manufacturing. A self-made man, in a sense. He inherited a very small business from his father and turned it into the global company it is now."

Queen Regina gave me a nod. "An accurate summary. His first love is his company. I have no idea why he and Giada decided to marry in the first place. They had nothing in common and spent practically no time together. She retired from modeling when she married him, but the marriage barely lasted two years. None of us were surprised when she filed for a divorce.

Her settlement was quite lavish. It felt more like a payoff to get rid of her."

Jamie was taking notes quickly in her native language. She flipped a page before asking, "Do you think the ex-husband is at all involved in the countess's death?"

"I can't see how he would be. The divorce was almost eight years ago, and they've had no contact that I know of. They don't even live in the same country. I tell you all this because you need to know where her current wealth came from."

"Ah. Got it. Please continue."

"After the divorce, she returned home, in a manner of speaking. Part of her settlement was a manor house on the sea. And when I say on the sea, I do mean right on top of the cliff that leads down into it. It's unnerving how that house is built. I could never relax in the garden, as I felt like any storm would suck the building right into the ocean. You'll see for yourself when you get there. She lived there until her death, with many an international vacation. Giada was not one who lived quietly. She had many friends and lovers over for house parties. About a year ago she became infatuated with Sebastian Barese, and they married after a whirlwind romance. I think both regretted it within four months. The marriage certainly seemed on the rocks after that. She moved in and out of his house so quickly, I'm not sure if anything actually became fully unpacked. They've lived estranged from each other for months, now. I'm told Giada even had a new lover."

So there was no attachment there, or at least not one strong enough to keep her from engaging with another man. Although it did beg the obvious question: "Did her husband know about the new lover as well?"

"I have no idea. They're not even living in the same town anymore. Perhaps he hadn't heard?" Regina canted her head in question. "You think jealousy might be the cause here?"

"At this point, we know too little to make any assumptions, but I would like to make some inquiries."

"I've his address as well as hers so you can look into it. Now, what I'm told is this: the day she disappeared, she had a house party with friends and her lover. I believe there were six guests in total. It wasn't a good day for Giada. She had multiple arguments with friends, her lover was pushing her to do something she disliked, and overall the house party was a very sour affair. She retired early. When people rose in the morning and didn't see her at breakfast, no one questioned it too deeply. But when lunch came and went, they started looking for her. They became alarmed when they realized the cars were all still in the garage and no one could account for her since the previous night. They reported her missing to the police, looked everywhere, but to no avail. It was all speculation until two weeks later, when her body washed ashore. The discovery of her body two days ago clinched matters."

I could tell this upset Regina by the bright tears in her eyes. She looked away, visibly trying to gain control over her emotions.

Khan lifted up on his back legs and rubbed his cheek against hers, purring. She petted him, saying softly, "Thank you."

Jamie reached out a hand and caught one of the queen's, squeezing gently. "Regina, I know this is cold comfort, but I promise you we'll figure this out."

"I'm handing this to you because I'm quite sure you will. And I have to entrust this to someone." She looked at Jamie, and I saw then a woman who grieved the loss of a friend.

"How did you know her?" Jamie asked.

"Oh, it was a simple meeting, at first. A little silly. We were at the same party once, and bored. I was a little tipsy, she was definitely drunk, and we hid on the balcony drinking and talking about men. Really, with the seventeen-year age difference between us, it might have seemed odd that we became friends. Giada was genuine with me, always making me laugh, and I found her to be a good confidant. I wish..." She sighed, eyes turning sad. "I don't approve of all of Giada's choices. She was cavalier with life, sometimes, but she was a good friend too. She didn't deserve murder, if that's what it was."

I didn't wish to ask this question, but needs must. "Do you suspect foul play?"

"I can't know for certain, but...well, Giada was quite wealthy and didn't attract the best of people around her. I don't know how they'd benefit from her death, but I can't rule the possibility out."

Jamie frowned slightly, and I could see her making mental notes. "This is a hard question for me to ask, but do you suspect suicide?"

Regina shook her head immediately. "No. She had far too many plans in place. She actively looked to the future. She wasn't one to hold onto something that caused her pain. Even if society frowned on her for it, she'd walk away from anything she disapproved of—like two husbands."

"Fair enough."

Something she said earlier made me wonder. "You said the house is uncomfortably close to the sea. So much so that there is a possibility she could have tripped and fallen over?"

"Yes, unfortunately." Regina's hands rose in illustration. "If my arm is the garden wall? Then my other arm is the sea. There's basically no distance. A few trees poke up along the outside of the wall, and their roots are exposed to the air, that's how little earth there is."

If she were drunk, or the night too dark or stormy for her to see, then could she have accidentally gone to her death? Interesting. I could see why this case was such an open question mark. Too many players, too many possible motivations, too many openings for things.

"We'll pack up today, get people organized, and head there first thing tomorrow." Jamie closed the notebook, tucking it back into her breast pocket. "I'm taking Niamh and Foster with me."

"Oh, that does make me glad." Regina's smile seemed genuine this time. "I spoke with both of them after the last case they worked with you, and they learned so much. They were eager to go out again."

"I'm taking them partially to train, but also because I have a feeling Niamh might come in handy. Her tracking skills are excellent, after all."

I could hear what Jamie didn't say. Giada Barese had hit the water somehow. Perhaps Niamh could find the path her body took on the way down. Just that might tell us something.

This seemed the right moment to leave, so I rose and gave my monarch a bow. "Rest easy, Your Majesty. We'll figure this out."

"Thank you, Dr. Davenforth." Regina paused before adding pointedly, "And do not think I have forgotten about making both of you kingsmen. I have not. We have been very busy and distracted of late, but I'm as determined as ever. We *will* properly discuss this once you've solved this case."

I objected stringently, "It's Jamie you want as a kingsman, not me!"

Her look said she pitied me as a fool. "First of all, Dr. Davenforth, I have been sorely tempted on several occasions to make you a royal mage—"

Alarm shot through my being as if I had tried to bottle lightning. What did she just say?!

"—your ability to be a kingsman is absolutely *not* in question. I would be quite relieved and honored if you chose to join those ranks. I do not speak entirely for myself, either. Several of my kingsmen have voiced similar hopes."

Jules Felix clapped his hands in approval. "Excellent suggestion, Your Majesty. I, for one, quite like the idea of Dr. Davenforth as a royal mage."

I looked at him as if he had lost what little common sense he'd been born with. "You of all people should know why I'm not qualified for it."

He regarded me as though I were the one who had lost my wits. "Because you're not the powerhouse I am? My dear sir. Who, precisely, helped us stop a pandemic in its tracks?"

Um.

"Who, precisely, thwarted a thievery attempt upon this very palace?"

Well, yes, but...

"And who, precisely, did Seaton turn to for help when the palace wards seemed to be faulty? And who figured out the cause and solution to it, no less."

He rather did have me there.

Felix turned to our queen and calmly stated, "I support your idea of making him a royal mage. We need this man's intellectual prowess, for one thing. For another, he's one of the few magicians I know who isn't an egotistical prima donna. He can work with all three of us without ruffling feathers, and that isn't something I can say for my fellow royal mages. I candidly speak for all of us when I say this: If you wish to appoint him, you'll not get any opposition from the rest of us."

Why did I have a sudden sense of inevitability about this?

Part of me was beyond flattered by this semi-offer. After a lifetime of being told I wasn't quite good enough, it was incredibly heady to hear both a queen and a royal mage tell me they would love it if I joined them. To have that kind of acknowledgement made my heart flutter.

On the other hand, I wasn't blind to a royal mage's duties, what their responsibilities were. The days where I had a routine, a schedule, and a comfortable evening in would be long gone. A royal mage was a first responder to magical crises, serving the country as a whole.

Did I want that kind of responsibility?

"I think the two of you have flummoxed him," Jamie said. She searched my face, a small smile playing around the corners of her mouth. "Maybe let him sleep on this? Because I think he'd be excellent—"

I twisted so fast, the vertebrae in my neck popped. "You do?!"

"—but it obviously isn't something he's thought about before," Jamie finished dryly. "So it's better to let him mull it over for a while. As for me, I do think it's time I joined the kingsmen. We're being pulled more and more on cases outside of Kingston. I'm slowly growing more comfortable with the world outside of this city. But if I commit, understand that I want specific people to come with me, and I'll need a team. There's no way I can do all of this on my own."

Regina didn't even hesitate, just nodded. "Yes. Done. However big of a team you wish. Do request Gibson be part of your team. The man will absolutely complain otherwise and never shut up about it."

Jamie grinned at her. "Cross my heart."

"Pardon?"

"Ah. I mean, promise I will. That idiom doesn't translate, huh?" Shaking her head, Jamie muttered, "I'm still finding some of those."

I was at the point where I truly wanted out of this audience and into a quiet space so I could think. I had no idea how to gracefully manage that, though. I just knew I had been overloaded.

Jamie slapped a hand to her knee. "Alright, we'll

get rolling. I'll give you an update in two days, okay?"

"I look forward to it," Regina said with relief. "Thank you."

"I'd say my pleasure, but this one promises to be a pain. Alright, cats, up we go."

While we'd been distracted, the Felixes had maneuvered their way to the floor for a wrestling match. All four looked up at us without comprehension, as if they couldn't understand why we would even contemplate breaking up what was a very fun activity.

Jamie was not moved by that look. She scooped up Clint and Tasha, tucking them back into her oversized coat pockets. I followed suit, putting Phil back into his perch in my scarf, noting that Khan was quick to rejoin his person.

We gave our bows, said our goodbyes, and I'd never been so relieved to be out of a meeting in my life.

Me.

A royal mage?

Did I want that?

I honestly had no idea. It had been so far outside the realm of possibility, I'd never considered it. Even as a child, it was obvious I wouldn't have the kind of power to warrant such a place in society. If I had any daydreams of it, I certainly couldn't recall them.

Jamie tucked her hand in the crook of my elbow and leaned in to murmur, "You really would be good at it. Don't close your mind off to the possibility, okay?"

"But if I'm a royal mage, what of you?" I protested.

"Ah. Is that why you're balking? If you're a royal mage, and I'm a kingsman, I guarantee we'll still work together constantly. This isn't a deterrent, darling."

"You're so sure you want to take the position, then?"

"I think I do. I miss playing with my adopted brothers here, honestly. And there's a lot more of the world I want to see. Being a kingsman is a good way to do it."

She'd be stunningly brilliant at it. But then, was there anything she wasn't stunningly brilliant at?

Patting my arm, she said, "Sherard wants to stabilize me before I go jaunting off to manors on cliffs. Come with me? Or do you want to go home and pack?"

I appreciated that she was giving me a graceful way of gaining a quiet place to think, even if only for an hour. "I'll go home and pack. Meet you there?"

"Sure thing." She sauntered off as if she didn't have a care in the world.

Phil's little nose poked me in the side of the neck. "Henri?"

"Yes?"

"If we stay here, I can play with Khan."

Well, I knew which way his vote swung.

Report 03: Possibilities

My friend must have been mid-project because he had diagrams pinned up on the walls and covering every imaginable flat surface. Sherard himself looked put together, dark hair combed back in a rakish fashion, so whatever project this was, he wasn't in over his head. He always looked like he'd been hit by a train when a project got overwhelming.

As Sherard finished stabilizing my core, I decided to catch him up on Regina's very interesting offer. Henri was too flummoxed by the idea to really know how to react. I felt he'd be brilliant at it, and I didn't want him turning it down because he didn't feel like he deserved it.

"Sherard, while we were in the meeting, something interesting cropped up."

He put his wand down, looking up at me with interest. "Oh yes?"

"Queen Regina informed Henri she wants to appoint him as a royal mage."

Instant delight bloomed over his face and he clapped his hands like a giddy child. "Yes! Ha, I wondered if that seed would bear fruit."

"What seed? Wait, did you suggest it to her?"

"Of course I did." He snorted, as if this should be obvious. "The man's a registered genius. We would have been in trouble without his help on numerous occasions. I realize he's excellent as a magical examiner, but it's truly a waste. So much of that work is run of the mill. Henri excels at not only the diagnostics of magic, but the *creation* of it. He has the right knack, the right imagination, to creatively problem-solve. And that's ninety percent of a royal mage's work."

"I completely agree. Apparently, Queen Regina does too, as she said he'd either be a royal mage or a kingsman. Either way, she wasn't giving up on having him here." Deciding this wouldn't hurt my case, I threw in, "And Jules Felix was in the same meeting and agreed Henri would be brilliant as a royal mage and cast his vote to have him appointed."

"I'm not surprised by that. Jules has a very high opinion of Henri." Sherard frowned, staring sightlessly ahead as he thought. "Which do you think Henri's leaning towards?"

"I'm not sure if he's got a preference at this point. He was so baffled by the offer, he didn't even know how to respond. His initial reaction, though, was that he didn't want to take on the role of royal mage if it meant he couldn't work alongside me."

"Now, that doesn't surprise me."

It didn't surprise me, either. We both loved working with each other, no question there. But Henri was also a little possessive of his time with me. Really, our work schedules were so insane that, if we weren't partners, we'd barely see each other. I certainly wouldn't choose to lose him as a partner.

I'd used the walk from Regina's garden to Sherard's office to think about this, and the wheels in my mind had been churning madly. Many a thing in Kingston was missing, in my opinion. Like paramedics. But there was only so much change I could suggest, so I ended up letting a lot of things go. This project, however, I could possibly get off the ground. Especially if I spearheaded it.

"Okay, so, here's the thing. I've noticed there is no governmental investigation department. It's why I'm called in as a kingsman consultant to begin with, right?"

His eyes came back to mine, and his expression said he was aware I was leading him somewhere but the GPS hadn't kicked in yet. "Right. And?"

"So, what if I spearheaded a department that was just that—investigations. Queen Regina already said I could have my own team, so why not make it an official department while we're at it? I'd have everything we needed in-house. Medical examiner, magical examiner, agents, the works. Henri could be the appointed royal mage to that department."

"Didn't you tell me that's what you were on your old world? An agent in a governmental investigation unit?"

"Right. I could recreate something similar here. Clearly, we need one."

Sherard thought about this for another second. "Who all would you invite in?"

"Henri, obviously, Colette, Foster, Niamh, Gibs, Marshall, and probably Weber part time. I'd love to invite Penny in, but I'm not sure if she'd be interested, now that she's made detective. Gerring's not senior enough to get in either, although I might be able to bring him on later."

"Hmm. Colette as your magical examiner?"

"I think we'd need one full time. Because while Henri can do the job, if he's functioning as my partner he'll be out of the office too much. The others will need to have someone on hand, right?"

"Right. It's funny, I thought if you understood magic, you'd be able to do what Henri and Colette do. But they analyze magic in an entirely different way."

"Different frame of mind," I agreed with a nod. "And I realize Marshall and Gibs can probably figure out how to do it, but Foster and Niamh aren't magicians. And if the department expands, like I expect it would, then we'll definitely need a magical examiner in-house."

"You've really thought about this."

I shrugged. "Ever since I had that initial conversation with Queen Regina over a year ago. And the more cases I worked, the more obvious this became to me. I miiight pull in a few other kingsmen, but I want to talk to them about it first. The ones I mentioned I know will be on board with the idea."

"I certainly am." His look turned shrewd. "Should I mention this to our good queen and plant another seed?"

"If you don't mind. Tell her honestly that I talked to you

about it, sound-boarding the idea. I'll put together a proper proposal and submit it to her along with names of who I want so she can run it past everyone else. And please, find a second to tell Henri that you totally support him being a royal mage. He's promised to think about it, but..."

Sherard nodded, understanding what I hadn't said. "No doubt he's been told that because of his power level, he'd never be able to hold a high position like this. But I stand by what I've always said. Henri Davenforth has a magical finesse, a genius that few can match. He can accomplish far more than I, some days, for all that I am more powerful. Frankly, we need someone of his intellect."

"Tell him exactly that." I was so glad Sherard was on board. I didn't think he wouldn't be, but Henri needed to hear these words. The man was so shy in some ways, it never would have occurred to him to be ambitious. Even handed the offer on a silver platter, he didn't know how to respond to it.

I wouldn't be mean and tell his mom about the offer. She'd skin him alive for even hesitating to take it. It would get him in a lot of trouble with her.

Sometimes, being an adult meant leaving unsaid the tempting thing. And it was super tempting.

I hopped off the table and gave Sherard a quick hug. "Thanks. I've got to talk to a million people and pack, but stay in touch, okay?"

"Sure." He gave the two cats a good scratch under the chin, and then we were off.

Since I was on palace grounds, and supposedly Foster and Niamh were as well, I chose to track them down first. I did coordinate some with them through the pad, finding out they were in the kingsmen common room waiting for me. I used to hang out there a lot when I first arrived, but I hadn't been back for months.

In those early days, my core had been so unstable, and my footing in this world so insecure, that they'd encouraged me to stay on palace grounds. Mostly because the place was packed with magicians. If something happened to me, there was always someone at hand to notice and help.

The kingsmen especially had liked having me here, hanging out with them, and I'd enjoyed the friendships I'd made. Now, it felt a little like revisiting an old playground, seeing Gibs waiting for me on the overstuffed couch next to a crackling fire. Foster and Niamh were talking to him about something before spying my entrance.

Thankfully, the room was warm compared to the winter day outside. It was half filled with people, although they'd shed kingsmen-red coats over the backs of chairs or hung them off pegs on the walls. A few of the kingsmen sat at tables, plowing through paperwork, while others hung around the kitchenette area with mugs of tea. I gave everyone a wave hello as I beelined toward the couch Gibs sat on.

"There she is." Gibs lifted his bulky body up enough for a quick hug, swallowing me whole as usual—Gibs dwarfed practically everyone. "What kept you?"

"Well, I got ambushed by a queen with an agenda." I gave him a wink. "Hold that thought. Let me handle business real quick. Niamh, Foster, our case is in Ashbluff."

Foster's foxy face screwed up in surprise. "Wait, I thought her body was found in Sheffield?"

"That's where she washed up, but her house and death occurred in Ashbluff," I confirmed. "There's a lot of questions surrounding the countess's death. We don't know the cause. It could be anything between accident and murder. We really have our work cut out for us. The countess was a friend of Queen Regina's, and our queen is really torn up about the whole situation. She wants answers. We're her task force."

Niamh gave a sharp nod. The Woodland Elf looked severe today, her blonde hair in a sharp bun, smoky makeup darkening her eyes. "I like a challenge."

"Oh, it's going to be that." I decided to warn her in advance. "Niamh, you especially are going to have a challenge right off the bat. We have no idea of the countess's movements the night of her death. According to the report, she had a fight with friends, went to bed early, and was never seen again. Her house literally borders a cliff. She hit the water somehow, but we don't know the entry point. As soon as we get to the house, I want you and Foster to scour the grounds and see if you can figure that out."

She gave me a firm nod, looking intrigued. "So you need my tracking skills on this one? Good. I'll do my best. This trail is cold, though."

"By a good two weeks. So it won't be easy. Just do your best. Needless to say, we need to make tracks and get up there. Train is probably going to be the fastest route. We'll leave first thing in the morning."

"Is it just us going?" Foster asked.

"Henri and Weber, too. We need to drop Weber off with the body in Sheffield and get a proper coroner's report. The first attempt was…" I paused, searching for the right word. "Lacking, to say the least. Anyway, we're hoping to drop Weber off on the way up and let him work his magic."

Tasha chose that moment to stick her head out of my coat pocket and inform Niamh, "I track too."

Niamh blinked at her, head canted. "It's a lot of ground to cover. If you want to work with us, that's fine. Clint?"

"I stay with Jamie," Clint disagreed. "I field cat the house."

"Honey," I said with a sigh, "the term 'field cat' is a noun, not a verb. You can't use it as a verb."

He blinked up at me as if he didn't understand the protest.

You know what, forget it, I wasn't getting into language semantics with a cat. That was a fight I had no desire to get into.

"Anyway," I said, moving us along. "After we get done talking here, go and pack. I'll look up train schedules, get us all tickets, and tell you when to meet me at the station. Be prepared to be gone about a week. I have a feeling we're going to have our work cut out for us on this one. We're not even sure what we're dealing with yet."

They both gave me quick assents, looking eager to get into things.

Good, okay, that was settled. I turned to Gibs, ready for Part Two. "Now. The thing Queen Regina ambushed me with was a reminder that she wants me to be a full-on kingsman."

Gibs let out a grin, looking as delighted as a leprechaun with a pot of gold and a double rainbow. "Did she? About time. You're going to take her up on her offer this time?"

"I am, under certain conditions. I want to develop our own department in the kingsmen ranks that deals specifically with investigations."

He didn't look at all surprised. "I think you've been heading in this direction for a while. I have to say, I approve. Who all will be in the department?"

"Well, now, that's the question. I want Foster and Niamh—"

Both of them startled, Foster pointing a finger at himself and asking in amazement, "Wait, me?!"

I gave him a droll look. "Dude. I have spent so much time training you. Why on god's green earth would I start over with some other random people? And you're good at this. Of course I'm keeping you."

The werefox looked delighted at this, like he'd never expected any of it. Apparently, I needed to praise my ducklings more.

"Same goes for you, Niamh," I told her. "You've got a knack for this. I'd like to keep you."

She smiled prettily, just as surprised and pleased as Foster. "I'd love to."

"Good. Now, as I said, you two, Marshall if I can convince him, of course you're coming, Gibs—"

His jaw dropped and he spluttered, "Me too?"

"Excuse you. You rope me into being a kingsman and then are surprised I want you on my team?"

His nose crinkled up before he grinned broadly. "You have me there. I'd love to. Who else?"

"Evans and Bennett, if I can convince them."

Gibs rolled his eyes. "That won't take much."

I shrugged, as I didn't disagree. Evans was like another

brother from my long-lost mother. Bennett was also a very good friend, and one I hadn't been able to work with since our pandemic case. I thought of them for a reason. They're very good at their jobs, they're great at adapting and learning new things, and they're fun to work with. Win-win all around. "I'll still properly ask them—assuming Queen Regina likes my idea and approves it."

"She'll happily do so, I think. You're not going to get much argument from her. But what about Davenforth?"

"Ah. That was the true surprise." I lowered my voice and admitted to the three of them, "She asked Henri to become a royal mage."

They looked at me with dropped jaws, then Gibs sat back with a huff of laughter, as if he should have seen this coming. "That's smart," he said approvingly. "He's one of the more talented mages this country has ever seen. And if you can wrangle it to where he's appointed over your new division, then you can keep him as a partner."

I winked. "You've got it."

Foster cleared his throat, looking between us uncertainly. "This is absolutely not meant as a disparagement against Dr. Davenforth, but…does he have the power level necessary to be a royal mage?"

"No, and he'll be the first to admit it."

Gibs shrugged. "But you have to keep in mind, whenever things take a turn from bad to worse, Davenforth seems to have the answer. He's now worked with multiple royal mages to counter some problem or other, and they all like him. Depend on him to help them find the answer. Our royal mages are powerful, no doubt. But he has the intellect and creativity they sometimes lack. I think that's why our good queen has decided to bring him properly in. I certainly think it a splendid idea, although not all might agree with her decision."

I hadn't thought of it, but the populace at large probably wouldn't understand the appointment. Some people would get it, but not all. It might mean pushback for Henri and be uncomfortable for a while. I didn't want him to suffer through that. Then again, he deserved the recognition, darnit. He was well trusted and liked, and he deserved the position.

Whether or not he'd take it, well, that was another matter.

I shook the thoughts and doubts off. "Even if he doesn't take the offer, I'll still have him as a partner. He's agreed to at least join the kingsmen ranks."

Gibs' brows shot into his hairline. "Has he really?"

"He said that ages ago, when I agreed to be a consultant. He's not shifted his stance since. If I go kingsman, so will he."

An unholy grin lit up my friend's face. "He'll have to get into shape for it."

I immediately put a finger to my mouth, shushing him. "Absolutely do not remind him of that before we can get him sworn in. I'm hoping he won't remember that part. The man already treats 'exercise' like a dirty word."

Gibs' grin did not waver.

I eyed him suspiciously, not sure what dark thoughts he was entertaining with such glee. I had a feeling I'd find out sooner or later.

I decided to keep moving before we got too sidetracked. "I'll put together a proper proposal on this when we get back. For now, we need to move. This case already has a lot of media attention, so guys, let's lay low with this as long as we can okay?"

I got nods, not expecting anything else, as no one likes reporters. I exited at that point, all of us going to our own living quarters in order to pack. I'd swing by the train station first for a schedule, figure things out from there.

Part of my brain kept chewing on the possibilities even as I walked towards a taxi. Was the countess murdered? Suicide? Accident? Even if I wanted to bet on it, I didn't know which way to go.

I really had to get more facts.

Oh dear.

what

Oh dear, I completely failed to think of the physical requirements for the job.

It will be fine, Henri.

I don't believe you.

I sure wouldn't lolol #exerciseisadirtyword

Report 04: My Scheming Partner

I scheme with only the best of intentions.

Oh, that's rich, coming from you.

The compartment was quiet, a comfortable sort of silence. The train rocked slightly back and forth as it carried us northward, the sun slowly rising to peek through our window. Jamie sat at my right, her head resting on my shoulder as she read through the police reports we had for the case. Her language skills were much stronger now after so many years on the planet, but she still came across the occasional word that baffled her. I served as her dictionary in those moments.

I was studying the coroner's report, as I could read through that easier than she. The Felixes were stretched out on the baggage rack above our heads, apparently preferring the loftier view.

We read—or, ostensibly, we both read, but my thoughts kept getting sidetracked. The report was dry as dust, which didn't help cement my attention.

Me. A royal mage. The mind boggled.

Truth told, it was still an odd concept, even after spending a good majority of yesterday thinking about it. I realized I had been called in for some of the bigger disasters in Kingston over the past few years, but that was mostly Seaton's doing. Had I made a good showing of myself? It wasn't arrogance to say that I had.

But did that really mean I had the ability to be a royal mage?

Jamie's head turned a little on my shoulder, her own reports dropping to fully rest in her lap. "So, what does the coroner's report say? Anything interesting?"

"Um." Despite having read three paragraphs, I had no recollection of what I'd read.

She seemed to realize I was distracted, and tilted her head back to look at my face. "Penny for your thoughts?"

I sighed, letting the report lapse to the side. "Jamie, tell me honestly. Do you think I have the ability to be a royal mage?"

"Yes," she answered without hesitation. "Anyone who knows you thinks that. I think the only person who doubts your ability is you."

"Well. That hits the nail quite squarely upon its head." I did appreciate her faith in me, though. It was a feather in my cap that I could wear with pride.

Her expression turned shrewd, and I mentally braced myself. I had no idea what she would say next, but it would likely give me a turn.

"I talked to Sherard about this, and he was gleeful at the idea. He told me he'd nudged Regina, hoping she'd agree with him and appoint you."

I blinked, briefly taken aback by this. "So the idea did come from him?"

"Initially, yes. Although you saw how Jules reacted. It's not just Sherard wanting to play with you."

I snorted, amused at the turn of phrase. Although it did make more sense to me now why this offer had come about. Seaton's opinion would carry a great deal of weight with our queen.

"I also mentioned to Gibs, Niamh, and Foster that this offer had been extended and they were not in the least bit surprised. Rather, hopeful you'd take it."

I stared at her, dumbfounded, the wheels and cogs spinning madly in my mind. "Truly? I didn't expect that."

"I also did you the favor of not telling your parents."

I winced, a brief shudder going through me. "Thank

you, dearest. If my mother found out I even hesitated over this, she'd wring my neck. I forever frustrate her in that regard. She has higher ambitions than I."

"Yeah, you're not the type," Jamie agreed with a fond smile. "You're just too humble for it. It's one of the things I like about you. And I'm not going to push you into this if you're really uncomfortable with the position. Regardless if you're an RM or not, Sherard's going to pull you into projects."

That was quite true. Although I felt better knowing she wouldn't be disappointed if I chose to pass on the position.

"But tell me honestly, is it that you don't have as much magical power as the other RMs? Is that why you're hesitating?"

"In part. A rather large part, really. Because I wouldn't be able to assist them much if something truly alarming happened. Magically speaking, I'd be as helpful as a boat anchor on land." I paused. Even though the words were a bit sour to the taste, I said them anyway. I needed this moment of honesty with her. "Also, I'm not blind to the possible reaction from the public. They'd question—and rightly so—why me? Why appoint me when I don't have the power as other royal mages? There might well be a public outcry and at the very least, quite a bit of political pressure in all the wrong ways. I do not wish to put myself into an awkward position."

"Ah. Yeah, you'd hate that. I think it might happen, to one degree or another. Maybe not as much as you're anticipating." Jamie pursed her lips, still studying my expression as if she could glean my internal thoughts. "But here's another perspective for you. The ones who will actually work with you want not just your magical genius, but your experience. Henri, you bring a lot to the table. You've been a magical examiner for a decade, you've seen things the rest of the royal mages haven't, and you have a perspective they don't. It's why Sherard brings you in, time and again. He needs that perspective. He needs your genius. They have enough power hitters in the palace to take care of things that need raw power. What they're lacking is problem solvers."

I could not argue, as she was entirely right. Jules Felix also had his own genius, but it was in a very specific area. Outside of his given field, he was severely out of his depth. And none of the royal mages could abide working with each other for any length of time. I recognized that part of the reason why Queen Regina wanted me was because I could get along with Seaton, Felix, and Vonderbank. That itself was a boon.

I turned this all over in my head, thought of what it would be like to hold that position. Aside from the public pushback, there was only one other objection that held true for me. "But who will partner with you?"

"You," she said comfortably.

I quirked a brow. "My dear, what are you scheming?"

"All the things," she promised brightly. "I want to create the equivalent of an FBI division here in the kingsmen ranks, appoint you as the RM over the division, and then bring in Colette as magical examiner, Weber as medical examiner, and keep all the agents I've been training off and on."

That was a great deal to unpack all in one breath. "I know we've spoken about some of this before, of which agents to bring in if you could do it—but Colette and Weber too?"

"We'll need someone dedicated in-house to handle all of the magical stuff, since you'll be too busy playing with me and Sherard to do it. Colette's great at it; she's proven that, and we all like her. Why not keep her?"

"I certainly have no argument. Same reason for Weber?"

"Yup. Out of all the medical examiners we've worked

with, he's the one with the best results. He's good at his job, easy to get along with, and flexible enough to work weird hours."

I saw her point. "I believe if you give Queen Regina a proposal with all of this outlined—including who you would like to have in the new department—she'd keel over in pure joy."

"Yeah? I mean, I give it good odds she'll like it, but you think so?"

"I am quite inclined to think that when she first offered you the position among her kingsmen, it was with the idea that you'd eventually create such a division. Her disappointment with you turning her down is otherwise disproportionate."

"Oh." Jamie chewed on that for a moment, looking blindly ahead at the muted carpet on the floors. "Huh. I guess I missed that. I was too panicked and wondering how to gracefully turn her down. Like, back then, in no way was I ready to do what she wanted me to do."

"At the time, I agreed with you. But you've stepped outside Kingston several times to work, and on national cases. I think you have a far better grip on this world. You're not the same woman you were even two years ago."

"Heh. No argument there. But then, you've changed too. You were quietly content to just go through your routine when I first met you. You'd be bored if we shoved you back into your lab now."

She might well have been right. I enjoyed the challenge of being her partner. Even the oddness of a police precinct couldn't compare.

Really, the only possible argument I foresaw was this: "Gregson will murder you if you take me, Weber, and Colette out of his station."

Jamie winced. "Yeaaaah not looking forward to that. At all."

I wasn't either. Finding a capable magical examiner

took almost a miracle to pull off. We might well have to borrow someone from another station to cover until Gregson could hire replacements. I had the feeling I'd be responsible for interviewing people, again. Still, I felt in my heart of hearts that this was the right move for her. Jamie was good at investigation. She had so much to teach that it didn't feel right leaving her in a police station. Not when she could do more. And I certainly didn't feel right about pushing her forward even as I dragged my own feet.

I looked at her, this woman who had survived the impossible and then proceeded to flourish. She'd been kidnapped by a deranged witch, broke free, and made a life on an alien planet. She did it with a smile on her face and a song on her lips. There was many a time I watched her and the daily courage she displayed, and stood in awe of her. If our roles were reversed, I was convinced I would not have fared as well as she.

Even now, she was once again embarking on a new adventure. Something that took courage on her part, as she tried to form something that did not exist on this world out of nothing but an idea and determination. She did so with an invitation and a hope that I might join her.

But she made no demands upon me.

How could I possibly just let her go ahead of me? How could I possibly hang back out of fear of what others might say? Would I really miss out on the opportunity to keep working with her, to be with her as she created a whole new division for the kingsmen, just because I feared rumors?

Phrased like that, it seemed a very imbecilic reason.

In that moment, the thought crystallized. I hesitated accepting the role of royal mage because it was outside my comfort zone. That was it, that was the true reason. That's why I dithered so strongly. It wasn't something I'd planned or thought to wish for, so I didn't have any motivation to take it.

But that, too, was the wrong way to look at it. If I was a royal mage, I could spend time with Jamie and Seaton on a routine basis. I could enjoy my friend and safeguard the woman I loved beyond all else. What better reason did I need?

I looked at Jamie, thought of the faith she had in me, and drew upon her courage. I'd need it, as this would be rocky in the beginning. But I could prove my own value in due course. Really, my priority should be her more than anything.

I said with a slight smile, "I think I should take it."

She blinked, not expecting this. "You sure? Don't say that on my account. I don't want to force you into something you'll hate later."

"I know, you never would. But really, the reason why I balked was that I feared leaving my comfort zone. And that's a substandard reason to make a decision."

"Oh. Yeah, fear-based decisions are never good ones. I totally agree."

The joy on her face told me I'd made the right decision. I'd adjust to the new role, and I'd be in step with her moving forward. I could never regret that.

I kissed her with soft affection, felt her joy as she kissed me back. It was a perfect, sweet moment. It left my heart warm, as if it were cradled in her hands.

"I'm really happy you're going to do it," she murmured. "Still want to sleep on it more?"

"I need to. I need to adjust to it all. And I think I want to wait until after this case is wrapped up to give an official answer."

"That's fair. Really, that might be best. I want to write up a proposal and submit it when you give your answer, so she's got all the pieces together." Jamie drew back, frowning a little. "Not that I have any idea how to do that."

"We'll ask Seaton. I'm sure he's written quite a few

in his time. We'll all pitch in to help you write it."

"Please and thank you."

"Well, I'm famished. Should we have dinner for breakfast?"

"Didn't you already get tea and a muffin?"

"That was not a proper breakfast," I protested. "I was too rushed this morning to eat anything substantial."

She eyed me sideways, eyes dancing with mirth. "Your hobbit is showing, sir. But sure, we can do second breakfast."

What was she on about? I understood the reference, but it didn't count as a second breakfast if I didn't get a proper first one, surely. Anyway, she wasn't fussing, so I led the way to the dining car. I took the coroner's report with me to pass along to Weber. I hadn't gleaned anything useful from it and doubted I would. He would be departing the train soon, as we were due to be in Sheffield in another hour or so. He'd need the report before we separated from him and continued on to Ashbluff.

Weber's compartment was three down from ours, and I stopped, giving the door a solid knock.

"Enter!"

Poking my head in, I found him seated on the bench, a newspaper in hand. Weber's white linen suit looked a bit creased from travel, and dark circles framed his eyes. I'd rarely seen him looking so exhausted. He was normally a man of energy.

"Are you well, Weber?" I asked.

"Exhausted," he admitted. "My daughter's teething three new teeth and has had us up most nights. I feel bad for my wife, leaving her on her own, but I'm very much looking forward to a full night's sleep tonight."

"Ah, that does explain it. You look fatigued."

"Oh dear. I'd hoped the suit would help mask that."

The contrast of the light-colored suit with his dark chocolate skin only highlighted the problem, but I wasn't about to say so. "I wanted to pass along the coroner's report before we head for breakfast."

Weber took it with a grimace. "I did look over this before it was given to you. It didn't contain much in the way of facts, did it?"

"No, that it did not." I gave him a wry nod. "Hence, you."

Jamie poked her head over my shoulder. "I didn't get to read it. What did it say?"

"Something along the lines of the body appearing to have been in the water for two to three weeks, cause of death unknown. Truly astounding how the doctor managed to stretch that into a full page. He noted two things of interest: one, there's only traces of water in her lungs. She didn't drown, so odds are she was dead before she hit the water."

Jamie made a noise of interest. "That is good to know. Anything else?"

"Only that her body carried a great many contusions, no doubt from the fall. She had multiple broken bones, but I expect that if she fell from a cliff's height." Weber touched a finger to the report and relayed, "Something else you'll need to note. She wore a nightgown and one slipper."

"So she was ready for bed when something happened? Or it happened really early that morning, before she could get dressed. That gives me a better sense of timeline." Jamie relaxed back on her heels to scribble a note in her notepad.

"I'll give you a verbal report to work from before submitting something formal," Weber promised. "Expect it, hmm, perhaps tomorrow? I want to go over her body very carefully. With her being in the water so long, there might not be much left for me to work from, but I want to be careful on this case."

"We appreciate that." And it was just as well, considering how dear this was to our queen.

Weber shook his head. “I suppose I shouldn’t have expected more. Sheffield doesn’t have a proper police station, much less a coroner on hand. A practicing doctor did the autopsy. Still, not to even run a toxicology report? I have no idea what I’m walking into here.”

I gave a glum sigh. “Neither do we.”

Report 05: Case, Start!

Even with our early departure, it took all morning to reach Ashbluff. We chose to eat lunch on the train, the easiest solution, as we didn't know the city. Henri was keen to hit the ground running, and really, so was I. We got off in the early afternoon and I took a moment to study the area as we alighted from the train. Much like Sheffield, the city of Ashbluff was a coastal town that attracted tourists. It wasn't large—maybe three or four thousand people in population—with picturesque houses of white stucco, red tile roofs, and flower gardens everywhere. With the blue sea right past the docks, and puffy white clouds in the sky, the scene was postcard perfect.

Except, you know, for the possibility of murder.

Why did I feel like I was in an episode of *Murder, She Wrote*? A seriously hard impression to shake. If a little old lady showed up on a bike telling me she knew who did it, I wouldn't at all be surprised.

Thankful, too. 'Cause I had no clue.

We went to a hotel first, a cute building named Seagull's Loft, and threw our luggage into our rooms. As usual, my Felixes earned strange looks, and I had to stop and explain what they were to our hostess. I had no doubt the cats would endear themselves to her soon when they started chasing mice away. That was usually how things rolled.

That settled, I met my people at the front door, asking, "Does anyone know where the police station is here?"

"I think we passed it coming in," Niamh informed me. "I saw the sign for it out of the corner of my eye. We need to go back down towards the wharf."

"Lead the way."

We passed many a local and tourist on the way to the police station. We probably wouldn't have garnered a second look from the locals, so familiar were they of strangers, if not for the cats. Phil was perched on Henri's shoulder like some sort of pirate's parrot, Tasha was lounging in my arms like the queen she was, and Clint wore his field cat vest, walking ahead of us like he knew the way already.

As we passed one house, a dog barked and charged the fence. It wasn't a territorial charge, more like a *whoa what's that!?* kind of charge. The barking was just noise, really, so I knew there was no danger.

Clint, however, whirled on his back legs, hissing and arching like a Halloween kitty. "Try me, dog!" he spat.

The dog stopped barking and whined, backing up a little.

Smart dog. Clint had no sense of size, really. I'd seen him attack things three times his size—and win. He was confident he could tackle anything that came at him. I didn't think he'd give the dog much in the way of mercy.

Because I feared for the dog, I shuffled Tasha and scooped Clint up too, letting him drape over my shoulder. "Leave the poor dog alone, Clint. He was happy to see something interesting. He wasn't going to do anything."

Clint hissed again anyway, clearly still in attack-kitty mode, because that's how he rolls.

Thankfully, the police station was at the next corner, well away from the dog. It was a modest sort of station in a building that made me think it had once been a pharmacy or a drugstore or something. It was only two stories tall, brown brick, with white window boxes and a blue painted door. If not for the sign on the front saying in solemn gold lettering that it was the Ashbluff police station, I would have mistaken it as someone's house.

We stepped inside and my earlier impression of a pharmacy was reinforced. A long counter ran the length of the back wall with floor-to-ceiling wooden drawers behind it. The main floor had precisely two desks arranged back-to-back, with uniforms sitting at them, diligently working on paperwork. The older cop was a weredog with more white than grey around his muzzle; the other cop a werebadger who was much younger and spry, the freckles dancing along his snout making him look twelve.

The older I got, the younger everyone else looked. It was a problem.

They both looked up as we entered, the younger cop springing out of his chair to greet us. "Hello, can I help you?"

Foster, bless him, flashed his badge as Henri and I both had our hands full. "Kingsman Foster, we're here to take over the investigation of Countess Giada Barese's death."

His expression cleared immediately. "Oh, the queen's task force! You made good time. Please, come in, come in. I'm Arco. This is my partner, Colombo."

Guys. Guys, at that moment, I needed serious prayers to keep my face straight. There was a weredog…who looked like a beagle…working as a cop named Colombo. Never mind the difference in spelling. I wanted to put him in a trench coat, okay? And give him a cigar. It was soooo tempting.

No one here would get the joke but me. Le sigh.

We all shook hands, introduced ourselves, and Arco was quick to grab chairs so we could sit. They were very welcoming, and I appreciated the attitude. Not every station took it well when someone else barged into a case.

Niamh settled in a chair and asked, "Is it just the two of you?"

"No, we're day shift," Colombo corrected her. "We've got two others who work night shift, and the doctor works part time as coroner. Mostly to confirm deaths for us."

"I see. Were you the ones called in when the countess was reported missing?"

"That was us," Colombo confirmed before glancing at me in consideration. "Detective, you don't mind me asking—you're the Shinigami Detective? The one the newspapers love to report on?"

I'd outlive this title someday. Today was not that day. "That's me."

"Pulled out the big guns for this case, I see. Not sure if there's any magic at play here, though." Colombo made a face. "We couldn't even figure out what happened, so proves what I know. Let me start with what I do know."

I pulled a notebook from my breast pocket, all ears, then had to shift Clint to the floor so I had room to write on my lap. He immediately transferred to the desk, sniffing curiously at a few files stacked on the edge.

Colombo eyed him sideways as he talked. He was clearly dying to ask questions but trying to be professional at the same time. Professionalism won out. "Countess Barese was a nice lady. A little high in her manners, but we didn't expect anything else from someone like her. Still, a nice lady. She'd stop and say hi if she was about. Didn't seem to have much luck with men, though. Seemed every time we turned around, she had a new one. The day before her disappearance, she had a house party. I've got a list of six guests there, including her latest paramour. The staff of the house numbers four."

So ten people in total aside from her. "You've got their contact information?"

"I do, all written down, along with their statements of what happened and where everyone was. Two of them are a married couple, should be easier to do follow-up interviews. Staff is still up at the house. The mother of the deceased has them helping her shut the place down and cleaning it. I think they plan to sell the house once it's cleared."

I couldn't fault them there.

"Now, everyone seemed to agree that Countess Barese wasn't having a good party or a good day. She got into arguments with every single person. It started with her lover, who was demanding something of her. Some said it was that she properly divorce her husband so he could marry her. The others said he was demanding money." Colombo shrugged, hands splayed. "Who knows what the truth is?"

Probably both. Giada Barese had a considerable fortune

in her own right, after all. I imagine her lover would like to get his hands on it if he wasn't a nice person.

"They'd planned to go down to the beach and have a picnic on the water, then do fireworks, but none of that materialized. They were too busy arguing with each other. The married couple actually went into town and did some shopping before returning to the house. I've confirmed that alibi. The others said they found their own pursuits, either going for a swim, or staying in to read. Either way, the last confirmed sighting I have for Giada Barese alive was about six o'clock in the evening."

"And there's no sign she was alive after that?" Henri asked.

Arco and Colombo both shook their heads.

"We can't find any evidence of it, at least." Arco tapped a finger on a discouragingly slim folder. "Here's our rough timeline, witness statements, etcetera. Colombo and I really worked the area, searched all over, and we know that she went over the cliff. We found her robe floating on the water. We searched the water quite a bit before giving up—she must have been carried away by the tides before we arrived on scene."

I had a limited understanding of tides, so I asked my better half, "How long would that take? For the tides to carry her out of the immediate area?"

"I would think anywhere upwards of six hours, depending on their search area," he answered.

As expected of my encyclopedia, he knew all. But then, he probably dealt a lot with tide questions, considering Kingston's proximity to the water.

"Her robe was in the water," Foster muttered to himself thoughtfully. "Where, precisely?"

Arco flipped open the folder and riffled through the first half of the pages before landing on one that looked like a rough sketch of the house and grounds. An X right off the side marked an area 'gardens.' "Here."

Interesting. Right on the other side of the garden wall.

I could see why both murder and accidental death were so much in question. With that entry point into the water, it could easily go either way. Suicide wasn't something I could rule out, for that matter, no matter what Regina thought.

"Anything else?" Niamh pressed.

Colombo hesitated strongly. "I tried to track her scent, but I didn't get very far with it. To be honest, her scent is very strong all over the grounds, I couldn't make hide nor hair of it. You're a tracker, correct?"

Niamh gave him a nod. "I am."

"Maybe you'll do better than my old nose. What I can tell you is this. I think she was in her bedroom, and then left it via the glass doors that lead out into the garden. The trail from her writing desk led straight outside. It got muddled once I was out there. But I'd swear she left through those doors—which makes sense, too, as the doors don't face anywhere else but the gardens. No one would have seen her go in or out of those."

Interesting. Okay, a little more info was good. I would let Niamh go over the grounds and then confirm that, though, before taking it as gospel truth.

"Anything else you can tell us?" I felt like I had very little to go off of, especially for a case that had been open for two weeks.

Colombo paused and thought. "I can't think of much else. We did notify the husband, Sebastian Barese, and he acted torn up about it. He told me he'd hoped to reconcile with her and repair their marriage. I got his whereabouts the day of her death, and he says he was visiting a Lady Dalris in Ciparis. He claims he didn't even know Giada was missing until a week afterwards. Oh, I also noted who her solicitor was. He's expecting you to call, although of course he'll need a copy of the death certificate on file before he can tell you everything."

I blinked at him. "You know who her solicitor is?"

"Sure. Only lawyer in town."

That's fair. "Okay. Thank you both so much for your

time. If we need help out there, can we call upon you?"

"Please do, Detective," Arco responded hopefully. "We don't like having the case so open like this, so if we can help, we'd love to."

"Good, I'll draw you in as I need you."

Niamh stood with the rest of us but requested, "Do you still have the found robe here in evidence?"

"We do," Colombo confirmed. "Care to see it?"

"Please." To me, she noted, "I only need a minute. I want to get her scent, and the scents of wherever she walked, off the robe if I can. Then I'll have an idea of what I'm looking for."

I waved her on. "Meet you outside."

Henri made a snap decision and said, "I'll come with you, Niamh. I want to do a magical examination, see if there's anything on it."

I didn't think the robe would tell me anything, especially not after being in the water for hours, so I took myself back out with the folder of information. Ten people in the house and not one of them saw her after six o'clock in the evening?

Either that was a very big house, or someone was lying.

Foster followed me out and we stopped on the sidewalk, looking at each other like, 'well, here we are.'

"Still want Niamh and I to go over the grounds?" he asked me.

"I do. I think Niamh especially might be able to figure out where she went after she left the house. Even if she went straight from bedroom to cliff, that'll tell us something."

"Fair enough. I do find it strange that she had so many people in the house with her that day and yet no one saw her."

I snapped my fingers at him. "Right?! I find that totally weird. She went into her room before dinner, but none of the staff thought to bring her a tray of food? No one checked on her after she had arguments all day? I mean, either she had really lousy friends, or someone's lying through their teeth."

"I'm inclined to think someone's lying. I can't get thirty

minutes of peace in my house without bribes, and I only have six people living with me."

I snorted. "I have two cats and still have no alone time."

Tasha rubbed up against my ankle and blinked pretty eyes at me, the picture of innocence.

I eyed her. "You're just as guilty as Clint, missy. Don't give me that."

Clint chose that moment to reascend my shoulder through the expedient method of just leaping from ground to shoulder, where he landed with an oomph. On both our parts.

I tacked on dryly, "Not to mention no personal space. Hey, bud. Why exactly are you perched on me?"

"Good view," my Felix informed me happily.

"Good grief, you're spoiled." I sighed and left him there; he'd only whine if I put him down.

Niamh and Henri rejoined us, both wearing interesting looks. I perked up hopefully. "Anything?"

"I've got her scent, and the scent of the sea," Niamh reported. "I have enough to go off of. There were traces of dirt, too? Which could have been collected as she fell, I suppose, but it was all along the hem."

That was interesting. I didn't think a fall would do that.

Henri offered, "I didn't detect anything magical on the robe."

"Okay. Really, all information at this point is good information. Niamh, when we get there, do your magic. I need to know where she was the night she died." I stopped and looked around consideringly. "How do you hail a taxi in this place anyway?"

Columbo. Columbo...books? Or one of your series?

Series of movies. When we get back, we're totally watching Columbo.

How DARE you have movie night without me!

oh stop pouting, you're invited too

Report 06: Base of Information

Giada Barese's house on the sea was grand indeed. It fit the style of this northern coast, with polished white stone, red tiled roof, a two-story building that seemed to stretch in all directions. The stark lines of it were softened by multiple decorations, greenery and ribbons that stretched along the balconies, over the windows, around the wrought iron sconces. It felt strange to see the house decked out for the holidays, considering what had happened to its owner.

Jamie and I went to the front of the house while Niamh and Foster split off, already going over the grounds. I hoped they'd find something helpful. So far, the folder in our hands contained very little in the way of useful clues. The Felixes were happy to romp off with them, exploring the grounds for anything interesting. I let Phil go, as he'd been cooped up in a train or a car for half a day and needed to run.

We knocked and got an answer shortly. A middle-aged gentleman with a rather pronounced nose and shirt sleeves rolled up to the elbow greeted us. His polite, professional smile looked strained. "Hello, we're not receiving visitors at this time."

"We're not that." Jamie pulled out a badge for his perusal. "Jamie Edwards, Kingsman Consultant. This is my partner, Doctor Henri Davenforth. We're here on the queen's behest to look into the death of Giada Barese."

His expression cleared immediately, although his

eyes turned bright with unshed tears. "Kingsman. Doctor. Thank you so much for coming. I'm Emilio Detti, the butler. Lady Giada was...an amazing friend and employer. We're all very troubled by her death. I want to know what happened to her."

"We do as well," I assured him gently. "May we come in?"

"Oh, I've left you standing here in the cold. I'm so sorry, do come in." He hastily stepped back, swinging the door open wide to let us through.

I stepped inside, blinking to allow my eyes to adjust to the dimmer interior. It wasn't that the house was badly lit—far from it—but the snow on the ground was blinding under the afternoon sun. As my eyes adjusted, I took in my surroundings with a quick sweep.

The house's interior was a perfect match to the exterior. It was a grand manor house meant for hosting parties, and no doubt had ten-plus bedrooms. The interior floor was a warm terracotta tile that matched the roofing tile in color, the walls a creamy white with ceilings hand stenciled in a floral motif. Understated wealth was not in evidence here—this place screamed luxury and wasn't afraid to showcase it with antique chairs and tables strategically placed about, priceless art hanging on the walls, and plush rugs spread across the floors that probably cost more than my apartment. The festive decorations were in evidence here as well, with bright ribbons and floral arrangements in every conceivable place.

Giada Barese might not have been born into wealth, but she certainly died with it.

Detti urged us through an arched foyer to a sitting parlor just to the right of the main door. Or I assumed it to be a parlor, until I entered and found that it was a study. With coffered warm wood ceilings, a chandelier that dripped crystal and light, the same coffee-colored tiles on the floor, and built-in bookcases of pale wood on all the walls, it was a book lover's paradise. Not something I expected to see in a former model's home.

Behind a large, rather masculine desk sat a woman in her late fifties, perhaps early sixties. Her greying hair was twisted in a simple updo, a white dress washing out her complexion and making her seem even more wan and pale than she might be. I knew her, although it had been many years since I'd seen her, and grief had aged her horribly. She looked up with a confused expression as Detti led us through.

"Detti, who is this?"

"Kingsman Jamie Edwards and Doctor Henri Davenforth, my lady," Detti explained with a wave to us. "This is Lady Lastra, Lady Giada's mother."

I approached her with an outstretched hand, having some sympathy for a woman who had just lost a beloved child. "Lady Lastra, I'm sorry that we meet like this."

She took my hand, held it with a searching expression. "You're Ophelia Davenforth's son, aren't you?"

"I am. Do you remember meeting me when I was much younger?"

"When we were both much younger, you mean. I haven't seen you since you were in your teens." She tried to smile but it fell flat. "Your mother mentioned you work for the police."

"I do indeed. Queen Regina has handed the task over to me and my partner to figure out what happened."

"Oh. Oh, that does my heart good. To know she would do that. I'm..." She looked down at the stacks of paperwork on the desk, her expression lost. "I don't know what to do. Really. I don't know what to do. She didn't exactly keep her estate in good order, you see. Giada was never good at paperwork. She was good with people, but not things like taxes. It's a bit of a mess. I don't know where to even begin to sort it out.

Or when to plan for a funeral."

Jamie came around to stand at my side, giving the woman a warm smile edged with sympathy. "Our coroner is examining your daughter right now. Once he's finished, which should take a day or two, we can release her to you for burial."

Her expression looked relieved. "Thank you...thank you, Kingsman. I appreciate that. And thank Queen Regina for me, too. She's always been such a dear friend of the family, and I know she was very upset at the news of Giada's death."

"She was...very upset," I agreed. "Hence, us. We have a great many questions that need answers. Are you up to them?"

"Yes, of course. Anything to figure out what happened," she whispered, her hands tightening in mine.

That was often the hardest part for a grieving mind. The mind struggled to make sense of the situation, to put some logical basis behind a loss so it could cope. To not have any answers must be mentally draining in the worst of ways. She could not heal from this until she understood something of it.

"We'll figure it out," Jamie promised her. "Here, let's all sit comfortably so we can talk. I'm going to shoot off a message to Queen Regina first, though."

I sat in an armchair next to hers, watching as she pulled out her pad and wrote a quick message to the queen.

We're at Giada's estate. Her mother is distraught. Giada's estate is apparently a mess and she doesn't know where to start. Can you send in help for her after we finish?

The answer was immediate: *Of course. Tell her to not worry about it.*

Jamie lifted her head and gave Lady Lastra a smile. "I reported to Queen Regina that you're struggling, and she said not to worry. She'll send someone over to help you as soon as we finish with our investigation."

"You told her through that?" She peered at the pad curiously. "What is it?"

"A new device, almost ready for the market." I held it up as I explained. "It allows us to send messages to each other almost instantly, much like a telegraph."

"Oh. Oh, how ingenious. I hadn't heard of those. And you can contact the queen directly?"

"We can, and we do, as she wants updates often."

"Then tell her thank you for me."

Jamie nodded and scribbled out a thank you.

Interviewing a parent about a lost child was always a delicate mission, especially with a woman I knew. I tried to phrase things in such a way to not upset her or put her on the defensive. "How was your daughter in the past month or so? Was anything troubling her?"

"She seemed in good enough spirits," Lady Lastra answered with a frown that denied her words. "Something about her health was bothering her. She mentioned going to see a doctor about it. But it didn't seem anything serious, as she was healthy to my eyes. She'd been getting into many fights with her current paramour, Felipe. Ah, that is, Felipe Iadanza. I could see the signs clearly, after so many of her boyfriends—she was getting tired of his demands and his ways. She was ready for him to go, I think. But he was making noises about marrying her and wanting her to get properly rid of her last husband."

Rocky relationship, it sounded like. And spurned men did not always respond well. I noted the possible motive.

Jamie made some notes, then asked, "Is Felipe the type to get physical? Is he in any way abusive?"

"All hot air," Lady Lastra replied with an immediate shake of her head. "He spoke pretty words but had no ability to follow through on any of them. It's why Giada was so frustrated with him. She wanted a man who could actually be responsible. I say that, but it's not like my own daughter was much better than he about commitments."

With two failed marriages, I chose to keep my comments to myself. "Did she have any enemies we need to be concerned with? What about her current husband—was he angry at all about the separation?"

"He's never had much of a temper. I can't imagine him getting violent with her. He even wanted her back, said he missed her."

"I have to ask, did your daughter feel the same way? Was a reconciliation being spoken of?"

She shook her head. "Giada didn't seem inclined to reconcile. She had no kind words to say about her husband. I know he kept trying, though. He often sent letters and presents, although Giada didn't pay them any attention. I'm sure his mother was glad of it too. She and Giada never got along. They bought each other pretty presents for the holidays, played their parts, and kept their distance the rest of the time. I think half the reason why Giada moved back to this house was to get away from the woman. She was very vocal about not wanting Giada as a daughter-in-law, and lamenting why her son chose such a woman. But I think I just described half the mothers-in-law in the world."

"It's universal, trust me," Jamie drawled. "Had Lady Giada heard anything from her recently?"

"No, I don't believe so. Things settled down when she moved back here, which was six months ago? Seven? I can't put an exact date to it. She'd only been married four months when she came here and just didn't go back."

Ah. One of those moves. "Anyone else? Anyone your daughter considered an enemy or threat?"

"No...really, for all her capriciousness, Giada was

well loved by most. We just couldn't hold a grudge against her." Lady Lastra's eyes fell to her hands, a tear escaping, her voice hoarse. "I can't see how anyone could stay angry with her long enough to kill her. I can't see her committing suicide, either. She was so full of life, with so many plans, and wasn't the type to stress about things. I really think this might have been an accident."

I reserved judgement. We really didn't have enough evidence to assume that yet. "When was the last time you saw her?"

"Oh, it was a good week before her death. She told me all about her house party and borrowed several of the unused fireworks from last year so they could play with them on the beach. She was in high spirits. Not that her party turned out as planned. Detti"—she nodded to the man in question—"tells me that the day of her death, everyone argued with her over something trivial."

"Yes, about that." Jamie's pen was poised over the paper. "What exactly were the arguments about?"

Detti sighed, shaking his head. "They truly were over trivial things. Iadanza was following her around the house, demanding she divorce Lord Barese, and something about paying off a bill for him. That was his usual line when tempers flared between them. With the others, it was arguments about using old fireworks, or what time they should go down to the water, or suggestions that she needed to get rid of Iadanza. It went round and round until Lady Giada didn't feel comfortable speaking to any of them. She went for a long walk on the beach to avoid them all, came back to the house at six, and gave us all strict instruction not to disturb her. She wouldn't even let me bring her a meal."

"I had wondered about that," Jamie muttered, making a note. "No one checked on her?"

"We knew better," Detti explained, although he looked pained to say it. "As sweet as she was, she had a temper, too. If she told you to do something, that's what you did. I had Sivi make up a plate for her and keep it on the stove, just in case she changed her mind later and hunger drove her out. But it never did."

Quite likely because she was dead before hunger got the chance. I carefully kept that opinion behind my teeth.

"Was this unusual?" I pressed. "For her to be so out of sorts with everyone?"

"Yes," Lady Lastra said instantly.

Detti hesitated, eyeing the mother sideways. He seemed poised to scoot back out the door rather than argue.

"That expression says otherwise." Jamie pointed her pencil at him. "Out with it."

Lady Lastra looked at the butler with surprise. "Giada wasn't the sort to just fight all the time!"

"Forgive me, my lady, but recently she was very out of sorts." Detti looked apologetic even as the words left his mouth. "She would come into these strange moods and take herself off for hours, wandering around the grounds. Sometimes she looked at us as if she didn't really know us. Then she'd lay down for a time and be back to herself again. I wasn't sure what was happening, but I suspect it was perhaps a touch of melancholy because she and Iadanza were fighting so much. I urged her to see the doctor, which she started doing, although I didn't see any improvements."

Lady Lastra looked at him in surprise. "What? She didn't mention any of this to me. She just said she was having dizzy spells."

"She had those, too. It's why she regularly saw a physician."

Lady Lastra was surprised, almost stunned. Her jaw dropped as if she had no idea about any of this.

What all had she failed to observe about her daughter? How reliable of a witness was she when she hadn't even known about this?

It also made me wonder about Giada, since her health wasn't stable. If she'd been in one of those moods that night, then could she have been so locked in her head that she misjudged the distance from the garden wall to the sea? I didn't know how plausible that was without seeing the area with my own eyes.

But it was a curious thing for Detti to observe. Why had her behavior changed over one paramour? She'd gone through two husbands and multiple lovers without this behavioral change, after all. Or was it a matter of culmination where the loss of yet another relationship affected her?

I'd have to ask Jamie. She'd have a better insight into the female mind than I.

"Lady Lastra, any chance she confided in someone about this?" Jamie asked hopefully.

Lady Lastra was still stunned but managed a shake of her head. "I can't think of anyone if she didn't even confide in me. Detti?"

"Perhaps her doctor?"

"Hmm. Okay, then that leads me to the next question—or, rounds of questions, I should say. I need to speak with all the staff and get a timeline down. We're hoping to narrow things down more than they already are. Lady Lastra, I realize you're trying to organize the estate, but can you leave that for a few days? I need full access to everything here, as it might shed some light on matters. I promise to give you control of it again by week's end."

She nodded in agreement. "Of course. Of course, anything to help. I can't do much with it at this moment anyway. What else can I do?"

Jamie stood and gathered her up. "Show me where her room is and let me supervise what you're taking.

I'm sure you'll need burial clothes, but I'll need to know what's gone to avoid confusion later. Thank you so much for cooperating, you have no idea how helpful you've been. Oh, and can you sit and create a list for me of any friends who might have been here the week of her death?"

"Yes, yes, of course."

I followed along, speaking to Detti as I did. "Arrange for the staff to meet us in the kitchen in perhaps an hour? One at a time, if you would. And let them know we have two other kingsmen searching the grounds and not to be alarmed."

"I will, Doctor." He hesitated before admitting in a lower voice, "I don't know if they'll find anything after two weeks, though. Multiple people have been over the grounds without anything untoward cropping up. But maybe a kingsman can spot something we can't?"

I gave him a game smile. "Deity of luck willing."

Report 07: A Fat Lot of Nothing

After seeing Lady Lastra out of the house, Henri and I retreated to the infamous garden bordering the cliff. It was immaculately kept, with hedges and low trees, little fountains, and stone benches to sit upon. Snow dusted the plants, but the stone had been swept clear.

And then, over the garden wall, nothing but sea. Seriously, Regina hadn't exaggerated. The wall followed the cliff edge—there was no separation between the house and a sheer drop into the ocean. Let me tell you, I couldn't begin to fathom why someone thought this was a good idea. Just standing here gave me the willies, as some part of my brain was convinced the whole thing was going to slide into the ocean any second.

Foster and Niamh were sitting on the wall, one leg seaside, the other on the garden's stone path, like two kids waiting to go play in the ocean. Even the cats were stretched out along the top of the thick stone wall, hanging out in the sunshine, purring away.

I shook my head, taking in the sight. "Is it just me who finds this garden really uncomfortable?"

"No, my dear," Henri assured me with a wide-eyed stare at the wall. "I do not know how anyone can relax in this space."

"Good, I can't either. Seriously, who thought this was a good idea to build a house right *here*?"

"It's a mentality I do not understand."

Foster lifted a hand in a wave as we approached. "Hello. Find out anything?"

"A fat lot of nothing, really," I answered with a grimace. "Mother couldn't think of a single person who wanted to kill her daughter. Doesn't believe it's suicide, either."

Henri added, "Detti, the butler, did mention that she might have been suffering from melancholy. Her moods had gotten strange as of late."

I eyed him sideways. "He thought that because she was fighting with her boyfriend. And he'd never seen her like that before—he said that, too. I doubt it was because of the boyfriend. It sounds to me like she was pissed off at him and tired of his demands. That's not going to make her wander around and act weird."

"You think not?"

"Men are very quick to assume women suffer from hysterics. They also like to assume those hysterics are because of a man. I assure you, most of the time, neither is true."

Niamh gave a snort. "Thank you, Detective, for putting that so plainly. I don't know why men like to believe that. It's rarely the case."

"You're welcome," I responded mock-solemnly.

Foster, being cute and young, looked between us with interest. "Really? But she was fighting with the boyfriend, right?"

I might have hope in getting this idea out of a younger man's head. Henri was listening too, so I tried to explain. "Look, when a woman gets upset with a boyfriend, she goes out with girlfriends, spends too much money, eats things she'll regret later, and works it out of her system. She'll eventually get rid of the boyfriend, too. What she doesn't do is act weird. What Detti described was that she would disappear for hours, look at them as if she couldn't even recognize her own employees, and take frequent naps. It was weird enough behavior that even she didn't understand it and went to see a doctor. That's not boyfriend troubles. That's something else."

"That, my dear, is a very good point." Henri looked enlightened and regarded the doors leading to the victim's bedroom with new consideration.

Niamh made an intrigued noise. "Wandered around a lot, you say? I'd wondered if that's what she was doing."

My eyes snapped to her. "What did you find out here, anything?"

"Oh, we found quite a bit. It doesn't make a lot of sense, but I hope context will help us figure it out." Niamh pointed to the glass bedroom doors. "It's an older trail, but Giada Barese came out of those doors and then wandered all around the grounds. It wasn't like she was just walking, either. She'd ducked behind bushes, under at least one car, behind buildings, and ended right here on the roots of this tree."

I looked at the scraggly ornamental tree that sat at Niamh's right boot. Ah, that's why she was sitting there. The tree sat on the outside of the garden wall, so precariously perched on the cliff that half of its roots were exposed to air. That wasn't much of a perch. Even a seagull would have to be careful how it moved there.

"From there"—Niamh pointed straight down—"she fell. Her presence vanishes straight into the ocean from here. Now, come a little closer, and look very carefully along the cliffside. You'll see what the local cops here missed. There's a slipper hanging off a little ledge."

I went to her side, carefully leaning over and peering down. It took a second—even my enhanced sight didn't immediately spot it—but sure enough, there it was, a baby blue house slipper that looked like it would fall off into the ocean at any second.

I let out a low whistle. "Niamh, great job. Seriously, a trail that old couldn't have been easy to follow."

"I lost it a few times, had to pick it back up," she admitted candidly. "I do think, by the way, that she lingered here. The stains on her robe make sense if she was kneeling or squatting here at the base of the tree."

"Yeah. Yeah, I can see why you say that."

Henri leaned in right next to me, peering through narrowed eyes. "I think I can retrieve that. Foster, can you give me some room?"

"Of course, Doctor." Foster immediately scooted over a good foot.

As Henri worked his magic to retrieve the slipper, I looked to my cats, who were giving serious attention to their sunbathing. "Well, anything to add, field cats?"

Clint's head came up and he regarded me with golden eyes. "She smelled funny."

"You're gonna have to clarify that one for me, bud."

"Funny, earthy smell," Tasha put in. "Like a plant."

"Haven't smelled it before," Phil added.

Foster tried to bail the cats out. "They said there's a distinctive smell in every place she knelt and touched, as if it was on her hands. And we only found it in those locations."

"Huh. A perfume, maybe? Or something the doctor gave her to calm her down?"

"Who knows at this point? We need her medical records to figure it out."

It may or may not have been important. But that could be said of almost everything we'd found today, so...yeah.

Henri's spell brought the slipper right to his hand, and he held it carefully. "It matches the robe we found perfectly."

"Matched set, huh? Okay. Let's bag and tag it."

"There's a glass shard in the sole, it seems? I need another bag for the glass."

Evidence was all about collecting everything at the scene, as you never knew what was useful or redundant until usually much later. "I'll handle that."

"Very good." Henri lifted his wand once more. "Let me see if I can find matching glass shards anywhere in the area. It could speed things along, as we'll have a delay in getting her medical records."

I waved him on, watching curiously. He grunted with satisfaction a moment later. "Well, this was a short trip. The glass shards are right there, at the base of the tree."

I levered myself over the wall enough that I could look down. Then I had to go cockeyed, hanging my head at an odd angle to see the glimmer of it lurking underneath a root. If I hadn't known it was there, I might have missed it completely, it was so well hidden. "Huh. Yeah, looks like someone dropped a bottle and it broke? Henri, can you grab those without one of us climbing over?"

"I can, yes. A moment." Henri disengaged the spell, reaching for another evidence bag to collect the shards into. "Well, we have conclusive evidence that she stood there before her death, at least."

"Yeah," I agreed thoughtfully. "I can't imagine she'd go far with glass embedded in her slipper, either. That would hurt, the soles aren't that thick."

Henri gave a satisfied grunt as the glass shards glided into his evidence bag. "There, done."

I turned to Niamh. "Did you notice any signs of blood?"

Niamh shook her head. "Blood has a very distinctive smell. I would know if it were here."

I looked once again at where Giada had been standing. Niamh described her going all around these grounds and hiding behind or under things. It sounded like she'd been pursued. She was running and hiding from something. With such a precarious perch here, where even a careless step would have sent her tumbling, an attacker could very well have scared her into death.

Foster canted his head, noting my study. "You think she may have been attacked?"

"Her movements certainly indicate she was running and hiding from something—or someone."

Niamh nodded. "I tracked her movements all over the place and she kept ducking behind things, or under them. Even her last perch was behind the garden wall. A simple push would have ended the matter. She might not have had the chance to defend herself. That said...there's no sign of any other person following her."

"Wait, so she wasn't being chased?"

"If she was, I can't figure out by what. Certainly not a person or animal. There's no other tracks but hers."

My eyes roved over the garden once more, trying to picture the scared young woman. "Seriously," I said, "was she just running scared, then?"

"It's the only thing that makes sense to me." Niamh spread her hands in a shrug. "Panicked people don't react rationally and her movements definitely look panicked to me. It could be that something scared her inside, enough to drive her out, and then she just kept running without realizing no one was actively chasing her."

I knew people did that, but still... "Okay, say you're right. No one heard her calling out for help? Surely she called for help."

"I would think." Foster looked at the slipper in the evidence bag. "If this person drove her from the bedroom, wouldn't it suggest someone intimately acquainted? Like her lover?"

"I think a lot of people would love to blame her boyfriend. No one seemed to like the guy. Still, that's not a good reason to charge him with anything. We have no proof he was the one." I liked him for it, though. "He had a lot of motive in my book. Sometimes, the obvious answer is the right answer. Statistically speaking, about eighty percent of all murdered women are killed by either family members or significant others, be that boyfriends or husbands."

Foster let out a low whistle, eyes going wide.

Niamh's head jerked back in surprise. "Really?" she demanded. "It's that high?"

"Yeah, unfortunately. Which is why I always look very carefully at the nearest and dearest. That said, this case smacks of being in the twenty percent. There's just too much weirdness going on. Let's interview the staff, see if any of them noticed anything."

I scooped up my creatures, who came into my arms like boneless noodles. Apparently, the warm sun on the rocks had baked all motivation to work right out of them. They were content for me to cart them around. Henri had to do the same with Phil, as he was not moving on his own either.

As we walked out of the garden, I looked at my better half and suggested, "Let's split up. Niamh can come with me and interview the staff, Foster with you as you do your magic thing, see if anything comes up. After, let's give Giada's room a thorough scrutiny."

Henri gave a nod in agreement. "Hopefully something turns up there. After we do that, we should return to the police station, put these in evidence lockup, and find dinner," Henri suggested. "That lunch on the train didn't go far. We'll also need to plan out the interviews for the house guests. I'm sure they're all back at their homes by now. Wherever those are."

I sighed. Day one and we already had a dozen interviews lined up. "We definitely have our work cut out for us."

I feel like you jinxed us by saying that.

I may have. I do that from time to time.
At least we have more clues now?

Yay clues.

I heard that sarcasm, don't think I didn't.

Report 08: No Two Stories the Same

I started with Detti, as I'd already been introduced to the butler and I had to start somewhere. We settled at the kitchen table, so I had an easy way to write notes, Niamh in the chair next to me.

Detti's expression made his round face look like a sad bulldog. He was trying to be professional, though, and help us, and I appreciated that.

I gave him my best smile. "Mr. Detti, thanks for this, I know it's hard. Right now, any information you can give me helps. I need an idea of what happened the day Giada died. Just start in the morning, work upwards from there. I understand she had a house party?"

He took the opening I gave him, nodding. "She did. Lady Giada loved having company over. It wasn't unusual for a friend to be over every week."

Niamh interrupted here. "Why call her that? Shouldn't she be Lady Barese?"

Ah. Good catch. I didn't always remember all the cultural rules—Henri was my safety net for that, so I was glad Niamh had the same instincts. Under etiquette rules, because Giada was born to nobility, she should be addressed by last name, not first.

"She hated the name," Detti explained. "Even mentioning her late husband or his mother made her upset. She refused to be called by it. We settled upon Lady Giada to appease her."

"I see. Thank you, please continue," I said.

"The guests were all good friends of Lady Giada's. We had Sophie and Arthur Li Fonti, Eva Graham, Raelynn Collins, and Atticus Williams all visiting. Of course, her lover, Felipe Iadanza was already in residence."

I jotted down the names quickly, trying to keep track. I'd need to speak with all of these people later, after all.

"Did they all arrive at the same time?"

"No, they arrived at different times over the course of the morning. None of them stayed at the house, either, they left again and returned in the evening. I'm not sure what the issue was, but almost as soon as Mr. Williams arrived, he and Lady Giada fell into a quarrel. I could hear the shouting even in the kitchen. Lady Giada stormed out afterwards, heading for the beach, and Mr. Williams left for town immediately as well. Mr. and Mrs. Li Fonti also left, I'm not sure where, although like I said, everyone returned by the evening. When Lady Giada did return, she was—well, I don't want to say ambushed, but..." Detti made a sour face. "Iadanza was practically lying in wait for her. They argued as soon as they laid eyes upon each other, ending with Lady Giada storming into her bedroom and refusing to come out again, not even for dinner. I didn't see her again after she went into that room."

"What time did she retreat to her room?"

"Early evening, I'd say around six o'clock."

"Was it common for Lady Giada and Iadanza to argue?" Niamh asked.

"These days, they did nothing but that," Detti answered with a sigh. "They were so silly with each other at first, giddy with new love, you know how it goes. It barely lasted a month after he moved in. It didn't take long for him to show his true colors."

Dun-dun-dun. I sensed something juicy. "You didn't like Iadanza, I take it."

"No one did," Detti assured me flatly. "He was the worst sort of man. All show, no substance. I think if Lady Giada hadn't been so heartbroken over her second marriage, she'd have seen him for what he really was. She certainly figured it out before her death. She talked to me about the best way to get rid of him."

Oh-ho. The plot thickened. "Did he know he was on his way out?"

"I think he sensed something. He kept pestering her about divorcing her husband and marrying him. He'd made an effort to be sweet to her again but it was too late, she'd seen his true colors. She'd have none of it when he tried charming her. It led to many, many arguments. I advised her to just throw him out, to have a policeman standing by in case he resorted to violence. I'm not sure why she delayed. Well, she was having her spells."

"The strange moods and dizzy spells you mentioned earlier?"

"Yes. Truly disturbing to witness, her spells. Do you have any idea how horrible it is to have someone you've known for years look at you with no recognition in their eyes?" Detti paused a moment to compose himself, clearing his throat. "The spells also interfered with her sleeping. She'd often wake at all hours of the night or not sleep at all, and be ravenous. We started preparing snacks for her, as she'd consume anything on hand if we didn't."

Now that was interesting. It kinda sounded like someone who'd gotten high and needed munchies afterwards.

Niamh picked up on this too. "Was she perhaps taking some kind of medication or drug that gave her side effects?"

"No, not to my knowledge. She had a sedative prescribed by her doctor, but that was the only thing she'd take. She'd tried something to help with the dizzy spells as well, but it didn't work. And Lady Giada was not the type for recreational drug use, she detested that sort of thing."

I didn't think a drug to make you sleep would cause munchies, but I'd definitely look into it. "Where's that sedative now?"

"On her bedside table."

I made a note. "Has anyone been in her bedroom since that night?"

"We tried to stay out of it, but there's been a few people.

Her mother, of course, Lord Barese came to collect a few things for sentimental reasons…" Detti trailed off, brow furrowed as he thought. "I can't think of anyone else. I locked it after she went missing, as I feared what Iadanza would do if he could lay hands upon her jewelry."

So the level of trust for her lover was that low, huh? Now that told me something. "I'll need the key to get in. I have to investigate that room."

"Of course." Detti pulled a keyring out of his pocket with a rattle and took a key off before handing it over.

"Where is Iadanza?" Niamh inquired. "You've made mention that he lived here, but I've seen no sign of him."

Detti's lip curled. "He took off shortly after Lady Giada went missing. No doubt because we were all so openly suspicious of him. He was packed and gone that very afternoon. I have no idea where he is now, but in my opinion, he definitely had something to do with her death."

"Your suspicion is noted," I assured him, a touch dryly. "Of the other house guests, do you know where they live?"

"I do. The Li Fontis are vacationing here in Ashbluff, they have a bungalow near the town center, and Mr. Williams lives near them. Both Ms. Graham and Ms. Collins are in Ginart."

Detti was seriously saving me effort and time by rattling that off. It's not like I could Google people or use the white pages, after all. "Thank you so much. Is there anything else you want to tell us?"

He sat there for a long moment before sighing, shoulders dropping. "I want you to understand that none of us on staff would have hurt her. Lady Giada was fickle, sometimes, but a generous and sweet woman. She was one of the best employers I've ever had. If we could have prevented this from happening, we would have."

The poor man really did look torn up about this. "I understand, Mr. Detti. Thank you. If I need help again, I'll call for you?"

"Please do, Detective. Please do."

"Right now, I need to speak to the next person."

"I suggest Sivi, as she needs to leave to take care of her son."

"Sivi, then."

Detti got up, leaving the kitchen to go and fetch the next person. I leaned into Niamh's side and muttered, "Wanna bet the lover did it?"

"No bet," she muttered back.

"Spoilsport." Statistically speaking, odds were good Iadanza was our man, even if I couldn't begin to prove it at the moment.

Sivi was a sweet-faced woman with a matronly build, wearing a maid's outfit of black and white, her hands twisted together nervously. Some people were nervous in front of cops no matter if they were innocent or not, and she might well be the type, so I just gave her a smile and waved her to the chair across from mine.

"Please, Ms. Sivi, relax. We're trying to establish timeline and get your take on the house that day. We'll get you out of here in fifteen minutes so you can go get your son, okay?"

She visibly relaxed, by about fifty percent, and gave me a tentative smile in return as she took the chair. "Thank you, Detective. My mother watches him, but she can't do it in the evenings, so I really can't stay here long."

"I totally understand. We'll make this quick. Now, I understand the day of Giada's disappearance, there was a lot of arguing going on between the friends."

"Oh, I don't know anything about that," Sivi denied, shaking her head. "The house was quiet, strangely so, as people barely popped in before leaving again."

Uh, what? "You didn't hear any arguments?"

"No."

"What were you doing throughout the day?"

"I was upstairs freshening up the bedrooms for the guests."

"Ah. So, say, if an argument was taking place in the front of the house, would you be able to hear it?"

"No, not at all. This house seems to swallow sound."

"You didn't see any of the guests, then?"

"Only Ms. Graham and Ms. Collins, as they came upstairs to claim their bedrooms and put their bags inside. They freshened up a bit and chatted with me about doing fireworks that night on the beach—which I thought an odd thing to try, as a storm was blowing in and it was incredibly windy—but they were so keen on the idea, I didn't have the heart to say so."

"Did they do fireworks that night?"

"No, it never happened. Lady Giada was shut up in her room all day and refused to come out. Detti said she'd argued with Iadanza, again. She often would seclude herself in her room and write in her diary when she'd fought with him."

It was funny, not a single person had spoken of Iadanza politely. No mister for him, huh. The way she said his name was like she'd spied dog crap on the floor, too. "Did you see her come out at all after she went in?"

"No."

"No sign that she might have snuck out to get a snack from the kitchen?"

"Nothing like that. I did make up a plate for her, after Cook made dinner for the guests, and set it aside in case she was hungry later. It was still on the stove the next morning."

Knowing what I did, Giada might not have had a chance to get to the kitchen before being scared out of the house. "When did Iadanza leave?"

"The very afternoon we realized she was missing." Sivi's lip curled. "He fled like a guilty rat. Detti watched him pack, just in case he tried to make off with any of the valuables."

"Anything strike you as odd that night? Strange noises, anything?"

"I really can't say, Detective. I don't stay here at night."

"Ah, right. You leave in the early evening and you're back here by…when?"

"Six am. I help Cook prepare breakfast and get the house running."

"Got it." I couldn't think of anything else to ask her, as she wasn't even here when things went down. "Thank you,

Ms. Sivi. If I have follow-up questions, I'll come find you."

She was just relieved to be done, I could tell, and barely gave us a smile before scurrying out.

"Not helpful," Niamh observed.

"Nope. Hopefully, next person saw something." I hopped up to go into the next room, where the staff was waiting in the dining room, and called for Tesfay, the footman. "Mr. Tesfay, come in please."

Tesfay was the youngest of the staff by a good ten years. He barely looked old enough to be out of high school, frankly, with some baby fat still lingering on his cheeks. He was the type to be homely-handsome—not ugly, just nothing to write home about.

He was also so nervous that he couldn't meet my eyes.

I tried not to be suspicious of him because of that alone, but innocent people rarely got that jittery around me. Then again, it could be because I'm the Shinigami Detective. That did set people on edge.

I pointed him to a chair and tried to show with my body language that I wouldn't eat him. This might have gone over better if Clint hadn't hopped up on the table and bent an unnerving stare at him.

Tesfay stared back, pressing into the back of his chair like he was trying to phase through it. "Why is it looking at me like that?"

Clint gave a sniff before assuring me, "No planty smell."

Oh, was that what he'd been checking? "Thanks, bud. Relax, Mr. Tesfay, he's a Felix. He helps us with investigations. Now, a few questions for you. On the day of Lady Giada's disappearance, where were you and what were you doing? Was it a normal day?"

He gulped, still staring at Clint like his face was in danger of being eaten off, but he did answer. "It was normal."

Not helpful, dude. Try again. "So what were you doing?"

"Uh, mostly helping the guests take their bags upstairs. Lady Giada had me dig out the fireworks from storage." He sat there, frowning like a kid who couldn't remember a math formula for a final test. "I can't remember doing anything in particular."

It was two weeks ago, granted. But still. He was too young for memory problems, surely. "So nothing out of the ordinary because you'd remember it? Okay. Were the houseguests in the house most of the day?"

"No, didn't really see anyone. Mr. Williams, he didn't like the look of the fireworks, so he went into town to buy new ones. I didn't see anyone else after he left. Cook said Lady Giada was having one of her spells and was lying down in her room, and the guests kind of fended for themselves after dinner that evening. I did fetch a light charm for Ms. Collins, as she said she's been having insomnia and wanted to be able to walk around, before going to bed myself."

Now wait a second, I thought Giada was in her room sulking because of a fight with her lover? Not because she was feeling off. "Are you sure it was a spell that sent Lady Giada to her room?"

"Well, that's what Cook said."

"But you didn't actually see her."

Tesfay shrugged, like any other bewildered teenager when pressed for answers. "Well, no."

Heaven preserve me from unreliable witnesses. "Thanks, Tesfay, you can go. Send Cook in, will you?"

He lumbered out and Niamh and I shared a speaking look. It was a different matter if Giada hadn't felt physically well that day, because the odds of her getting dizzy and falling into the ocean on her own went up. It didn't explain why she was running around like crazy at night, though.

Cook looked like she sampled a lot of her own cooking, if you catch my drift. She seemed like a generally happy person, as there was a lot of laugh lines around her eyes, but right now she was in mourning clothes, her face drawn. She sat heavily, making the poor wooden chair creak in protest, and her eyes were already full of tears.

"Oh Detective, you don't know our Lady Giada, but please don't think she'd take her own life!"

Um. I didn't say that?

"She was such a warm, caring person," Cook rambled on, already picking up steam. "You know, she hired me when I was having the worst luck, almost losing my own house, and it was only because of her generosity that I was even able to pick the pieces backup after my own dear husband's death. That was two years ago, you know, and even when she married that no-account husband of hers, she didn't let me go, just let me stay in the house and—"

Yeah. This interview might take a hot minute. Hopefully she knew something, though, otherwise I'd be sitting here for the next hour without a thing to show for it.

Report 09: Lifestyles of the Rich and...Noble

yeah that failed

Were you trying to quote something??

The staff interviews gave us an idea of timeline and who to interview next, which I could only hope would give us better info, because they really hadn't seen much. It also wasn't clear if Giada had retreated to her bedroom because she was feeling ill or because she'd lost her temper with Iadanza.

Either way, I wanted to really search her room and see if there was a clue there that other people had overlooked. She'd run out of there in the middle of the night in nothing but a robe and slippers. Something happened in that room. I just had to figure out what.

I set Niamh and Foster to searching the office, and Henri and cats went with me to her bedroom. I found the door locked, which was a good sign, as that meant very few people had been stomping all over trace evidence. I unlocked the door, pulled on my trusty work gloves and started on one side of the room, Clint walking the perimeter of the other.

The room was something I expected from a woman of this status: very large, with open space on all sides of a king-sized bed that sat smack in the middle of the room, framed on either side by large French doors leading out to the garden. The furniture was delicate in appearance, a soft dove grey, and it was the epitome of the rich version of 'beach vacation.' I'd seen something similar on an HGTV episode once, I was sure of it.

I went through her clothes first, getting a sense of what she normally wore. It all looked like designer labels in strong jewel tones. She'd been a model once, and it showed in her wardrobe choices. Based on what we'd gathered from her friends and family, Giada liked being pretty and took good care of her health.

"Bottle of sedative," Henri informed me, holding it up from her nightstand. "Looks like it's about half empty."

"So she was using it regularly."

"Seems that way. The dosage is...rather substantial, more than I'd use for a woman of her size." Henri frowned at the label. "For that matter, I wouldn't feel comfortable taking this dosage myself."

"Really, that strong? Was her insomnia that bad?"

"A very excellent question to ask her physician. If it was, it's strange that no one else remarked upon it except Detti."

Henri went about bagging and tagging that, then pulled out a wand and went around the room, doing his usual diagnostics. He was looking for any trace amounts of blood, or magic, and I left him to it. I was looking for something else entirely. Some sign of forced entry, or signs of a struggle.

Nothing about this room indicated anything violent had gone down, though. Detti said no one had cleaned in here, so it wasn't like it had been straightened up. There just wasn't anything markedly out of place.

Clint came back to me with his nose all wrinkled up. "Jamie."

"Yeah, bud?"

"Something smells."

I sank down onto my haunches, head canted in question. I'd learned to pay attention when Clint told me that. "Yeah? Can you describe it for me?"

Those purple ears of his moved back and forth, catching and dismissing errant sounds even as he thought. "Planty," he finally said. "It smells planty."

"Same smell as the trail's?"

"Yeah, same."

"Well, well, well. Ain't that interesting. Let's ask the staff later if there used to be plants in here that they took out."

Clint hopped up onto the nearest chair, which was

pulled slightly away from the desk. The desk was definitely something that saw regular use. I say that because it didn't have delicate, cute things sitting on it. There were books, letters tucked into the top cubbyholes, wax stamps and seals, and traces of ink on the light grey top. Giada liked to use this desk, and it hinted something important might be in here.

I pulled some of the letters out first, skimming through them. About half were from her estranged husband, begging for reconciliation. I wondered if she wrote him back? She kept them, for whatever reason, so I definitely needed to follow up with him. I tucked those into another evidence bag and labeled it. The other letters were from various friends, one from a brother, and I made a mental note to go through them more carefully and add them to our interview list. It never hurt to contact every person in a victim's life. People really didn't understand just how much they knew, sometimes.

That exhausted the top of the desk, so I started opening drawers. The main drawer immediately proved interesting. It was pretty jampacked with odds and ends, but the center of the drawer was perfectly empty, the space rectangular in shape.

"Something sat here," I observed.

Clint poked his head over the edge of the drawer. "What?"

"A book of some kind. Maybe a diary? The staff said she wrote regularly in one. But something sat here, and recently enough that the stuff in this drawer didn't shuffle around. Hmm. Okay, that needs to be followed up on as well." I opened the side drawer next to it and noted a similar phenomenon where the back of the drawer was packed with random crap, but the front of it was neatly sectioned off. "Annnd something is missing from here, too. How interesting."

Clint leaned in to get another sniff. "Planty."

My eyes sharpened on him. "Plants again? Inside the drawer?"

"Yeah."

"Weird. Also interesting. Keep that scent in your nose,

my friend. And tell me if you smell it again." I could smell it too, now that he'd pointed it out. It wasn't something that rang a bell for me, just earth and vegetation. I pulled out my magic specs and took a good look around the inside of the drawer, but whatever this was, it wasn't magical in nature. Absolutely nothing stood out. I put them away again, now more curious than ever. Just what was this stuff?

"Henri, anything strange about this desk?"

Henri came over, did another spell, then canted his head at the result. "Nothing magical, at least. No sign of blood, either."

Phil leaned in from his perch on Henri's shoulder, nose going a mile a minute. "Planty."

"Look, when I have two cats telling me the same thing, something's weird." I looked around the desk. "If there's a strong plant smell here, then it means something was here to cause it. Something that's been moved. Was it just taken out and Detti didn't think to mention it? Or was it important?"

"A good questi—" *Knock, knock.* Henri cut himself off, turning to the door.

Detti leaned inside, expression caught between being apologetic and aggravated. "Sorry to interrupt, but there's a reporter outside that simply will not leave. She's trying to force her way in, in fact."

I groaned. Ah, the bane of my existence had decided to grace me with its presence. How lovely. "Right, I'll go out and deal with them. Detti, quick question, was there any sort of bouquet or plant here by the desk?"

Detti looked at the desk, puzzled, then shook his head. "No, Detective, nothing of that sort. Why?"

Well now I'm just curious. "Never mind. Thanks."

Henri leaned into my side and murmured, "Don't murder them, my dear."

"Don't tempt me," I muttered back, already striding for the door, Henri following.

I made it to the front of the house in record time, mostly because I didn't want a reporter sneaking in and taking pictures of something they shouldn't. I could hear her before I saw her, and I groaned in true grievance as I hit the main foyer.

King was here.

I ask you, oh fate, what have I done to piss you off? Huh?

Of all the reporters, I hated her the most. It wasn't the oh-so-prissy way she dressed, or the mousy way she talked like she had rodents in her family line. It was the way she persisted in making up a story that had very little to do with the facts. This case was already sensational enough without ad-libbing, but I just knew she was going to twist it all out of proportion the minute she could lay hands on a typewriter. She was that kind of malicious.

No helping it. No one else here was qualified enough to drive her off. I kept Clint in hand—he liked to go attack-kitty on King—as I stepped through the front door. "King."

She paused, no longer arguing with Tesfay, who was physically barring her from entering the house. Her lavender hat sat askew on top of her head, so they'd really been tussling before I came out. "Detective. Well, well, why are you here? This is very outside your jurisdiction."

I really didn't want to say this. But if I didn't, she'd try to report me, and that would just get all sorts of things muddled. "I'm here as a kingsman consultant. Now, leave."

She whipped out her camera, took a step back, and snapped a shot of me.

If I broke her camera, it'd be totally understandable, right? Right?

I tried imagining explaining this to the higher-ups. Even in my head, it didn't go well.

"King, for the love of everything holy and unholy." I groaned, eyes rolling. "What good does my picture do for you?"

"A great deal," she purred. "Now, Detective, do tell me why you're on this particular case instead of someone else? Like the local police."

"Lady Giada, as a member of the aristocracy, falls under

the jurisdiction of the kingsmen," Henri interrupted smoothly. "Especially since her body was found in international waters and washed up ashore in a different city, it was deemed unsuitable for the local police to handle this investigation. Does that answer your question, Ms. King?"

Oh, nicely put, partner. I gave him an admiring look. He was so smooth about side-stepping the real reason.

"Is there question, then, on how Lady Barese died?"

Yeah, no, we're not playing the twenty-questions game. No point, she'd just misquote me later anyway. "We're not discussing an open investigation, King. Leave now."

Her mouth went flat, eyes like chips of ice. "You'll have to provide answers to the public, Shinigami Detective. You can't avoid that."

"How about when I have answers, I'll give them? Right now I only have speculation and a lot of weird facts. Good day, King."

She didn't like it, she really didn't, and she tried one more foray. "Was her lover, Felipe Iadanza, the one who murdered her?"

"Good *day*, Ms. King," Henri said with authority.

Thwarted, she growled in disgust, gathered up her skirts, and stomped off.

Did I think I had seen the last of her? Absolutely not. She was just retreating to make me think that. When I least expected it, she'd pop up again. Like a mosquito.

I asked Henri, "Is it bad that my main motivation for solving this case is to shake King off my tail?"

He snorted in dry amusement. "Understandable, if nothing else. Come, back to work."

As I followed him back in, Clint whispered to me, "Next time, I attack-kitty."

I high-fived him because that? That was the best idea ever.

Jamie! Do not encourage that behavior.

I, of course, have no idea what you mean.

Report 10: House Party

I can no longer use those words without the Super Junior song popping in my head.

Don't you dare start singing it. It gets stuck in my head.

This is my house party!

HOUSE PARTY!

This is my house party!

COME ON NOW!

I hate you both.

All of the interviews yesterday and searching Giada's bedroom didn't lead to anything. Unfortunately. We had a whole new round of leads to follow up today, though, and I was determined to find something that made sense of the clues I'd already been handed. I also needed breakfast first because the little grey cells were not awake.

Henri, Niamh, and I were sitting at breakfast in our hotel's restaurant, mostly finished, when my pad lit up with a call. I fished it out and saw Weber calling me. Oh good, more clues! Or at least, I hoped that would prove to be the case.

I accepted the call and answered with, "Weber, tell me something good."

"*Detective. I've finished my examination if you're ready for an oral report.*"

"Would love one. We're short on clues at the moment."

"*I can confirm that the deceased was dead before she hit the water. There's trace amounts of water in her lungs, but the alveoli isn't damaged enough for this to be a drowning. I'm confident in saying she was dead before she hit the water. The sea-life did a rough job on her—I suggest a closed-casket funeral—but a few interesting things to note. One: her neck, shoulder, arm, one leg, and four ribs were broken. All from a strong impact—I think from her fall. Two: her underclothes were all intact and there's no sign of sexual abuse. Three: I saw no sign of defensive wounds. She's bruised, but in all the wrong places.*"

"So she wasn't attacked, that's what you're getting at."

"*I can't find any sign of that, no. I'm afraid I can't tell you much else. She wasn't pregnant, either, by the way. I did a basic toxicology panel on her, but whatever was in her blood is long gone now, if she took anything.*"

"Thanks, Weber. Any trace elements on her hands?"

"*Nothing that I could find. Again, the sea-life did a number on her soft tissue, not to mention being in the water for two weeks probably washed away any trace evidence.*"

"I figured, but had to ask. Anything caught in the clothing?"

"*Nothing of real interest. There were a few shards of glass embedded in the sole of the slipper. I tagged those, although I'm not sure if they'll help in any way. The only other thing I did find strange was her nightgown didn't match her slipper, as it was blue and the slipper pink, but make of that what you will.*"

We all startled a bit and looked at each other. One pink slipper and the other blue?

"You're certain it's pink?" I inquired.

"*Yes, why?*"

"We found the other slipper she wore that night and it was blue. Same as the robe. Why the mismatched slipper? Are you sure the sea water didn't somehow change the color?"

"*Oh, the seawater did damage, but the nightgown color remained more or less identifiable. This was definitely pink.*"

Niamh asked, "Was she in that much of a rush to get out of her room that she didn't realize she'd put on mismatching slippers?"

"I mean, she was running around in a nightgown and robe. Obviously she was in a tearing hurry." But more than I anticipated, if her slippers didn't match. I wondered if they were the same style, something easily confused in dim lighting? "Weber, you said glass shards. Green glass shards?"

"*Yes, as a matter of fact. Oh, does this make sense to you?*"

"It matches with the other slipper. It had green glass in the sole, too. Do us all a favor. When you send up that report, send the clothing items with it."

Likely being in the sea would have removed any and all

trace evidence, but I wanted Henri to test it, see if there was something those clothes could tell us.

"*I certainly will. I'll send it up by train today. Is there anything else I can do?*"

"Just a death certificate is all I need from you."

"*That, I can complete and send along with the clothes.*"

"You've given us some good information," I assured him. "Thanks, Weber."

"*You're more than welcome. Good luck.*"

"We'll need it. Can you release the body at this point for funeral rites?"

"*Certainly. She can't tell me anything else, really. I'll fill out the necessary form and release her for transport. Just tell me what address to send her to.*"

"I'll message it to you later, after I confirm with the family," I promised. "Thank you. Have a safe trip home."

"*I will. Keep me updated, will you? I'm invested in this case.*"

"I certainly will." I ended the call and replaced the pad in my pocket.

Henri had a look on his face that suggested he was thinking hard. "Well, this does and doesn't answer a few questions. I really wish Weber had said yes, she'd been stabbed, definitely murder. At least then I'd know what I'm looking at."

I nodded in sour agreement. "Cause of death would be helpful in this case. This is too open-ended to give us a solid answer. Well, Henri, pick your poison. Interviews or go looking for Iadanza?"

Henri drew in a breath and let it out slowly. "I think, in this case, Iadanza. Niamh will have a cold trail to follow and might need some assistance. With everything said on the man, I truly suspect he was involved somehow, and it'd be better if we could lay hands on him quickly."

"Totally agree." I turned to Niamh, checking in with her.

She gave me a nod. "I'll try to pick up his trail from the house."

"Okay. I guess that means Foster and I do interviews with

the house guests."

"Good luck, my dear," Henri offered wryly. "Hopefully someone will have a vital clue to hand you."

"If that happens, I'll eat both shoes." Witnesses were terrible, but still, you never knew what someone else knew. Sometimes, too, just the disconnect between stories told you where the gaping hole was.

I used our hotel's phone to make calls and get interviews lined up. Everyone at Giada's house party was of the idle rich—except her lover, an artist. I took the artist part with a grain of salt as I'd seen no evidence of even a sketchbook in Giada's house. An artist without any tools of the trade? Kinda weird.

Foster and I headed out to our first interview. Sophie and Arthur Li Fonti had a nice little vacation house on the opposite end of town from Giada's. It was very much a summer bungalow, not meant for parties, but something for a relaxed vacation. The driveway was lined with seashells and neatly trimmed hedges, the yard tiny but perfectly manicured. Someone kept up with the place.

The taxi driver stopped in front of their house and I leaned in, touching his shoulder.

"I don't anticipate this to be more than fifteen minutes, can you wait?"

"Of course, Kingsman," he assured me brightly.

"Thanks." It was odd hearing people address me as a kingsman. I wasn't that—yet. But I was functioning in that capacity so chose to roll with it.

Getting out, I went ahead of Foster and knocked on the door. He'd had a little practice with the staff yesterday, but I'd stay lead and let him watch and observe.

A pretty werefox maid wearing a sensible dress and apron answered the door. "Yes?"

"I'm Jamie Edwards, Kingsman Consultant. I have an appointment with the Li Fontis?"

"Oh yes, they're expecting you. Come through."

She took our coats, hanging them on a rack nearby before

leading us in. The small foyer led into a larger, brighter room that was predominantly windows, a hearth with a fire in it, and comfortable chairs and sofas. Definitely a hangout spot.

"Kingsman Edwards, my lady," the maid introduced.

A woman—presumably the lady of the house—stood to greet us, her eyes taking me in curiously. She had quite possibly the darkest skin I'd ever seen on a person, ebony black, her soft dark hair a perfect match. She was, in a word, stunning, and the bright yellow dress she wore emphasized it. She looked to be of an age with Giada, somewhere around her thirties, as did the man seated next to her.

"Kingsman Edwards, do come in. This is my husband, Arthur."

Arthur was as pale as his wife was dark, the epitome of a cream-and-milk complexion, with ruddy freckles over a hawkish nose. Not a bad-looking man at all, and his smile was charming as he shook my hand.

"Kingsman," he greeted cordially.

"Hello and thank you for speaking with us. This is Kingsman Foster."

More hellos went around before Sophie gestured us toward a couch. "Please, do sit. Tell us how we can help. Giada's death was just dreadful, perfectly dreadful, and I'm... still quite torn over it all."

She did look upset, the way anyone would when losing a friend. Arthur did as well, his face tight and pinched.

"You don't suspect suicide, do you?" Sophie asked uneasily. "Because I don't think Giada would."

"Right now, we don't suspect anything. We don't have enough facts to even guess. It's why we're speaking to you. We need a better understanding of what happened that day, of your impression of what was going on. I understand the house party was meant to be a fun day at the beach with fireworks?"

Arthur nodded immediately. "Yes, that was the plan. The plan was shot down rather quickly once we arrived, though. She and Felipe were constantly fighting and he'd already started an argument with her that morning. When we arrived, she looked ready to call it a day, and wasn't really in the mood for company, although she tried to put on a good face."

I nodded. So far, that lined up with what Detti had told us yesterday.

"What were they fighting about?" Foster asked.

"That, we're not really sure on." Sophie glanced at her husband uncertainly. "We only caught the tail end of it."

"I imagine it was the usual," Arthur opined. "Felipe only had two things he seemed to talk about."

Sophie rolled her eyes. "Yes, that's true enough."

I gave them a smile. "Do fill me in."

"Felipe is an artist," Arthur informed me, tone so droll that it was clear he didn't actually mean those words. "As much as I'm an artist, anyway, and I can't draw a reliable stick figure. He had the supposed artist's temperament—dramatic. He was constantly going off about something, passionate and high-tempered. We have no idea what Giada saw in him that made her take the man on, but she did seem to have terrible taste in men."

"Truly," Sophie responded with a sad smile. "She loved to be in love, but I'm not sure she knew what to do once she was in it. If that makes sense."

"It does. I know many a person who fits that description. So you don't think he was an artist?"

"No. Or, at least, I never saw him draw a single line. And he didn't even speak of painting or sculpting or any of that. He moved from patron to patron. That's how Giada met him—at a house party of one of his former patron's." Arthur frowned a little, brows drawing in. "I think that was almost four months ago? They fell into each other rather quickly and he basically moved in with her within the month. And then started treating her like a patron instead of a lover, constantly demanding she pay some bill or other for him."

"This wasn't usual for Giada," Sophie commented. "Usually, the men she gravitated to were very established in life. Well to-do, or hard working. I think she was initially under the impression that Felipe was a good artist who was just having trouble selling his work and was between good luck. She knew painfully well what that was like. It wasn't until recently that she realized it was something of a sham. She spoke to me about getting rid of him, but she wasn't sure how to do it or if she was being too hard on him."

I kept my pencil poised over my notebook. "When did she talk to you about that?"

"The week before the party." Sophie paused, counting things out on her fingers. "Yes, I think that's right. I'm not sure who all she pulled into her confidence, but I advised her to get rid of him. Really, her husband was so much better for her. I told her that, too, suggested they should reconcile. But she hated her mother-in-law, and her husband refused to move far from his mama. Moving back to him would have meant putting herself back in that woman's sphere, and she wasn't willing to do it. Not that I blamed her. Still, she agreed Felipe was more of a headache than he was worth. I think she was seriously considering giving him the boot after the house party."

"I heard Felipe wanted to marry her?"

Arthur snorted in dark amusement. "Yes, that was the other thing they liked to argue about. Felipe was forever going on about her divorcing her husband so he could marry her. She never would commit to it. We're not sure why, really. She didn't seem motivated to patch things up with her husband, so why hang onto him? But she'd made no move to end the marriage. And neither had he."

Considering she'd divorced the first husband readily enough, I found that interesting. Why the hesitation? What did I not know? It was often these hidden things that shed light on the picture as a whole.

"Do you think Felipe realized he was on the way out?" I asked.

They both nodded without hesitation.

"Oh, definitely." Sophie's face drew up in a grimace.

"Under the yelling, he was clearly upset and afraid. I don't know that he had a place to go if Giada threw him out. He'd burned several bridges already."

I couldn't wait to talk to him. Assuming he'd talk to me. "Alright, so let's start at the beginning and walk through the day. I need a timeline of who was where. You came to Giada's house at what time?"

"Just before lunch," Arthur answered. "I want to say about eleven. We meant to have lunch with her, plan things out for the evening, but we didn't really get a chance. We did eat lunch—her staff laid that out for us—but there was so much contention between her and Felipe, it became a bad atmosphere very quickly."

"It didn't help when Atticus arrived," Sophie tacked on, rolling her eyes in clear exasperation.

Foster was taking his own notes and glanced up to clarify, "Atticus Williams? One of the other guests at the house party?"

"Yes. He came straight in and asked about the fireworks for some reason. When Giada told him they were leftovers from last year, he went on and on about how they probably wouldn't work and why had she even bothered with them, why hadn't she bought new? He demanded she go into town with him to see if there were any to be found. He was annoying in the extreme. I think Giada was ready to bash a vase over his head."

Arthur tempered this with, "Atticus has these moments where he hyper-fixates on something. He never really means anything by it; sometimes he just fixates on things until they're 'fixed.' I agreed he had a point—some of the fireworks might not work after being stored a year—but they'd all been kept dry, so odds were most would. But the minute I said that, he went off again about how we needed something new, and I think Giada took it as me agreeing with him. It upset her, and she stormed off, going who knows where."

"Atticus felt bad about upsetting her." Sophie shook her head. "He does get into those intense moods. I told him she'd already had a rough morning and that he needed to drop the matter, but he went into town instead to see if he could buy fireworks on his own. He said he'd meet us on the beach later that evening."

"So did you see him at all the rest of the day?"

"No, not really. None of us made it down to the beach that evening. He came back for dinner at...roughly six?" Sophie checked with Arthur again, nodding when he did. "I believe that's right. He was all aflutter that we hadn't gone down, but I told him none of us were in the mood to be out there, and he finally gave up on the fireworks. He ate dinner with us, then went to the parlor and played chess with Arthur for a while."

"Atticus is always a good challenge, and we were there for a while."

I realized they'd skipped ahead so drew them back. "Back up a little for me. Atticus came in around lunch and then left. What did you do after that? And when did Raelynn Collins and Eva Graham arrive?"

Sophie answered easily, "Oh, they came in together, right around when Atticus did. We'd planned to have lunch with Giada, you see. But when it was obvious Giada wasn't willing to sit and eat with us or plan things out, they chose to go down for a walk on the beach. Arthur and I were uncomfortable in the atmosphere of the house. We chose not to stay, either, so we went into town to shop before returning to have dinner."

"Not to a better mood, though." Arthur smiled sadly. "When we came back for dinner, it was to find Felipe and Giada in another argument. They were screaming so badly at each other that I couldn't pick out more than one word in three. I'm not even sure what they were quarreling about."

Sophie grimaced. "Really, it was probably the usual. Giada divorcing her husband and marrying him. Why he thought screaming such a thing at her would win her over, I have no idea. Anyway, once they noticed us watching, they broke off the fight. Felipe stormed upstairs, and we didn't see him again. Giada locked herself into her room at that point. We ended up eating dinner without either of them. We were all set to stay the night, so we chose to do so—hoping, I think, that she'd wake up in a better mood and we could salvage the party. But when we awoke the next morning she was nowhere to be found, and the more we searched, the more desperate it looked before we called in the police. They only confirmed our worst fears."

I had some sympathy for her, as that had to be a nightmare. "I'm so sorry. Can you confirm what time you both went to bed, and what time you awoke?"

"Oh, somewhere around ten in the evening, I think." Sophie tacked on, "Well, I retired then. Arthur did the same but then left."

"Couldn't sleep," he explained. His smile looked a little strained, eyes fixated on mine as if he were trying to sell me on a story. "Too restless. I got up so I wouldn't disturb her and went back to the parlor. Just whiled away the time there reading before I felt tired enough to sleep. I want to say it was about midnight when I returned to our room. Slept until nearly nine the next morning."

I made note of all of that. It gave me a better sense of where these two were, at least. I also made note to verify what he'd just told me, as the man was acting a little cagey, and I wasn't sure why. "And you didn't hear, see, anything?"

"No, I'm afraid we didn't." Sophie looked as if she mentally kicked herself for that. "I'm normally a light sleeper, I would have heard something if Giada was up."

I found that a strange comment, as Giada was on the ground floor, the guest bedrooms on the second. Sivi the maid had said she couldn't hear anything from the ground floor if she was upstairs, but I let the comment pass.

"But...well, that night was especially windy. We almost feared a storm would blow through, although it never materialized. It was so noisy outside, I fear it drowned everything out."

Ah. Now that made more sense. Why had no one heard anything? The wind covered any noise Giada made. Sivi had mentioned it was windy that day, but she was the only one who had, so far.

"Do either of you know of anyone who would want to hurt her?"

Both paused and thought about it before Sophie finally said, "No. I really can't think of anyone. Giada was hard to hate—she was too charming for that. Even those she chose to cut out of her life would rather reconcile with her than hurt her. I can't imagine who would want to hurt her."

Arthur sat up a little straighter. "You think someone did?"

"I honestly don't know at this point. We've got more questions than answers, but I have to look at the possibility. You both have been so helpful, thank you. I have one more question for you. Do you know where I can find Felipe?"

"I'm afraid the only contact we had with him was through Giada. I have no idea where he is now."

No one seemed to know where the man was. The address he'd given the cops was my only clue and I wasn't sure how viable it was two weeks later, especially if he was so transitory. I hoped Henri and Niamh caught Iadanza before the man left town altogether. "Got it. Are the two of you planning to stay here for a while?"

"Yes, until we have an idea of when Giada's funeral will be. The family doesn't live too far from here, you see," Arthur explained. "Why? Do you need us to be nearby?"

"In case I have follow-up questions, yes, if you don't mind."

"Not at all. We're in no rush to get back home," Sophie assured me.

"Thank you." We made our goodbyes and walked out into the brisk air. It was always colder near the sea, and I felt it keenly as I wrapped my coat around me.

As we headed for our waiting taxi, Foster noted, "It doesn't seem like they know anything or had anything to do with Giada's death. They're honestly sad and disturbed by it."

"I agree. Something about Arthur, though...he's hiding something. He was acting a little cagey. I want to double-check his whereabouts. I have this nagging sense he was lying to us."

"A serious lie?"

"Not sure. Could be innocent, could be he's nervous talking to a cop, who knows? Still, I want to double-check. I just found his behavior odd. I have no idea if he's our perp, or what his motive would be, but no one's given me a motive for Giada's death so far. Even Iadanza profited more from her living than her death, unless this was a crime of passion. I keep interviewing people hoping to get a motive. And maybe, just maybe, someone saw something they don't realize is important." I paused with my hand on the car door and looked at him. "Sadly, I'm kind of banking on it. There's just nothing about this case that even hints at what happened."

"I don't think you can go back to Queen Regina with an 'I don't know,' either." Foster shivered as if someone had danced across his grave. "I just got chills imagining it."

"Yeah, I'd rather not. Reporting that I haven't figured it out yet makes me uncomfortable." I opened the door and climbed in, glad the cats hadn't come with me for the interviews. They'd be bored hopping from one place to another, talking to people. Besides, they were of better use trying to track down Iadanza. Knowing them, they'd already challenged Niamh on who could find the man first. "Alright, next interview. Let's see what Atticus Williams has to say."

Atticus wasn't far, just a few streets over, so it was a quick hop, skip, and a jump to his house. He was also in a cute bungalow with a perfect yard, similar to the Li Fontis except for the color of the house: a creamy yellow with blue trim and door. Unlike the other two, who waited for me to knock at the door, he was hovering next to the window, watching for our arrival. I barely got to the door before he yanked it open, words tumbling over each other.

"Kingsman Foster and Edwards, am I right? Of course I'm right—the red uniform gives it away. Do come in out of this cold. I'm Atticus Williams, of course—you knew that. Come in, come in, I'm most keen to speak with you."

Who spiked his Sprite? Seriously, he was almost bouncing in place, looking like an affable hobbit on speed. The three-piece suit, bushy sideburns, and pudgy body strongly reinforced that impression.

Stepping in, I found the house to be far more pleasing than the Li Fontis'. It was more lived in, with books stacked on every surface and the furniture looking inviting and cozy. I saw a haphazard attempt at holiday decorating—really just some greenery tacked onto the mantel and a box of decorations sitting nearby. He'd clearly lost motivation partway in. At his urging, I settled into a chair near the fire, Foster next to me. Atticus plopped into what was obviously his favorite armchair, immediately tucking a blanket around his legs.

"I really can't stand this cold," he fussed as he sat, his tenor voice not matching his looks whatsoever. "I get chilled easily. Now, do tell me what I can help you with. Giada was a dear friend. I'm so upset with her death, truly upset."

His eyes were a touch bright saying this, and he had a hard time meeting my eyes as he confessed the sentiment. I felt a twinge of sympathy for him. I knew how hard it was to lose a friend. "I'm so sorry, Mr. Williams. I know this is hard. I'll try to be brief. Can you give me an outline of events the day of the party?"

"In retrospect, I could just kick myself. I really angered her, and I didn't mean to, I was just anxious for things to go well. I arrived early that morning for the party and talked to her about the fireworks we'd use that night. I was concerned they wouldn't function properly, and then we'd all be disappointed. She was already upset—likely because of Iadanza—and my questions to her only tipped her over the edge."

I interrupted him. "Why do you suspect it was because of Iadanza?"

"Oh, he kept storming into the room, huffing at her with this manner like she'd done something to upset him on purpose, and then storming out again." Atticus rolled his eyes heavenward. "It was just like watching a toddler throw a tantrum. I asked her why she put up with him, and she assured me she wouldn't for much longer. Iadanza overheard her, as he stormed back in and they started screaming at each other. I left to give them privacy to sort it out, but when I came back down again, I tried to follow up with her about the fireworks. It was the wrong tactic. She wasn't in the mood to be rational, and when Arthur chimed in, it set her off badly. She stormed off, and we ended up eating lunch without her. I was still worried about the fireworks, so I went out at that point and tried to buy some new ones."

So far, this more or less matched what I'd been told. He came in earlier than the Li Fontis realized, but I didn't care about that. "And after?"

"Hmm, I returned for dinner, only to see them in another row. They broke things off just as I entered, so I'm not sure what it was about, but I didn't see either Iadanza or Giada the rest of the evening. They both shut themselves up in their rooms. We ate dinner at the house, I think hoping Giada's good humor would be restored by morning."

"What did you do that evening?" Foster prompted.

Atticus thought for a moment. "My hopes for the fireworks proved in vain—no one was inclined to go down. A storm was coming in, too, so we chose to stay in. Arthur and I played a game in the parlor. The ladies were chatting over wine, I think. I eventually retired to bed."

"About what time?"

"Oh, ten or so? I did read for a while in bed, as I had a riveting book, so I would say I fell asleep somewhere close to midnight."

I noted down the time. "You didn't leave your room at all?"

"No."

"Hear anything?"

"Just the wind. It was loud, rattled the windows a few times."

"What time did you go back downstairs?"

"The next morning, somewhere around nine? We all gathered for breakfast. We didn't see Giada, but she's a habitually late riser, none of us thought it odd. We passed the morning just idling about until lunch was served. Still, Giada didn't make an appearance and that did worry us enough to check on her. It was then..." He paused and looked upset all over again, reminded no doubt of that morning scene. "It was then that we realized Giada wasn't in her bedroom, or anywhere to be found. We immediately split up and searched, of course. Much good that did. She was already gone, wasn't she."

It wasn't a question. I didn't try to answer it. "Mr. Williams, you've been helpful. Thank you. Can you tell me if she had any enemies?"

"Giada? No. Well, I know her mother-in-law didn't like her, but I can't think of anyone who hated her to the point of hurting her."

"Was she frank about that, then?"

"Giada was not a person who could keep secrets," Atticus assured me dryly. "Everything she thought, she said."

"What about Iadanza? What do you know about him?"

"Frankly? Very little. He wasn't one I would choose to associate with, and if not for Giada, I wouldn't have. He's a very...well, shallow person, to be honest. We had no common ground to speak on aside from Giada. Iadanza chose only to court her favor and had little to say to the rest of us."

"I see." Iadanza really wasn't doing himself any favors by not making friends with his lover's circle. It did leave me with the problem of how to find him, too. "Thank you, Mr. Williams. I'll likely have follow-up questions for you."

"Of course. Please, let me help in whatever way I can."

"I appreciate the offer." I stood, we said goodbye, and I went straight back into the taxi.

Foster closed the door and settled into the seat next to mine. "He wasn't really all that helpful. Aside from verifying the other two's statements."

I sighed, cursing our luck. "Sometimes, that's as helpful as witnesses get."

Report 11: Someone is Lying

"Well, that was a bust," Jamie informed me as she sailed into the room. She stopped long enough to put an arm around my shoulders, hugging me lightly in a hello, before turning and dropping into the chair near mine.

"What was a bust?" I inquired.

"The interviews. No one saw anything helpful, if you exclude multiple witnesses saying Giada and Iadanza had massive fights. Twice," she answered with a grimace. "I've now interviewed all of the house guests and my hopes for a vital clue are sunk like a pirate ship. The only one left is the hated ex-lover. Speaking of, did you find Iadanza?"

Niamh took a chair near Jamie's, looking just as disgruntled. "Sadly, no. He has no means of support with Giada's death, so he's literally hopping from place to place, mooching off of whoever will let him stay as a guest. He's changed houses four times in the past two weeks. And the last house had no idea where he went. He'd gotten into an argument with the lady of the house and stormed out."

"Fiery, isn't he?" I murmured. Truly, what a temper.

"Also stupid, when his temper flares. I understand that he has burned a lot of bridges because of it." Jamie rubbed a tired hand over her face. "You couldn't pick up his trail?"

"I tried. He boarded a train. Tracking someone in a vehicle becomes guesswork unless I can lay hands on the precise vehicle. The train he was on is long gone. I need to find another starting point for him."

I'd tried to aid Niamh's search as much as I could, but we had no other reference point for Iadanza. There was too much in question regarding the man. It was frustrating in the extreme, as he was a key suspect in this case. I knew Niamh felt the frustration keenly, but I had no immediate solution for her.

Niamh grumbled out a curse, slouching further into her chair at the table. "Who knows where he is now? I'm becoming more certain he had something to do with Giada's death, just because of how hard he is to find right now. It almost feels like he's running."

"Or desperate. If he has no means of support, he must be scrambling for one now." I wasn't quite ready to point fingers yet. Everything we had against Felipe Iadanza was hearsay, at best, after all. And focusing too hard on a suspect often blinded you to other possibilities.

"Heh, true."

I looked over at Jamie and Foster. "Was that truly the only thing you discovered? That Iadanza and Giada fought the day she died?"

"Yes and no. We did get a timeline for the day's events, which more or less corroborates with what the staff told us. That no one saw anything was the general consensus. They did their own thing, went to bed around midnight, didn't come down until the next morning." Jamie shrugged, a hand splayed. "Two people acted sketchy: Raelynn Collins and Arthur Li Fonti. He acted dodgy when he said he got up and went to the parlor, although I don't know why. I can't confirm he was doing something else. So far, no one else left their beds after they got into them. Raelynn Collins said she went to bed at midnight and slept through the night, but Tesfay the footman said he had to give her a light charm because she has insomnia and often gets up.

When I asked her about it, she looked all flustered like she didn't know how to respond to me and just said she'd been restless before midnight, but once she was in bed, she slept solid. It was odd how they couldn't answer a simple question."

"Hmm. That deserves looking into. Did they give you a timeline for Iadanza's movements?"

"Sorta. Everyone said that after he fought with Giada the second time, they both locked themselves in their rooms and didn't come out again."

I took note of that with interest. "Separate rooms?"

"Yeah, they weren't sleeping together. Or at least, not that night. I want to follow up and see if that was typical. If Giada had already moved him out of her bedroom, the relationship was definitely on the rocks."

Foster's ears twitched back and forth, his manner thoughtful. "It really does look like he did it."

"Foster, you and Niamh search his room. I believe Detti had it cleaned after he was basically thrown out, but let's make sure he didn't leave anything interesting behind."

"Sure thing."

Niamh gave a shrug, her expression musing. "If it was a case of murder by her lover, don't you think he'd have tried to come up with a better alibi?"

"He's not been described as smart, though," Foster pointed out. "Murder of passion?"

"We can't rule it out," Jamie agreed. "If he's stupid enough to argue with his lover when she's on the verge of throwing him out of the house, then he's probably not the sharpest tool in the box when he's mad. Man, I wish we had an idea of where he was."

Niamh swore, "I'll find him, one way or another."

"Don't break your brain doing it," Jamie advised. "We might need to put out a notice to all stations and network this."

It was not a bad thought. I'd do so later, after we

finished eating. Finding Iadanza was something of a priority and with a two-week head start, the man could be in a different country for all we knew.

"Going back to the house guests, we found the store where Atticus bought fireworks, and they confirmed part of his story. Found two stores that remembered Sophie and Arthur's stopping in to shop. It doesn't help us much, but we can confirm where they were during the day," Jamie shared.

Foster tacked on, "I wish we had a way to confirm their night movements. That would be more helpful."

"Tell me about it."

I told my better half, "I've fetched the death certificate and clothing evidence. Evidence is in lockup at the station."

Jamie perked up. "Oooh, that means we can finally interview the doctor and lawyer. Awesome sauce. I'll try calling them today, see if we can interview them tomorrow. It's late in the day now, they're probably ready to head home at this hour."

"True enough."

"I'd also like to go back and look at Giada's bedroom again. Something was off about that room, and I didn't get to figure out what before King pulled me out of there. If I can just sit in there uninterrupted, maybe I can figure it out." She flopped back in her chair, groaning in vexation. "Nothing makes sense right now. I can't find a single person who wanted this woman dead. We can't even figure out if her death was on purpose or not. This whole case is strange."

"Well, we're in the early days yet. We'll overturn some clue soon enough." Usually the first round of interviews told us very little, but it was important to get that foundation work in place so we had some kind of framework. Otherwise, nothing made sense when we did get the right pieces handed to us.

"Food," Jamie declared. "I really can't think

anymore on an empty stomach. Dinner, anyone?"

We all agreed the idea to be a good one, and I for one was quite famished, so we retreated to the front of the hotel where the dining room was. It wasn't very busy at this early hour, and we found a table near the fireplace, which we all appreciated after a full day of tramping about outside.

A waiter came and took our orders, and I was pleased to order every hot dish they had on the menu. Truly, the wind today had been cutting in the extreme. Despite the heavy coat I wore, it sliced right through to the bone. Even the Felixes had felt it despite heating charms. They were now ensconced in front of the dining room's fireplace, intent on soaking up as much heat as they could.

Jamie tapped a finger to the table after the waiter had left, drawing our attention to her. "Okay, change in subject. Can you two do me a favor and list out what training you received when you came on board as kingsmen?"

Both of them blinked at each other, and then Jamie, as if not sure where this request was coming from.

"We can," Niamh confirmed, brows drawn up in confusion. "But why would you—oh, for your proposal."

"Right. I realized earlier today that I really don't know what all you guys are trained to do. Like, how much were you officially trained for, how much do you just pick up on the job? I know what I've had to teach you, but it doesn't really give me a baseline, if that makes sense? And part of my proposal has to outline what training I'd need to put anyone in the new department through before they'd be able to work in the field."

It was a thought I hadn't considered, but of course she was correct. I hadn't been able to turn my mind to either her offer or mine with all we'd done today, but she clearly was able to multitask better than I.

Foster was eager and quick to agree. "I'll make you a list of training tonight. I even promise to make my handwriting legible."

Jamie snorted a laugh. "That would help, yeah. Thanks."

It did bring up a question I hadn't thought to ask before. "What training did you undergo?"

"It's really a list," she answered with a reminiscent smile. "Becoming an agent takes twenty weeks, and it's an intense twenty weeks, let me tell you. We're trained in academics, case exercises, firearms training, operational skills, the works."

"Operational skills?" Niamh asked with keen interest.

"Tactics, operations planning, coordinating witnesses and informants, surveillance, undercover operations, intelligence work, etcetera."

I'd known some of this but not all. She'd been trained in tactics? "You plan to train everyone in the new department in the same skills, I take it."

"I mean, they kinda need to know all of that. It all comes into play. Think about when we had that pandemic case. How we handled that was all operational stuff."

True. I couldn't fault her logic. "Still, dearest, that means you'll have to develop a twenty-week course and find instructors for all of it."

Jamie winced. "Trust me, I know. It was the first thought I had after I realized the gap. It won't be easy to do. I can teach some of it, but if I'm to work cases and get this thing off the ground, I can't be a full-time instructor."

"No, you won't have time," I agreed immediately. "Really, you shouldn't try to head the department, either. It wouldn't be the right use of your time or skills."

Foster protested, "Wait, why shouldn't she? She's the one creating it, right?"

Jamie, however, knew what I meant. Her eyes were on me as she gave a slow nod. "You're right. I'm not an administrator. I need a good manager to keep track of the department, someone who can sit behind a desk all day and keep people moving."

My darling Jamie was many things, but content to sit still was not one of them. She thrived best in the field, where she could move and keep things in motion. She was a good instructor, hence why many came to her to learn, but she never sat them down at a desk to teach them. I'd seen this play out too many times not to realize where her strengths and weaknesses lay.

"I'm not sure offhand who would be the best person for this," Jamie murmured thoughtfully. "I want to say Gibs, but he hates being at a desk as much as I do. He'd murder me if I put him up for this."

"My dear, you don't need to solve every problem or fill every position in your proposal," I advised her. "They need the structure, to understand the logistics and budget for what this will take. Leave filling the positions up to them."

"Eh. Good point, I may be getting ahead of myself."

We paused when our food arrived, and I was quite happy to tuck in. I think we were all famished to one degree or another. Conversation dropped to a lull as we invested ourselves wholly in the excellent dinner in front of us.

As Niamh slowed, her fork stilling on the plate, she looked back up with a thoughtful expression. "Detective, you said case studies. But what case studies would you use to teach people?"

It was an excellent question. "I can think of several."

"Like that ridiculous charms case where the guy poisoned half the city?" Jamie offered with a wry smile. "Or the one where we had thieves trying to circumvent heavy-duty wards? Or the case of the locked-room mystery where a royal mage was murdered? Trust me, I have plenty of case file studies on hand—even written down."

Knowing precisely what she was referring to, I objected, "You can't mean to share my own notes for educational purposes!"

Her arched eyebrow was both amused and challenging. "I'll trim it down to the pertinent info, and I won't give them the conclusion. It is a learning tool, after all—they'll have to figure out who did it."

I was only partially relieved by this. Mostly because I didn't trust her sense of mischief.

Foster looked back and forth between us with rising confusion. "What notes?"

"He calls them notes, but they could fill a book." Jamie leaned forward in confidence. "Since our first case together, he's been writing detailed notes on each case. It makes for very fun reading."

"You say that as if you yourself don't add whole chapters to it. And notes on my chapters," I muttered, already resigned to this.

"Some of it's way too personal; he'd never agree to publish it, which is a shame. The unclassified cases make for a wild read and would probably sell well."

I recognized that she mostly teased me with this possibility. Still, I kept my voice firm and my eyes level with hers as I said, "No."

"See?" Jamie shook her head, still with that teasing grin. "He's adamant. But for the purposes of training, I can trim it down to where it's just the facts of the case."

Foster's eyes went upwards, and I could see him remember the first case he worked with us. "The train robbery would be a good one, too. We really had to think on that one."

Niamh held up her hands. "Wait, wait, go back to

the one where the royal mage was killed in a locked room. How did you even begin to figure that one out?"

Jamie fell into describing the case, the nuances and questions we had to solve. I acquired Phil in my lap at some point during the retelling. Foster chimed in with his own questions. I mostly observed as Jamie gave them both a sampling of what her coursework would entail. After working with her, learning from her, they were quick to ask the right questions. I watched and felt like I was seeing some glimpse of the future. Future agents would learn just like this and become far better prepared for difficult cases, helping them achieve justice for those wronged.

Well, maybe I wouldn't mind if she used my case notes.

I was reviewing whatever she wanted to use, of course. For that matter, Seaton wouldn't be allowed any of them. When put together, those two were often far too mischievous for their own good.

Our hotel owner was very invested in us solving such a high-profile case. When I requested a room for investigational purposes, he immediately showed me to a back room that doubled, I thought, as a party room. At any rate, it had two tables lining the walls, small round tables in the middle, all lined with chairs, and a corkboard on one wall to pin things to. I thought it rather perfect. We retreated there after dinner to confer with each other and get the timeline down.

I'd picked up some butcher paper on the way in tonight, and Foster and I pinned to the board and wrote what we knew of the timeline. My Felix chose to bask in front of the pot belly stove in the corner as we worked, tail twitching idly as he supervised our efforts. Foster took a blue pen, I a black, and we both wrote out the timeline of movements for each of Giada's friends and her staff, side by side for easy comparison.

As we worked, Foster said, "I'd hoped interviewing them would shed some light on this, but...it doesn't look like my prayers will be answered. Doctor, if you had to guess, do you think this was murder or accidental?"

"I don't even feel comfortable guessing, truth tell. We just don't have enough facts." I looked at the timeline, my mind whirling with possibilities. The strange movement of Giada the night of her death, with her running all over the grounds, kept teasing at my mind. As if that was a vital clue I just didn't have the right perspective on. "I do feel like something was chasing her."

Niamh, sitting behind me, pitched in, "But was she having an argument with her lover, trying to avoid him? Or was this something else?"

Jamie grunted in agreement. "It's strange, isn't it? Something pushed her out of her bedroom so quickly that she put on mismatching shoes, she runs around like a crazy person hiding, but we have no hint of what it was. Or who it was. I know no one liked her lover, that he was arguing with her, but do you think he was the one chasing her?"

"It's a very good possibility," Niamh pointed out. "Both Raelynn Collins and Eva Graham described him as a man ruled by his passions and emotions. If he was upset enough with her, he might have been chasing her about. In which case, this could go either way, murder or accidental."

Foster's ears went a little flat, looking perturbed. "Detective Edwards, your earlier statement still bothers me. Eighty percent of women are really killed by family or a lover? Is it really that high?"

"Sadly, yes."

"Domestic abuse is just as high, and often linked." I sat down next to him, looking at this man who suddenly seemed so young. I forgot, sometimes, that Foster was only in his mid-twenties and a kingsman for a little over a year. He still had much to learn about the darker aspects of the world.

"I really don't like that number, sir."

"None of us do, I assure you. Jamie has a whole campaign to put proper self-defense weapons in the hands of women, and she teaches self-defense classes. If you'd like to join her, to help fight that wave of abuse, she'd welcome your aid."

Jamie nodded in fervent agreement of this. "Ooh yes, please do."

Foster sat with that for a moment before nodding firmly. "Yes. Yes, I'd feel better if I fought against that. My own family is very loving and supportive. All families should be that way."

"Very true." Really, Jamie had done well choosing to keep Foster as one of her ducklings. She had clearly seen his character before I had. He would make not only a good investigator, but a sensitive one, and not a man dismissive of a woman's plight.

"Alrighty. Your very excellent timeline now has names, descriptions, impressions they have of each other. All good stuff, here. I like it, but does that mean you're done and we can add our bit in?"

I was glad Jamie appreciated the work. Sometimes the hardest thing to keep track of, when you had this many witnesses, was remembering who said what. How they viewed each other. People individually were unreliable narrators, but if enough people agreed about one another's personality, it became more reliable. Sometimes, it's what drew a second glance and the right questions, as well.

"I am." I turned, handing Jamie the pen.

Niamh was already frowning, as if something had piqued her interest. "Hooo."

We all immediately perked up a little.

"What, what?" Foster demanded hopefully. "You see something?"

"Rather, I should see something, and it isn't mentioned…by either party. Raelynn Collins said she was restless before midnight and wandered around the main rooms, reading in the parlor before finally going to bed? It's interesting, because Arthur Li Fonti said the same thing. He was in the same room, at basically the same time, and yet he made no mention of seeing her."

I pursed my lips and looked at our timeline with renewed interest. "And she made no mention of seeing him. Well, now. And what might those two be hiding?"

Jamie pointed authoritatively at the board. "My money's on an affair. Who's with me?"

We all raised our hands. Because, really, that was the obvious motive for not mentioning the other person.

Unless…

"Either an affair or…they did something?" I tilted my hand back and forth. "It's equally possible they were behind Giada's death and they're covering it up. Still, I would think they would alibi each other. Why not mention the other person at all?"

"I asked this question right in front of Sophie Li Fonti," Jamie pointed out. "Her husband is not about to admit he was hanging out with another woman, alone, around midnight, where there were no witnesses."

My raised palm acknowledged the point. There would be no excuse or reason for a man to be alone with a woman at night unless something was afoot. "So either murder or an affair. Motive? I can't see why they would kill her."

"Maybe it's both?" Niamh offered. "They were

having an affair, Giada knew, hence they had to kill her? They don't bring up the other person because they don't want us to know they were together."

"Alright, so if they're having an affair, were they actually in such a public space as the parlor?"

"Ha, I bet they weren't. Why would they both say the parlor and not mention the other? Because they didn't get their stories straight to begin with. They both mentioned a public room, something innocent looking. If anything, I bet they were in Raelynn Collins' room." Jamie tapped a finger to her notebook, clearly thinking hard. "She wasn't sharing a room with anyone, and it's on the opposite side of the house where the couple was staying. Although they could have been somewhere else, I suppose. Anyway, we know they weren't where they said they were. Hmmm. Now, Sophie Li Fonti mentioned to us that it was extremely windy that night. So much so they thought a storm would blow in, although it didn't ever hit."

"Even with them about in the house, you don't think they'd have heard anything?"

"I seriously doubt it, if there were strong winds. Hmm, this really looks suspicious, though. These two were maneuvering around for a rendezvous in the middle of the night and still didn't see Giada leave?"

"Can we appreciate," Niamh drawled, "the gonads it takes to still meet up with your lover while under the same roof as your wife?"

I gave a sour grunt. "Guts or stupidity, I can't decide which. I favor stupidity."

Jamie offered me a high-five, which I accepted with a light smack against her palm. She liked it when I did the Earthian mannerisms with her, as if I was in on the joke. Of course, the other two watched us curiously, not getting the significance of the movement.

"Although," I added, "we will still need to talk to Raelynn and Arthur again, see if we can get them to admit to it. And make sure they weren't part of the murder somehow. Niamh, could you track Mr. Li Fonti's movements to Ms. Collins' room?"

"Of course," she assured. "Easily."

"We'll use it as proof later, if we need to."

Jamie sighed. "Right, well, let's write down everything else we've learned this morning and see if it matches up. And then...I guess we still have to track down where Felipe Iadanza went." Jamie shook her head. "What bothers me, more than anything, is that I have no framework for him." She frowned at the timeline as if it had personally failed her on some level. "Who are his friends? Family? Where is he from? Like, the man's acting as if he's some deranged butterfly, just floating about where the wind takes him, but he has to be from somewhere."

True, most people of interest or witnesses not only had a connection with the case, but connections elsewhere. We knew how they tied into society, what their social relationships looked like. But with Felipe Iadanza, his only known connection was with Giada. Aside from that, people only had vague information. Supposedly, he was an artist. Supposedly, he lived with patrons before falling in with Giada. None of those were facts we could prove.

"Is that important?" Niamh asked, looking between the timeline and Jamie.

"Vital," Jamie answered firmly. "The problem with cases like this is that you can't go with the obvious answer. You can't assume you know all the players involved. We have no witnesses to Giada's movements the night of her death; we literally have no idea what happened. Is it probable the people in the house that night were responsible for it? Statistically speaking, it's pretty high. But it's equally possible someone snuck in and out and we have no idea who that person is. No one even saw Giada running around like a chicken with her head cut off. It's entirely feasible someone else snuck in unawares."

She made a very valid point.

Jamie held up a finger. "And, I'll warn you guys of this right now: nine times out of ten, the reason why a case goes cold is because you failed to talk to the right person. Not everyone knows what they know, if that makes sense. They don't always come forward to talk of their own initiative. I've gone cold on my leads many a time, and every time it happens, I've gone back to the drawing board. I once found my killer because I interviewed the victim's father about who all her friends were—and then interviewed all of her friends, who then led me to a whole other subgroup of friends no one had mentioned before. And it was in that subgroup of friends that we found the man who murdered her."

Foster let out a low whistle. "That wasn't obvious in the initial investigation?"

"I had no clue who this dude was up until I did the third round of interviews. You see what I'm getting at? Right now, we cannot assume we have all the players involved. There's other people we probably need to interview. They may or may not be directly involved in Giada's death, but they may also know something we don't—or know of someone we don't." Jamie cocked her head, a twinkle of challenge in her eyes. "Alright, let's make this a training exercise. We'll start with the victim. Who was directly connected with her that we haven't spoken to yet?"

Niamh answered readily, "Husband."

"Good. Who else?"

"Mother-in-law," Foster tacked on, his brow furrowed. "Her father. Does Giada have siblings?"

"She does, and we should speak with them too. Who else?"

Niamh was smart enough to start making a list as

they worked.

As I observed, I couldn't help thinking about how good Jamie was at this. She was truly a woman of many talents, I was not blind to that. The gift that might well serve this society best was her ability to teach what she knew. She was patient, knew how to explain things, and never supplied all the answers. There always came a point where she made her students think and reason for themselves. 'Critical thinking skills' was how she defined it.

Jamie worried on some level that Queen Regina might not take her proposal of forming her own division well. I had no doubt it would succeed, and it would do so based upon moments like these. Queen Regina wanted more detectives among her kingsmen. She wanted them to be another Jamie Edwards. And if Jamie emphasized the training of the kingsmen in the proposal, I had no doubt it would be signed off on as soon as our good queen could get a pen into her hand.

Speaking of training…you realize you will be one of my trainers?

Why me?!

You volunteer me for work, I volunteer you for work. That's how I roll.

…warning taken.

Report 12: Bad Smell is BAD

I ate a hearty breakfast at the hotel's dining room before going up once more to Giada's mansion. I figured I'd need food to sustain me, and Henri was always down for breakfast. I was very keen to get back into Giada's bedroom. That plant smell and the open space in her desk bothered me and I wanted to figure out what was missing.

Niamh was trying to track down anyone who knew Iadanza or Giada and getting interviews lined up. Foster was tackling the bedroom Iadanza stayed in with a fine tooth comb, just in case the maid had missed something. Henri had specific questions to ask the staff, so Clint and I tackled Giada's bedroom. First task, find the remaining slippers that matched the ones Giada wore that night and tag them for evidence. They'd be good to use for a cross comparison. It was a simple matter to find them in the base of her wardrobe, so it took me all of five minutes to get that sorted.

Alright, desk. Give up your secrets.

I tugged my gloves on a little more firmly as I went for the right-side drawer in the desk. This one had even more letters all bundled together with ribbon and shoved inside.

I adored letters. They were like the pre-cellphone equivalent of social media. They told me all sorts of fun things like who people were, who had dirt on who, activities, places she'd gone, etcetera. I got lots of good info from letters. And diaries were the bomb diggity if I could lay hands on those. I didn't open anything as I didn't want to disturb things quite at this point. I did lean in and take a deep breath, though, trying to figure out if the plant smell was stronger inside the drawer. It seemed to be.

Why...would a plant smell be inside a drawer?

You know, I ask myself a lot of weird questions while working on a case, but this one had to rank right up there. I sat back on my haunches, looking over the room again. Something still teased at me, something off.

But I didn't see what drove Giada out of this room. There wasn't so much as a hint of a struggle. Between my heightened senses and Clint's, we should have picked up on something if there was a physical reason. I think. Pretty sure.

I stood, taking the letters out of the drawer and tagging them for evidence. Something was in the drawer that made me sneeze, and I had to quickly turn my head and sneeze into my hand to keep it from hitting the letters. Aw, crap. Well, those gloves are toast. I pocketed them, pulled on a new pair to finish bagging the letters. The other drawers just had empty places, pens, ink spills, that sort of thing. Nothing of note. I wanted to know what had been in this side drawer, and the middle one, but that was a question for Detti.

Standing at the foot of her bed, I tried to put myself in the dead woman's shoes for a second. I'm upset—I've had a bad day all around, arguing with friends, arguing with my lover, and I've had it. I sequester myself in my bedroom. And then...what? She couldn't get on Facebook or Twitter and rant, so what did she do? Write in a diary? Write to a friend or relative? I didn't see a letter on the desk, but things were missing, so maybe someone posted something for her? I'd have to look for a letter, just to see if one existed.

Alright, so maybe she wrote something. Maybe she just paced and ranted to herself. Maybe she walked in the garden. Was she so upset that she didn't notice the mismatching slippers until she was already outside?

I went to the wardrobe, like I was putting on shoes and a robe, then retreated to the bed. I stood there, looking around the room, and still saw nothing that would trigger flight. Changing directions, I went to the glass doors and pulled them open, looking out over the garden. A breath of fresh air knocked the plant smell in my nose out for a second, which I appreciated, but it didn't bring me any answers.

"What did you do that night, Giada?" I murmured under my breath.

"I ran," a female voice answered clearly.

I turned sharply. Sitting on the end of the bed was the slender form of Giada, blinking sad, dark eyes at me. I recognized her from the portraits hanging around the house, although she didn't look all pretty and made up now. She wore the same nightgown, robe, and mismatched slippers as she had when she died. Which was strange—why would she be wearing that when those clothes were in evidence lockup?

And she was kinda see-throughy?

So, look, I couldn't see ghosts on Earth. Right? Right, didn't see them there. I'd started seeing ghosts here on this world, which was cool but creepy, but I can't say that I've gotten used to it. She was probably a ghost. Probably. I didn't have my magic specs on, so I wasn't sure if she was illusion or ghost, but I'm going with ghost. So...the thought splintered and disconnected, the logic failing before it could reach a conclusion. Whatever I thought, I still saw a transparent dead woman sitting in front of me.

I...was seeing a ghost. Uh. Um. No thanks?

Really, hard pass on that.

I blinked, hoping she'd go away. She persisted in existing.

My mouth was dry but somehow it found its way around words. "You ran?"

"I ran," she repeated, still looking at me with those dark eyes.

"From what?"

"From everything. You see it too, don't you?"

The world took a slow spin around me, and as it spun, it changed. The room was no longer light and friendly. Shadows lingered in the corners, and a chill trailed along my skin. My mouth felt like cotton, sticking together in a way that made me long for water. It was kinda spooky, like she'd brought the sense of a graveyard into the room with her. I felt like I'd just entered a haunted house, which was kinda cool, but also disturbing.

"Jamie?" Clint's little paw tapped at my leg, and he was up on his hind legs, looking at me in concern. "Jamie, what's wrong?"

"You don't see her?" I asked him quietly, still not taking my eyes from the figure on the end of the bed.

"See who, Jamie?"

"The ghost. Giada's ghost."

He stared up at me, then towards the bed. "Nothing's there."

"She's sitting on the bed. You don't see her?"

"No."

He now looked even more worried. Aww, poor baby was scared of the ghost. I might have thought this was kinda funny, but he didn't. I didn't want him scared. "Clint, go to Henri."

Clint looked relieved at this suggestion. "I'll go get him!"

He was out the door like a shot. Seriously, air vacuumed in his wake. I had no idea how he thought Henri could help in this situation, but I was glad he was out of the room. I couldn't figure out whether to scream or laugh hysterically.

I faced Giada again. She may have been alarming, but I at least wanted to ask her questions. "Can you tell me how you died?"

She looked at me for the longest moment before finally speaking again, the words hollow and forlorn. "I fell from the cliff."

"Were you pushed? Or did you fall accidentally? I don't know if you were killed or not. Can you tell me?"

"The water was so cold," she responded as if she couldn't hear me. "I didn't feel it, though. Not then. I wasn't alive when I hit the water. I still feel the ground crumbling underneath my feet as I went over. Why did I move into a house so close to the sea?"

"Lady, I've been asking that same question ever since I took this case, trust me. Because this looks cray-cray to me."

I heard the rapid sound of footsteps and the puffed, labored breathing of someone not in shape. I turned to see Henri running toward me, red in the face, with three cats bounding ahead of him.

"Henri," I greeted with surprise. "You're running. Do you know how long it's been since I've seen you do that? But slow down, don't scare her. I think she's willing to talk."

He slowed but wasn't paying any attention to Giada. Just to me. "Who's speaking, Jamie?"

"Giada. She's sitting right there on the bed." I turned and found that she'd actually moved. She was by the stone wall now, looking out over the water. "You're not one of those crazy ghosts who reenacts their death over and over again, are you? Don't go jumping back into the sea, please."

Giada ignored me completely.

Henri closed in, his hand lightly touching my arm. "Dearest, look at me."

He sounded really perturbed. "She's a little weird, huh?" I asked, trying to focus on his face. "I'm not sure if I'm equipped to deal with ghosts. Maybe she'll talk to you?"

"Your eyes are fully dilated. And your balance is off—you keep swaying. Can you tell me if you ate anything strange?"

I blinked. Then blinked again. I didn't get it. "What?"

"Out of this room first."

He put an arm around my waist and physically hauled me out of there. I went, because if Henri was being forceful, something was really wrong. Admittedly, I didn't want to stay with the crazy ghost who wasn't making sense anyway.

It's funny, I didn't think of Henri as particularly strong. We're of similar height, and physically speaking, I knew I was stronger than he. But he had moments, like now, when adrenaline kicked in and he surprised me. I mostly went along with him because of the surprise. And why not? I liked Henri.

"I like you too, dearest. Stay with me."

"Am I talking out loud?"

"Yes, you are. It's fine, just stay with me. And tell me, did you eat or drink anything in the past hour? Since I've seen you?"

"Nope!" I was proud of that. For some reason.

Henri didn't like the answer, though. He looked more concerned.

"Is that bad?"

"I don't know at this point."

"Where are we going?"

"The kitchen. I need to run tests on you if we're to figure out the answer."

"Answer?"

"To why you're acting strange?"

I blinked at him. "Am I trippin'? Duuuude. That's so unprofessional of me. What did I do that for?"

"I don't think this is voluntary, dearest." Henri's expression turned grim. "Which is rather the problem. But I will figure this out, rest assured."

"Okay." I smiled at him sunnily. As long as I wasn't in trouble—and I didn't have to talk to Giada—I was cool.

You know, this is hysterical in retrospect.

I don't find this funny yet.

Neither do I.

Why?

Turn the page and read for yourself.

Report 13: An Unwelcome Surprise

Seeing the most level headed, practical woman of my acquaintance act as if she'd imbibed a recreational drug alarmed me right to my marrow. Jamie was not the type to imbibe anything and chase some artificial high, so I knew this wasn't on purpose. She wouldn't be that irresponsible, especially working a case like this. But it left me the question of what was wrong—and what had sent her spiraling into this state in the hour I hadn't seen her.

I sat her at the kitchen table and thanked any deity that came to mind that she was amenable to following my direction. She was clearly undergoing hallucinations, but she wasn't paranoid or combative, and I was grateful for that small mercy.

"Uh, no, absolutely not." Jamie stared directly at a blank corner of the room. "You're creeping me right out. Go away. Henri, make it go away, it's not listening to me."

I had no idea what she was talking to, but it seemed to unnerve her, which in turn unnerved me. If she decided to run from whatever it was, I would not be able to either catch or restrain her. Thinking quickly, I promised, "I'll put up a protective ward in a moment. Let's get settled at the table first."

"Yeah, okay." Jamie made a mean face to the corner, keeping a wary eye on it as if it would bite at any moment.

"Clint, tell me again what happened," I urged him

even as I readied several things out of my bag.

"She searched the room with me. Then stopped and stared at the bed. Said Giada's ghost was there." Clint sat on the table next to Jamie's elbow, staring at her in worry. "I didn't see a ghost, Henri."

"I don't think a ghost was actually there."

Jamie frowned at both of us. "She was too. I was talking to her. She didn't respond very well to questions, though. I mean, seriously, is it too much to ask that she tell me if she was murdered or not?"

"Clint, think carefully," I urged. "Was there anything she imbibed? Anything she ate or drank?"

Clint shook his head.

This must be a contact substance, then, somehow. It narrowed my field somewhat.

Tasha and Phil came barreling in from outside, and I stopped them with an uplifted hand. "Wait, both of you. I need you to do something quickly. Phil, go find Mr. Detti and tell him Giada's bedroom is strictly off-limits. No one is to enter. Tasha, I need you to retrace Jamie's footsteps, but don't enter the room. I need to know if she was somewhere else other than that room."

Both Felixes gave me a firm nod before sprinting back out, already on task.

I blessed them for it and urged Clint, "Keep her occupied and focused on you."

Clint gave me a serious nod, then put a paw on Jamie's shoulder, bringing her attention to him.

"What is it, bud?"

I let their conversation flow over me, worry beating at my chest like a drum. I didn't know what this was. Her core seemed stable, nothing obviously wrong. I did a basic scan on her anyway, trying to find any abnormalities that touched her aura, making sure all was well, and the results came back as normal. Well, as normal as she ever was. I didn't know what to test for, why she was in this state. With the things

Belladonna did to her, I always exercised caution with Jamie's physical health. While her reactions to things were largely predictable, there were moments I was utterly caught off guard.

This unfortunately seemed to be one of them.

Not knowing what to do or where to start, I tried putting some semblance of order into this examination. There couldn't be anything magical to her reaction; the immunity spells Belladonna used prevented that, and Clint would have been able to sniff out any spell or charm. I had seen nothing on the magical spectrum either on Jamie or in the bedroom. Alright, so chemical.

I always kept basic ingredients to test with on me at all times, as I never knew what would come in handy when I was in the field. I carefully swabbed the inside of Jamie's mouth with a glass scraper I kept for this purpose.

She blinked at me, all doe-eyed innocence. "Whatcha doin', Henri?"

"I'm testing your saliva."

"Yeah? Cool beans."

Seeing her sit here so docilely, allowing me to maneuver her body as I wished, alarmed me even further. 'Jamie' and 'obedient' didn't belong in the same sphere of existence.

I had to shake that feeling off, focus on the problem. I couldn't afford for panic to erode my thought process. I took my sample and then dropped it onto six charm papers. All stayed white, the neutral reaction to saliva.

Alright, so not a common chemical.

On the off chance I was wrong, I scraped just the barest hint of skin off her hands, then tested for outside magical traces on the sample and her clothes. Clint pointed out the gloves she had worn right before she started acting strange, so I tested them with various spells and diagnostics. Everything came back either neutral, nonexistent, or benign.

None of that was reassuring. My anxiety over the situation ramped up with every negative test result. All it meant was that I wasn't asking the right questions. And Jamie was still sitting there, acting strangely and...and...I couldn't accept the situation as it was. I couldn't accept I didn't know the answer.

I may well have been too emotionally compromised to think clearly, and I could think of only one other person I trusted to call. I yanked my pad out of my pocket and plugged in Seaton's number.

He answered rather promptly. "*Hello, what's—*"

"Portal to me now," I interrupted curtly. "There's something wrong with Jamie and I can't determine what it is."

Seaton's answer was both alarmed and succinct. "*Coming.*"

True to his word, he was at my side seconds later.

Jamie jumped a little. "Whoa! This is some trip. Heya, Sherard, did you transport down from the mother ship?"

Seaton frowned at her before demanding of me, "What is she saying?"

"I don't know and that's partially the problem. She's acting as if she's consumed some sort of hallucinogenic. She swore to me not fifteen minutes ago that she was conversing with Giada's ghost. But I can't determine what she's come in contact with."

Jamie frowned at Seaton, her brows screwed up in worry. "You're wearing red. That's not good, man. The red shirts always die. Maybe let's get you something blue to wear, yeah? Blue shirts survive."

My heart sank. She was starting to make even *less* sense now. Just what had she come into contact with?!

"Have you pulled samples from her?" he demanded, waving a hand to indicate the various dishes arrayed on the table.

"Skin cells and saliva," I answered frankly. "Her

clothes, as well."

Seaton drew out his wand and threw several diagnostic spells at the same samples. Then he grunted, reading off the results from his notebook. And they were interesting results. He'd performed a broader spectrum test than I, and I realized my mistake in assuming something almost immediately.

"The plant." I pointed to the green dot listed out among all the other results. "There were no plants in the room she was in. That should not be there."

"Planty smell," Clint confirmed with a nod.

My eyes snapped to him. "What?"

"You smelled something like a plant in there?" Seaton demanded.

"Oh yeah, the planty smell." Jamie's voice turned singsong. "So weird Clint picked up on that. No flowers or vases in there. Said it wasn't coming from outside. I smelled it inside the drawer. Who puts plants inside a drawer, am I right?"

Clint elaborated with a worried eye on Jamie. "Don't know it."

I looked at Seaton, not sure if this made any sense. Why would a strong plant smell come from inside a desk and be one of the things Jamie's aura had absorbed? It had only registered as a weed in Seaton's initial diagnostic. And I didn't know why that would feel so important, but it was the only thing in that initial scan that didn't make any sense. It gave me something to question and focus on.

"Keep testing her," I urged him. "I'm going back into that room to figure out what plant it is. It may or may not be the reason why she's acting like this."

Seaton was already lifting his wand. "I have her. Go."

Clint raced ahead of me and, for the second time in the past hour, I found myself running. I crossed paths with Tasha as we went barreling back down the hallway. She'd been running for the kitchen when she saw us and abruptly turned, now running alongside me.

"Jamie only went from front door to bedroom, nowhere else," Tasha reported in her high-pitched voice.

"Thank you, that confirms things a little," I panted. I wasn't sure if it was my own lack of stamina or my panic that caused me to be so short of breath, but I didn't appreciate it, either way. Breathing was vital in this moment.

Phil stood guard just outside of Giada's bedroom door, and I spared him a thankful smile before heading straight inside. I went for the desk, as did Clint, still guiding me.

"Sniffy in middle drawer"—he indicated which one with a jerk of his chin—"and right drawer."

I promptly opened both, and used yet another glass rod to scrape out the sides of the drawer. Then I put it into a glass tube, running it through a quick diagnostic spell. "Reveal Elements. Define with name."

The results wrote themselves out on the label adhered to the glass tube. *Sand, trace minerals, jimsonweed. Common name: devil's snare. Common weed with white tubular flowers and seed pods. Warning: Leaves and seeds contain potent alkaloids.*

In other words, this thing caused hallucinations.

I swore, threw everything back into my bag, and immediately snatched up Clint, hauling him out of the room. It was a miracle he hadn't been affected, too.

His claws sank into my jacket as he demanded, "Henri, okay?!"

"No. That desk is firmly off-limits from now on. The room itself is." I quickly vacated the room and shut the door firmly behind me. Clint leapt free of my arms so I had a free hand to work with. "Come with me, all of you."

I puffed as I jogged back towards the kitchen, out of breath and stamina, but determined to get back to Jamie and Seaton.

Seaton looked up sharply as I entered, his wand still poised to run another test. "I can't determine what's wrong with her."

"The plant is jimsonweed," I reported, setting my bag down and bending a little at the waist as I struggled to get my breath regulated again.

"Jimsonweed—you mean devil's snare?" Seaton's jaw worked for a moment before he burst out, "Isn't that used to induce hallucinations in ceremonies?"

"Sometimes, yes. I believe so. I have no idea why it was found on the insides of Giada's desk drawers, but that's what Jamie's reacting to. It was mixed in with sand, so I believe it was part of a drying powder."

Seaton's alarm grew. "But jimsonweed can kill people if used in the wrong dosage!"

"I hope that because she only came into trace amounts of it, she'll be fine, but..." I trailed off and looked at Jamie with worry. She didn't react in predictable ways to things. It's why anything new was so alarming. This had affected her so quickly—and with such potency, despite it being a trace amount—I didn't dare trust she would be fine.

"We need to take precautions. I want to do a stringent cleaning spell on her clothes to remove any other trace amounts. If we can get her into a shower quickly, that will also help." Seaton gestured vaguely towards the bedroom. "I want to clean wherever she found this."

"That's evidence," I negated immediately. "But putting a ward up around the room to prevent anyone else from stumbling upon it is a good idea."

"I'll do that, then. I think we should keep her under careful watch until this passes."

I fully agreed. "She's been reading a particularly

interesting book recently that—"

"Oooh, is it read at work day?" Jamie bounced in her chair. "I can totally dig that."

Clearly, I wouldn't have to work too hard to distract her. "That's right, dearest. Let Seaton clean you off, you can soak in a hot tub of water for a while, and we'll settle down and read after that. You can continue where we left off."

"*The Murder of Roger Ackroyd*," Jamie said with a dreamy look. "First time I ever read it, you know? Loved the adaptation with David Suchet, though, man's an amazing actor."

Seaton let her babbling go, doing the cleanup spells with both efficiency and possibly more power than necessary. I wasn't about to say a word about it. As soon as he was finished, I told Clint, "Show him where the room is, please?"

Clint gave me a paw salute and hopped lightly off the table.

I got an arm around Jamie's waist and once again hauled her up, directing her out of the kitchen. "Alright, dearest. Let's get back to the hotel and you can read to me."

"Doesn't Sherard want to hear the story too?" She pouted, the expression making her look a decade younger.

"I'm sure he does, he just has to do something first. He'll catch up with us momentarily." I didn't pause, forcing her to stay in step with me.

"Oh. Okay. I'll do my best voices for him. My French accent sucks, but them's the breaks. Not that you guys would know the difference anyway. Heh. That's funny. Why is that funny?"

I wouldn't be able to focus at all on the story. My concern for her was too deeply entrenched in my mind. But hopefully, this would pass soon and without damage to her.

We just had to ride this out.

nope still funny

.... *I give up.*

also it pains my soul that you didn't catch the red shirt references

have I not shown you Star Trek yet?

Star what?

well I'm fired

Jamie's Additional Report: Yikes

I don't know how people who do drugs for fun manage it. Honestly. I had the worst hangover after the jimsonweed wore off. I felt tender, too, like a Mack truck had run over me—and then did it again for giggles. Like, there was no part of me that had any desire whatsoever to repeat this experience.

I napped, riding the low, and woke up grouchy. Seriously, this sucked. And I would have to write a report on what happened, too, which sucked even more. Additional paperwork added insult to injury.

The hotel room was nice, at least. Henri had gotten a fire going, keeping the room nice and toasty. My nightstand had a box of chocolate creams, my Kindle—fully charged—and a tall glass of water. And, of course, curled up on the bed with me were Clint and Tasha; one alert and watching me, the other snoozing away.

I gave Tasha a good scratch under her chin. "Your turn to watch me?"

"Yeah." She blinked up at me, those golden eyes studying me carefully. "See ghosts still?"

"No, hon, I think I'm off the trip. The world looks normal again. Thank god." My mouth felt like a war of cotton balls had clashed, with casualties resulting in sticky residue that clung to my tongue. Gag. The water and chocolates looked amazing, and I promptly drained half the glass before selecting a chocolate. Mm, orange filling. Perfect.

My better half really did know how to take care of me. Even when I threw him curve balls like this one.

I may have been high as a kite, but I still remembered Henri's panic. I really had scared him. Sherard, too. Granted, when things went weird around me, they went *really* weird, so I didn't blame them for reacting strongly. Hopefully they wouldn't hold it against me, though.

Clint woke up from his siesta and regarded me with those big eyes of his. He must have seen I was mostly back to normal because the only thing he said to me was, "Message Henri."

"Is he still working?"

"No, next door."

Ah. If he was afraid of contamination, he might well be changing clothes and washing down. I sure would be in his shoes. I pulled the pad closer to me and shot him a message. *Hey, I'm up. Wash your hands like you've murdered the rightful king at your wife's urging and you're now getting rid of the evidence.*

Not two seconds later, I kid you not, he was lightly tapping at my door. "Dearest?"

"Yeah, I'm decent, come in."

Henri slipped through the door, looking concerned—but not relieved—to find me upright and talking. I wasn't sure if I should be insulted by that or not.

He came straight for me, looking me over carefully, his hand at my forehead. "How do you feel?"

"Back to normal. Ish. Really, I feel like roadkill. The aftermath of that trip is not fun. But I'm not seeing ghosts that aren't there or feel like the room is contorting, so there's that."

He did not look entirely sold. "Your message to me didn't entirely make sense, though."

"What? Oh. *Macbeth* reference. I forgot, you haven't seen that one yet." I waved it away. "Not important, I promise I'm good. Really thirsty still, though."

"I'll fetch you more water momentarily." He sat on the side of the bed, his hip pressed against mine, hand brushing lightly against the side of my face.

I felt the light, sweet tingle of his skin against mine and

turned my face into it, kissing his palm. Sometimes, Henri absolutely disarmed me by being so tender, and I had to take a moment and not become a puddle of mush.

"I scared you," I murmured against his skin.

Henri's voice was husky as he answered. "You did. Badly. I do not fault you for it, as I know it was not intentional and there was no way to guard against it. Even though you wore gloves, you still came in contact with it."

I cast my mind back to what I'd done around that desk. "I leaned into the drawer at one point and inhaled, trying to figure out the scent. I have a bad feeling I sniffed this crap."

"Ah. That would explain your strong reaction, if you ingested it directly."

"This must have been what was affecting Giada," I muttered darkly. "I mean, look at what it did to me. It would explain why she was acting so weird."

"I agree."

"There were missing things in that drawer, too. I think that's where the devil's snare came from—those missing things. I just got the trace residue of it. Ugh, thinking about this is giving me a headache."

"We'll properly investigate it tomorrow when you're up to the conversation."

"Henri, I have a really bad thought."

"I'm not surprised. What?"

"Giada wasn't just writing in her diary at that desk. She was writing letters too."

Henri's expression told me he was way ahead of me. "I know. Letters going to all and sundry with poison ink. Seaton and I realized the same thing earlier. If it helps, anyone handling the letters would get a very mild dose, barely discernable. Unless they licked the ink right off the page."

I snorted at that mental image.

"I don't think we need to worry about them. Really, there's not much we can do about it. We have no idea who Giada wrote to, and whoever it was, it happened two weeks ago."

"Yeah, water under the bridge."

"Precisely. Now, rest. The answers will wait for us." Henri shook his head, letting it go. There was a strain around his eyes, and I could tell he needed a good hour of no people to recover from today.

"Me getting a high today was really inconvenient." I paused and rephrased, "And by that, I mean it's like saying Godzilla is a minor nuisance to Tokyo. I did *not* want to get high. Like hard pass on that. I'm glad I didn't get too paranoid or do something stupid like jump over the cliff."

"Trust me, I was very aware of all the dangers and grateful you were docile instead. This might well be a vital clue, but you're not in any state to discuss it. I think it's fine to leave the case for today. Rest, regain your equilibrium, and we'll sort the fiasco of today out tomorrow."

"That's seriously one of the best offers I've had all month." I looked at my Kindle with longing. A full afternoon of reading and eating chocolate. Someone pinch me, I might be in heaven after all.

Henri's face relaxed a smidge into something that may have been a smile. "I'll fetch you more water. Do you feel like you can eat something? Food will help your body process the jimsonweed."

"I'm actually starving. Food sounds great."

"Excellent. A moment, then." He leaned in and kissed my forehead, the kiss like gossamer wings against my skin, and then left, leaving the door cracked behind him.

I warmed under all the attention. Henri was pretty demonstrative, all told, but he was always a touch sweeter when crap hit the fan. Maybe I could convince him to curl up on the bed with me, spend the afternoon reading and petting cats. I couldn't think of a better way to recover from this morning.

And I would seriously consider what I'd learned today in that bedroom. The information was vital—I had that gut feeling—but brain.exe failed to respond. I'd have to think about it when I had actual brain power to work with.

For today, at least, I gave myself a break.

I feel like this entire insert was just Jamie bragging about Henri.

Nah. Well, maybe a little. Mostly it was me, hungover.

It was a lovely afternoon, though. We read quite companionably until dinner.

See, you ARE bragging!

We just need to find you someone. Then you won't be jealous. Are you having trouble finding a soulmate?

I have trouble finding a matching sock.

Report 14: Devil's Snare

I sat at breakfast with Jamie, Seaton, and our two kingsmen. Everyone seemed relieved Jamie was back to her usual spirits. Not more so than I, of course. If nothing else, my lover was a very resilient woman. While this reassured me, it also frustrated me. I did not like to see her in such a state; I doubted any man would.

I tried to let that feeling go, as I had no ready target to unleash my frustrations upon. I needed a clear head to figure out why the jimsonweed was in the drawer to begin with.

The breakfast served in the dining room of our hotel was excellent, with crispy toast, perfectly flavored eggs, and kippers grilled to perfection. It did much to restore my mood, and seeing Jamie eat without care was an extra boon. The dining room was a busy place; more than one person took advantage of the delicious fare, and people moved all about our table. A buzz of noise filled the air, both from the myriad conversations, but also from the birds cawing at each other from outside the glass windows.

I took the morning paper with me to the table, flipped open to the second page—and swallowed a curse. There, in the corner, was Jamie's picture with the very unflattering headline of: "Shinigami Detective Hard At Work—Or Was She?"

The article went on to allude that Jamie had taken a recreational day, in every sense, with a hangover in the afternoon. It was close enough to what happened I had to wonder, just who had Ms. King's source been? Only the people in the hotel and Giada's house would even know that Jamie had been affected.

"Henri?" Jamie looked me over with concern. "You look ready to yeet someone into the sun."

I growled out a choice breath. "If by yeet, you mean throw, then you're quite correct. Ms. King has been at it again."

"Oh for the love of..." Jamie's head dropped back for a second. "Alright, let me see it."

I handed the article over and watched her face as she read it through. She looked as thoroughly aggrieved as I felt, and ready to punch the reporter. (I actually didn't put the last one past her.)

"May her soul hang on the devil's bedroom wall and rot," Jamie growled before slapping the paper closed again. "How did she even know about this?"

"She has a source somewhere, clearly." We might not ever figure out who, but I truly wished we could somehow remove this particular thorn from our sides. Ms. King was truly a hinderance, especially on high-profile cases like these.

Foster cleared his throat, more to draw our attention as he poured himself another cup from the teapot. "Detective, I'm glad you're feeling better today."

Jamie put the paper aside and mustered up a smile for him. "Trust me, so am I. Thanks for taking over and letting me get my feet back under me. What did you discover?"

"Ah, well, we confirmed the affair." Niamh rolled her eyes. "It was almost anticlimactic, really. We called on Raelynn again and confronted her about the mixed-up timeline. She panicked and blurted out a confession that she and Arthur Li Fonti have been seeing each other for months. Apparently, no one knew about it."

Foster muttered, "I found that last part hard to

believe. People are never as discreet as they think they're being. We tried to follow up with Arthur again as well, but couldn't catch him. We can keep trying him if you wish."

"I confirmed with Tesfay the footman that the two of them were actually in Raelynn's room," I interjected, "not the parlor, so I don't think it necessary."

"So they really weren't as discreet as they thought." Jamie shook her head, rolling her eyes heavenward. "I maintain the man's stupid for cheating on his wife under the same roof, but what they do is their business. Good work, guys, thanks. At least we have that confirmed."

"We were glad to do it, especially with what you suffered yesterday." Niamh leaned forward, her eyes studying Jamie in a sweep. "How are you?"

"Much better today, thanks. Anything's an improvement over yesterday, though." Jamie grimaced. "Afterwards, I didn't have two brain cells to reliably rub together. I ended up reading manga. That was the only thing my brain could handle."

"Tell us more of what you experienced," Foster urged. "I know it wasn't pleasant for you, but I feel like this is a break in the case."

"Me too, trust me. I understand why Giada was acting weird and running around the house, even though Niamh didn't find any signs of someone chasing her. I was paranoid on this crap." Jamie rubbed at her chin, eyes narrowed. "I felt perfectly fine. I didn't realize anything was off at first and I should have."

That wasn't boasting on her part. Jamie's senses were roughly twenty-two percent more efficient than the average human's. If anyone could detect something through smell, it would be her. "You had no idea anything was wrong, then?"

"No, not a freaking clue. Not until I saw Giada sitting on the edge of her bed wearing the clothes she died in. That's what made me realize something was up." Jamie gave something of a shiver, the motion not at all exaggerated. "I got Clint out of the room because I was worried about him."

Seaton leaned forward slightly, drawing her attention to him. "Did it feel that real to you?"

"I had absolutely no suspicion it was a hallucination. It was so real that I actually asked her who killed her." Jamie pressed fingertips to her temples as if a headache threatened. "That's from a trace dose, too. I can't imagine what a full dose would do to someone. Did anyone figure out how she ingested this? There's something missing out of the drawers—is it linked?"

"We looked into it," Niamh assured her. "We're not sure yet what was in those drawers, but RM Seaton went with us throughout the property as we investigated."

Jamie regarded her friend with interest. "Sherard, you were investigating with them?"

"I could hardly do otherwise, as I was quite determined to figure out what had happened to you." Seaton's expression promised mayhem once he had a proper answer. "As I reported to you, I couldn't find any trace of jimsonweed anywhere on the property. Even the surrounding beach and roadside leading up to the house had no trace of it. Wherever she came into contact with it, it wasn't near her home. I did determine it was relatively fresh. Perhaps a few days before her death, I would say."

I pursed my lips. "That timing is fairly suspicious."

"Isn't it?" he agreed. We exchanged a look that spoke volumes.

"It would make sense with her movements that night," Niamh said slowly, staring very intently at her eggs. "If she were in a paranoid state—and I imagine she must have been if she'd been given a proper dose—then it would explain why she ran around all over the grounds that night. She probably did think something was chasing her."

"How she ingested it, that's my next question," I said. "It was in a dry, powdery sort of form inside the drawer, darkly stained. Was this a powder she had mixed in with a drink on purpose? Or like Jamie, was this coated on something, so that Giada ingested it or absorbed it through the skin?"

Foster cleared his throat. "Forgive me, Doctor, but I'm still not clear on what this is even used for. I only know that it's a hallucinogenic drug. Is this readily available?"

"Yes and no. Jimsonweed is actually quite a common weed. You've probably passed it hundreds of times without even looking twice at it. That said, few know how to properly distill the bulbs of the plant and create the drug with it. It's typically used in Ciparis for religious ceremonies and, in a full dose, is known to be lethal. It's certainly not something to trifle with."

Jamie let out an *oooh*. "So is this specialized knowledge? Can we search for people who know about it?"

"Hmm, I'm not sure. It's common enough in Ciparis, or so Colette once told me, but I'm not sure how widespread the information is here. Or how one would even go about acquiring it. It's not so uncommon, however, that someone who likes recreational drugs would be ignorant of it."

"Rats. So maybe not the lead I want it to be." Jamie frowned at the ceiling as if it had personally offended her.

Niamh glanced between our faces and asked uncertainly, "Is it possible that Giada was using this for recreation?"

"It's entirely possible," Jamie mused thoughtfully. "Although she was clearly getting it from an outside source if she was. She'd had a hard day, her friends were being jerks, her lover was fighting with her.... I could see why she might take a hit to relax. On the other hand, I don't want to make assumptions she did this on purpose and then miscalculated the dose. Detti said once that she hated recreational drugs, so this could be something that was done to her. If she did this to herself unwittingly, that's one thing. If someone planted this stuff in her drawer, it's another."

Foster sipped at his tea before offering, "So the odds of her being poisoned are higher than this being something she'd done to herself."

"Looks that way to me. Henri, when you interviewed the staff again, what did they say?"

I rolled my eyes expressively. "I truly wish people were better witnesses. What was described to us as dizzy spells were quite more severe than they initially let on. Giada was acting paranoid or running away from them, only to return hours later looking pale and dizzy. She'd take random naps, then wake up hungry and alarmed with her own actions. It wasn't as simple as we were initially led to believe."

"That sounds exactly like me yesterday. How long had they observed this behavior?"

"Months," I informed her, shaking my head. "It was apparently the thing that sent her routinely to her doctor, too. Every time she had an episode, she'd see him the next day."

"Ah. Really, Detti could have been clearer about that. He made it sound like a health problem, not something weird going on. So this wasn't done on purpose. At least, she wasn't doing it to herself. She wouldn't be seeing a doctor about this if she knew the root cause."

It gave me hope that we might be able to make some sense of this yet if a professional had examined her. "I moved the interviews of the doctor and lawyer to today. Both are eager to speak with us. I want to know more about this and the medical records might well shed some light on it. Also, it raises the question of dosage. If this had been going on for months, then the beginning dosage must have been quite mild."

Seaton nodded in agreement with me. "I was about to say that very thing. The reason why jimsonweed is used only in religious ceremonies is that too much of it can kill you. They use it once, maybe up to three times per person, before they say no more. It must have been an incredibly mild dose in the beginning if Giada survived months of contact with this substance."

Giada must have been quite a strong, determined woman in her own right to withstand it. It was a wonder, really, that she survived it as long as she had.

Niamh made a face. "She was acting this crazy and they put that down to arguments with her lover? I can't make the logic connect."

"There is none." Jamie's mouth went into a flat line of anger. "You know, the more I learn about Giada's life, the more I feel sorry for her. I don't think anyone was properly in this woman's corner. The minute I went down, acting weird, I had four different people and three cats who closed ranks around me. She should have had that, too."

Jamie's expression was a touch sad. I put a hand over hers, giving it a light squeeze. She was all too correct—Giada Barese did not have the support she should have. I have no doubt her family loved her, but they didn't seem to know how to support or protect her. Was it a lack of empathy? A feeling that she somehow deserved such treatment since she had made her own bed? I had no idea of the root cause. It was a sad thing to observe, however.

Jamie flashed me a quick, thankful smile. "I'm fortunate, and grateful to all of you. We can't do much about Giada's life, but let's at least figure out if she needs justice. Sherard, you said you can't find jimsonweed anywhere near her place. That smacks of someone putting it there. Figuring out how they were getting it into Giada on a regular basis might tell us a lot. The other question I have is, why bother?"

I pondered her words. "Good question. Whoever did this must have gone through quite a bit of trouble. The jimsonweed was planted for...what purpose?"

"To make her look crazy?" Foster suggested, arrested with his cup midway to his mouth. "I've seen estates be passed onto a conservator under those kinds of circumstances."

"Possibly?" Seaton's head canted in thought, his face drawn into a frown. "I believe the Barese family's finances are in good health at the moment, though. I can't see a court appointing anyone but family over her estate."

"Ah, but if she'd divorced her husband and remarried her lover, then we might finally have the right motive for Felipe Iadanza." Jamie's smile was not at all nice. Sharks had friendlier expressions. "He was desperate to marry her. And a husband would get first dibs in that kind of situation, I would imagine."

Now, that was a distinct possibility. I saw only one problem with the theory. "Wouldn't he have been too impulsive in this case, though? She hadn't agreed to either divorce her husband or marry Iadanza, so poisoning her now would have only unhinged her at the wrong moment. Then again, he's constantly described to us as being ruled by emotions, so perhaps he misstepped."

Niamh's eyes were sharp on Jamie's face, evaluating her. "You're sure it's Iadanza?"

"Eh, maybe, maybe not. I can see him trying to play with her mind, to manipulate her into what he wanted, since she wasn't keen on marrying him. We've heard that from multiple sources. Also, no one thinks of him as being very bright, so it's possible he got the dosage wrong and hit her too hard with it that night."

"Too desperate to save himself, so he pushed her over the edge with a high dose?" Niamh nodded slowly, taking this in. "It would make sense of her flight that night, how erratically she was running around."

"Nothing was actually chasing her, but she was too paranoid to understand that."

"I think this was done to her as well. Giada's behavior doesn't make me think she was doing this to herself. It does match with what her siblings said of her." Niamh glanced at Foster, who nodded thoughtfully. "When we interviewed them yesterday, they were both adamant it couldn't be drugs. Giada hated any sort of addictive substance and avoided them completely."

"Yeah? Then I'm even more inclined to think it wasn't on purpose. There's something else that makes me feel that way too." Jamie put down her fork in order to illustrate with her hands, fingers shaping a rectangle in the air. "The open space in one of the drawers was about this size. It looked distinctly book-shaped."

"A diary," I murmured.

She turned to me, brows lifted in question. "You see where I'm going with this?"

"I do. The inside of that drawer was covered with jimsonweed. Her drying powder was apparently laced with it. There's no need to take her diary if she was using the jimsonweed recreationally. But if someone was planting it there, in a place they knew she used routinely, then there's every reason to take it—to hide the evidence of it being there in the first place."

"Bing bing! Get the man a cookie."

Seaton sat up straighter, voice growing excited. "That drawer wasn't the only one that had suspicious open space to it. The middle drawer also had a void, the rest of it crammed full."

"Noticed that, did you? She kept a lot of letters and such in the desk as well. Also, there's no pen set on her desk that I could find. It was that nagging thing I couldn't put my finger on—hard to see what's missing, sometimes. But if she wrote in her diary routinely, and letters, then she had to have a pen set on that desk. Where is it?"

"Ahh," I intoned with satisfaction. "That was it. That bothered me too."

"You're sure it was the drying powder?" Jamie asked of me.

"The jimsonweed was mixed with sand and trace minerals. What else can it be?"

"Then it really was in that set. Crap, we've got to find it."

I agreed wholeheartedly and only hoped that a simple location spell would do the trick. Alas, I doubted it, but I'd try it anyway now that I knew what to look for.

Jamie's mind had already moved ahead, her eyes narrowed in thought. "I think, really, that we're looking at a murder—a very carefully crafted murder. It could well be that the killer didn't intend for Giada to die—maybe look crazy. And it was her paranoia that made her crawl over the wall and accidentally fall off." Jamie shrugged. "But something in those drawers would have tipped our murderer's hand. That's why certain things were pulled out."

Niamh practically vibrated in her chair. "Let me look for it. Whatever was in that desk. I really want to lay hands on it. We need some physical evidence."

"Good," Jamie encouraged. "You and Foster do that. Go talk to the lawyer too, then read through the letters I did find, make note of friends she contacted recently, interview them too. Actually, Sherard, can we keep you a bit longer?"

"You can't drag me out of here," Sherard promised her firmly. "I portaled home last night, packed a bag, and now have a room here. Just in case you come across more jimsonweed while investigating, I'm staying nearby."

Jamie gave him a sweet smile. "You're the best. Thanks. Can you do something with the letters so they're not hit with a jimsonweed high like I was?"

"Of course, consider it done."

I hadn't known he had intended to stay, as I only just crossed paths with him here at the breakfast table, but I wasn't surprised by it, either. Seaton was as close to Jamie as a brother and would not stand anything untoward happening to her. I may have panicked yesterday, calling him in as I did, but I couldn't find it in myself to be embarrassed by my reaction. Calling for his help was a necessity on an emotional level; he would have been distraught to hear about this later and not have been able to aid her. It might well take both of us to safeguard her until this case was solved.

Foster's tone lilted up hopefully. "RM Seaton, if you would go with us when we investigate the room once more?"

"I'll need to, to let you in through the ward," Seaton answered with a reassuring nod. "And I wish nothing bad to happen to either of you, so I'll be happy to assist. Having one friend unduly poisoned is quite enough for this case. I will not stand for it to happen a second time."

"Exactly what I was about to suggest. Thanks, Sherard." Jamie looked to me, suggesting, "While they're doing that, let's talk to the doctor. I need those medical records. I also really want to talk to Lady Lastra. I want her take on all of this. She seemed to know her daughter better than anyone. I want to know what was in that desk. I bet Mom can tell us."

It was entirely reasonable but would mean a trip to the next town over, as the family did not live here. "It's less than an hour away. I'll call and see if we can arrange an interview this morning."

"I'd really like to talk to the husband, too. Get his take on this. Those two were the only ones that Detti allowed in Giada's bedroom after she died, so if anyone took something out, odds are it's one of them." Jamie pursed her lips thoughtfully. "Something about the husband bothers me. Giada was quick to get rid of the first husband when she got tired of him, but held onto the second even though she wouldn't live with him."

"Perhaps there was something else going on?" Niamh offered. "I've seen couples argue over joint assets."

"Maybe? They were certainly wealthy enough to buy things together, but I'm not sure if they did or not. I dunno, it's why I want to talk to the man. Something held them together, I just can't figure out what."

"If they were about to reconcile, then it could be another motive for Felipe Iadanza," I noted. "He might well have gone mad with jealousy if he knew she would not accept him."

Jamie's mouth screwed up in a grimace. "I do not underestimate what an angry, jealous person will do to another in a fit of rage. Niamh, Foster, after you guys track down whatever was in that drawer, go to the station and see how our APB to the other stations is going. We put that out yesterday; I was hoping for a sighting by now. He's got to be *somewhere.* Either running or in a shallow grave, but one way or another, we need to find him."

"Shallow grave, eh?" Seaton gave her an amused look.

"The man likes to seduce other men's wives," Jamie pointed out sardonically. "I doubt Giada was the first."

"Good point. We'll look for him." Seaton rubbed his hands together like the cheerful maniac he was. "I have some excellent seeking spells. If the police can't locate him, perhaps I'll give it a go. I'm sure it'll be a brilliant game of Felix and mouse."

Oh dear. What had Jamie just unleashed?

"And on that cheerful note, I'm going to find my cats. And get ready to go interview a grieving mother, again." Jamie stood with a grimace. "And update a queen. Ugh, too many conversations I don't want to have today."

I sympathized. Sometimes, a detective's job was nothing more than speaking to every single person involved. I didn't know how Jamie did it. I felt my soul start to shrivel inside my body after the fourth interview in a single day. It was far too much socialization for me. The one thing I could help her on was, "The Felixes are out sunbathing on the terrace, I believe."

"Yeah? Alright, let's see if something fast and rodent-y has caught their attention or if they're still being good. I do not lay my money on them being good." So saying, she strode for the balcony doors.

I didn't bet on them behaving, either.

Niamh and Foster both excused themselves, leaving Seaton and I alone to finish up breakfast. I fortified myself with more tea, as this day called for such.

Leaning in, Seaton murmured to me, "She looks much better this morning."

"I do believe she's back to her normal self. Thank magic."

"I'm relieved. I can never quite predict what she can handle and what will take her down. Then again, the jimsonweed is entirely natural, so her defenses have no immunity to it."

"True. I did realize that, belatedly. At the time, I was too panicked to really think along those lines."

"Hmm, I don't blame you. I wasn't entirely clearheaded myself. Usually, even when something takes her down, she can still remain logical and in control on some level. Watching her senses take a turn gave me one as well." Seaton shook his head. "But I'll linger as long as I can. Just tell me you have something of a solid lead."

I gave him an apologetic shrug. "Sorry, old chap. Wish I could. As you heard during the breakfast conversation, we're still trying to determine if Giada's death was deliberate or not."

"But you think the lover did it, don't you?"

"We think he had motive, but we have no proof. Really, we have no proof that anyone did it. There are absolutely no witnesses to Giada's death or any evidence linked directly to it that wasn't on the body itself."

Seaton stared at me, a man waiting for the punchline. "I'm beginning to see why Queen Regina sent you and Jamie."

"Don't you? This case is tricky in multiple ways."

"Well. Doubly glad I'm here, then. Maybe I can tease a solid lead out of the lineup of suspects you have."

"I certainly won't turn down the help. But aren't there duties awaiting you at home?"

Seaton waved this off. "It'll be fine for a few weeks."

"Weeks! Don't jinx us, man. I don't want to be up here for weeks."

"Days?"

"Days is better. Hopefully it'll take days. We're coming up on the holidays, after all, and I'd prefer to be with family."

Hopefully. I did not find myself holding my breath, however.

We should have bet on it. Clint and Tasha got distracted chasing mice.

And Phil?

Watched them from the terrace, like the disapproving old soul he is.

You're telling me he didn't chase a single one?

He will neither confirm nor deny. But I did find him on the terrace.

I suppose that's truth enough. And the other two?

Turned into a competition of who could catch the most.
I understand Tasha won. Clint is now pouting.

Report 15: Death Certificates Open Doors

The doctor's office was a quaint building, white board and blue shutters with a black door and gold stenciling labeling it "Dr. Heathrow's Clinic." When Jamie pushed the door open, a little chime alerted, though I saw no bell. Ah, the charm was there next to the door, I saw it now.

The front foyer was a small square space, a receptionist sitting behind a single desk with rows of file cabinets behind her. Jamie stopped there, flashing a badge for the woman. "Detective Edwards. I'd like to speak with Dr. Heathrow."

"Of course, Detective, I think he's expecting you."

We waited for only a moment before she was back, holding open a door that led through to a private office. "This way, please. I'll fetch you a hot cup of tea."

"If you would be so kind." Heating charm or no heating charm, the tea would be welcome.

Dr. Heathrow stood just inside the room, offering a hand in welcome. "Detective Edwards, is it? Charles Heathrow, pleasure."

Jamie shook hands with him as she introduced me. "This is Dr. Henri Davenforth, my partner."

"Pleasure, Doctor. If you don't mind my asking, these are some very unusual creatures you have with you. They are...?"

Clint, as always, was eager to answer the question. "I field cat. My name is Clint."

The good doctor blinked down at the purple cat

stretched across Jamie's arm with open astonishment, his bushy grey brows kissing his receding hairline. "Good deities, how astonishing. You're sentient?"

"Yes," Clint answered forthrightly.

"They are Felixes," Jamie explained patiently, as she always did. "Constructed by RM Jules Felix. They're really meant to be a magician's familiar, but I've got three because Jules likes to field test things with me. They enjoy the investigation process, too. It's a win-win."

"Quite astonishing. Well, do come in, please let me know how I can help you." He waved us to two armchairs in front of his desk.

It was a well-appointed office and one that saw much use. I took note of the stacks of files on his desk, the file cabinets lining the back wall, and a few things that made me think he saw particular clients here for examinations. It was not a true examination room, however. Something he did for VIP clients, perhaps?

Jamie settled in the leather armchair, relaxed and in control of her own space. "We're here regarding the death of Giada Barese. I have a death certificate on me if you need to see that first?"

"I will, just to keep formalities in line, you understand."

"I do, and thank you for keeping things legal." Jamie produced it from an inner pocket, which he examined with an obligatory read-through before handing it back. Folding it back into her pocket, she continued smoothly, "What can you tell me of Giada's health before her death?"

"Physically, she was in the peak of health in many ways. Giada did a great deal of swimming, dancing, and light sports to keep her body fit. She was one of my better clients about being wary of how much sugar she consumed. It wasn't until recent months that her health began to worry us. She started having spells—

random, disconnected events that I couldn't find a pattern to. The episodes included paranoid behaviors and vivid hallucinations, followed by extreme fatigue and hunger. She started a log with me, to show when she had these episodes. We tracked both environmental and situational factors, everything from what she ate to who she was around when they happened. From what we could tell, they happened most frequently in the evening, sometimes lasting until one o'clock in the morning. They were always triggered at home. There were no other common factors. I ran several tests on her but couldn't pinpoint the source."

He didn't sound dismissive of it. The doctor, at least, had believed her. I was strangely relieved to know that at least one person had. "Was this log something that she continued to do up to her death?"

"No, she stopped some weeks ago. I have it here, with her records."

Excellent. I loved data such as that. "Did her episodes increase in frequency?"

"No. They did, however, seem to increase in strength. Her symptoms turned from mild to something almost unmanageable. It wasn't from something she had directly digested, as I tested her mouth and stomach contents several times."

"Was she taking any kind of medication to help with the symptoms?"

"She was, a tonic to help detox her system and keep her calm. It had less than stellar results. Also a sleeping tonic to help her rest better at night. I wasn't sure what to prescribe, to be honest. Not without knowing the cause." In a confidential tone, Dr. Heathrow admitted, "We both feared it might be her lover poisoning her. The relationship was on the rocks and everyone knew it."

I had to question this. "Was this a theory you entertained from the beginning?"

"No, in fact. It wasn't until about two weeks before Giada's death that we thought to track who was near her, to see if this was done by someone close to her. It was also about that point her relationship with Iadanza had hit rock bottom. Giada had him stay with friends for a few days at one point to test the theory, but she still had two episodes. If he was the cause, it wasn't something he actively had to do."

"Did you have any suggestions for her?"

"We'd actually scheduled for her to see a specialist the very week of her death. She was set to travel into Kingston for a very thorough magical examination. I felt it the only recourse. *Something* was affecting her, but I couldn't determine what, and with the frequency of her spells? It was only a matter of time before something untoward happened." Dr. Heathrow winced, regret open on his face. "Which, unfortunately, it seems we were too late."

His reaction seemed interesting to me. "You believe she had one of these spells, and that's what killed her?"

"Word around town was that she fell into the ocean. I believe it entirely possible that during one of her hallucinations, she would mistake the sea for something else entirely. Her episodes were incredibly vivid to her, to the point that she could not discern reality from make-believe." Looking at us both firmly, he said, "I do not believe this was an illness of the mind. I tested for that upon her first visit to me regarding this matter. It was not a mental illness. I will stand in a court of law and swear she was not suicidal. Giada was fighting for her life and sanity. She was in no way in danger of losing that battle, either. If she fell into the ocean, it was by accident."

Or by intent of another party, but I did not want to say that aloud. The closer we kept the truth, the more room we had to negotiate with.

Jamie gave him a reassuring nod. "For the record,

Doctor, I do not believe it was suicide either. A lot of strange things happened around Giada the night before her death. I will get to the bottom of why and how she died, but I think suicide is not the answer."

He visibly relaxed, shoulders dropping from their defensive clench. "Thank you, Detective. I'm relieved to hear that. I feel like I failed Giada somehow. I still don't know what was wrong with her. If I missed something obvious, it will be a regret I take to the grave."

I personally did not fault him for missing the jimsonweed. It was a strange thing to test for, especially from a woman who hated recreational pursuits. He'd already arranged for a specialist to give her a thorough examination. What more could he have done? "It is through no fault of yours that she died, Doctor. I assure you of that. Do you mind if we take a copy of her medical records with us?"

"Please do. I wish to keep her original file," he said with a thankful nod to me. "As a reference, really, just in case I see another patient with these symptoms. And please, if you ever discover what was wrong with her, do tell me. I do not want to see these symptoms again in another and see them go down the same path."

With those words, I realized I had to rescind my earlier opinion. He was entirely correct—without knowing what Giada suffered from, how could he safeguard another? It would no doubt come to light in some newspaper article in the future, but those accounts often got the details wrong. Did I want to trust a reporter to lay out the facts correctly?

The idea gave me chills.

I glanced at Jamie, her eyes finding mine in the same moment. Our communication was entirely silent and unanimous.

"Doctor, I assume doctor-patient confidentiality still stands with you in regards to Giada?" I inquired, knowing full well the answer.

"Yes, of course." He sat up straighter, eyes locked on me. "You know. You know what was wrong with her."

"I know what we discovered in her bedroom," I corrected him. "I believe it was the root cause, yes. We do not know who put it there or how it was transferred to her. Some of this is still under investigation. I tell you so that if you see these symptoms again, you know how to respond."

"And tell us," Jamie piped up.

Dr. Heathrow nodded immediately, eyes bouncing between us. "What was it?"

"Jimsonweed," I said.

"*Jim—!*" Heathrow's jaw dropped and he spluttered. "That has hallucinogenic properties?!"

"It does. Usually only used in certain cultures for religious practices, although I've come across it twice as a magical examiner in connection with a case. Some people are stupid enough to use it as a recreational drug. Used incorrectly, it can lead to death. We found traces of it among her things."

"Actually, it got me," Jamie added with a grimace. "It's not a fun trip, I can tell you that. And I only got a trace dose."

Heathrow sank back into his chair, a hand over his eyes. "Great deities above and below, I didn't even suspect that."

"If she'd made it to your specialist, I think they would have quickly figured it out. Do not be hard on yourself. I tell you because we have yet to figure out where it came from and how it came to be in her bedroom. If there are others suffering from the same symptoms, it might well lead us to her killer. So tell us immediately if you see this."

He lowered his hand, his expression now one of fierce resolve. "I swear to you I will. Thank you for telling me this. It would have haunted me for years. I appreciate that you normally wouldn't say this in an open investigation. I won't breathe a word to anyone else until you find her killer. She was killed, wasn't she?"

Jamie gave a shrug. "That's my working guess. She was worried enough about these trips to come and see you, which means she didn't know what was going on. Someone planted the jimsonweed in her room. Even if the intent wasn't murder, it ended with her death."

"That's murder in my book." Heathrow shook his head, agitated and angry. "Giada was a beautiful woman. Somewhat shallow in her appearance, but still, a kind person. She didn't deserve this. I don't know how much more I can help. Take her medical records. Here, the top page"—he reached for her file, opened it, and flipped it around so we could see for ourselves—"has a list of dates and times for every episode. I have a more detailed summary of each in her own hand in this file. She was methodical about tracking this. Will it help?"

I immediately took the file from him, my heart singing with joy. Data. He'd just given me a thick folder of data. It was neatly recorded in columns, the dates, times, even durations all listed out.

Jamie snorted. "You just made him super happy, Doctor. I can tell from his face. This may well help us crack open the case. We really do not have enough credible information of what was going on with Giada leading up to her death. Just witness accounts, and those are shaky at the best of times. Thank you for this."

He seemed glad to hear those words. "I hope it does. I would hate to fail her even in death."

"Trust me, you didn't fail her. As far as I can tell, you were the only person who took her situation seriously. Everyone else was brushing it off as man trouble. Which pisses me off, not going to lie. So, thanks for being that one person." Jamie stood, arranging Clint over a shoulder to free up a hand. "Thank you, Doctor. If we have follow-up questions, we'll be back."

Dr. Heathrow shook her hand in a strong grip, then mine. "Thank you for coming. I feel better knowing you're on her case. The best of luck finding her killer."

"Thank you." I gave him a smile as I tucked the file under my arm. "We're going to need it."

Report 16: Diaries

The Lastra mansion was grand indeed, but I could see signs the family did have money struggles from time to time. Queen Regina had mentioned that the Lastra family had highs and lows when it came to wealth. Giada had been born into poverty and then married into riches, or so I'd been told. I kinda saw signs of that as Henri and I rode a taxi to the Lastra mansion. We passed multiple abandoned buildings on the estate. Obviously abandoned. Not enough money to keep all of it up, eh? As we got closer to the house itself, everything else was well kept, the grounds mowed and impressive. There was quite a bit of festive décor along the windows, doorways, and wrapped around the lights, greeneries and bright ribbons.

Not to mention the white ribbons of mourning.

We were taken over the paved driveway straight to the front door. Clint nestled in the crook of my arm, with Tasha riding in a front pocket, as was their habit. How they decided on all of this, I did not know. I was not privy to the conversation. It was my duty to haul cats around, not to ask questions.

Henri stepped out ahead of me, then turned to give me a hand down, which I appreciated. There had been a recent rainfall and the weather had turned colder, making things icy and slippery in the worst ways. Balancing two cats and getting out of a narrow taxi door could be harrowing at times. I probably didn't need the help. I appreciated it anyway.

A butler answered the door before we could even ring the bell, looking rather stiff and uncomfortable for some reason. He greeted us with a shallow bow, really more a nod of the head than anything.

"Detective Edwards and Dr. Davenforth to see Lady Lastra," I identified for him.

"My lady is expecting you. Please come through."

We followed, only pausing long enough to shed coats and hand them over to a footman before continuing. Clint finally decided to use his own paws and walked at heel like a faithful dog. Tasha wanted to be in my arms, though, in a better position to survey the scene.

We were not shown into any formal receiving room, but into a morning room made mostly of glass. what warmth from the sun coming in and reflecting throughout the room. I'd been in enough rooms like this to recognize this as the lady of the house's personal room. The light furniture, pastel fabrics, and flower arrangements everywhere readily gave it away.

Ensconced in a chair near the fireplace sat Lady Lastra, looking rather the worse for wear. She had a thick blanket across her lap, high spots of color in her cheeks, and a handkerchief clutched in one fist. Still, she greeted us with a wan smile.

"Detective, Doctor, do come in. Pray excuse me, I've come down with a nasty cold."

"I'm sorry to visit you when you're sick," I said. "I wasn't aware."

"I'm quite determined to help you with my daughter's case, in whatever form I can. My cold is not so severe to stop me." She waved us to a settee nearby. "Please, sit. I'll have tea brought out to you immediately. It's dreadful weather outside."

"Strangely enough, it was nice in Ashbluff. Cold, of course, but clear skies. Funny how dramatically the weather can change even over a short distance." I took the seat, arranging both legs and cats as I did without much thought.

Henri sat with me, our hips pressed lightly together. "Lady Lastra, I can offer you an anti-sickness charm before I leave. It will do much to restore your health overnight."

"Thank you." Her smile brightened a notch. "You're always so kind and thoughtful. I called your mother, you know, after I knew you were on this case. I caught up with her and all you've been doing. I understand the two of you are courting?"

"We are," Henri answered comfortably.

"How splendid. It's always such a lucky thing, to find someone you truly like. I'm quite pleased for both of you. My own children seem to struggle with that. But you two must be well matched if you can both court and work with each other."

I gave Henri a quick wink and enjoyed his grin in return. "It's because we work so well together that we wanted to try dating."

"I consider myself a fortunate man that it's going so well."

This smooth talker. I'd reward him for that line later. Shaking my head, I turned my mind back to business. "I just have a few questions that have cropped up. I promise we'll be quick so you can rest and get better. First, did Giada keep a diary?"

"Oh my, yes," she answered without hesitation. "Giada was incredibly consistent with it, too. She wrote daily in her diary without fail, often whole pages about who she met, or what she did, or what thoughts she entertained at the time. She had done that ever since she first learned how to write."

Lady Lastra's hand came over to rest on the stack of books sitting on her side table. Most of them looked at least twenty years old. "I still have the ones from her youth. I've been re-reading them as my heart allows, reliving those happy days. Why do you ask, Detective?"

"There's evidence of something book-shaped and a stack of something missing from her desk drawers."

"Oh." She blinked at me, brows drawing together. "Oh dear. I can't explain that. I haven't had anything removed from the room except the day you were with me to watch, and when Sebastian came over."

"Lord Barese came to visit?"

"After we discovered that she was...that she wasn't just missing, he came to me and asked if it would be okay if he took some small memento from her room." A tear tried to come to her eye, but she wiped it away with the handkerchief and continued, determined to keep her emotions in check. "He was so distraught, poor man. He did love my daughter, and keenly. I didn't have the heart to tell him no. But I'm not sure what he ended up taking."

"But as far as you know, the diaries were always there?"

"Yes, I think so. Are they important?"

"I'd love to read them," I answered honestly. "It'll give me a better idea of her days. Second question. Tell me more about Giada's relationship with her husband and mother-in-law."

"It was never really good," Lady Lastra admitted. "Sebastian seemed to sweep Giada off her feet at first. He's very charming when he puts his mind to it, and they had a mutual love of socializing and parties, so it was easy to be in each other's company. It wasn't until after they were married Giada realized her mistake, I think. Sebastian is the type to not really settle down with anyone. He kept flirting with women even after they were married, and whenever she confronted him about it, he'd pass it off as just conversation. It sparked many arguments between them."

Oh yeah, I bet. I'd certainly be hot under the collar if my man was doing that. Not that Henri ever would. "Was that what broke their relationship?"

Lady Lastra leaned in and offered, "Giada suggested he was doing more than flirting. I think he actually did keep a mistress on the side. She was too upset to really talk about it."

The plot thickened. If hubby was cheating, no wonder Giada ditched him. "Was their conflict the reason why Lady Barese didn't like her?"

"No, I don't think so. She's one of those mothers who believes no one is good enough for her son. Giada complained to me often that Lady Barese was spiteful to her. She bullied

Giada whenever she could, to the point that Giada spent most of her married life outside the house as much as possible, taking trips to keep her distance." Lady Lastra rolled her eyes expressively, a sigh slipping out of her mouth. "Really, she should thank any woman willing to take him on. Sebastian is both frivolous and unreliable. He's not good husband material."

"So really, when Giada left him, you were relieved?"

"I was, yes. Sad that she'd once again had a marriage fail on her. Still, I'd rather she leave Sebastian than stay with him."

"She left him six months ago, but did she say she would divorce him?"

"She threatened to do so several times. I don't know why she hesitated with Sebastian, when she didn't with her first husband. I know Sebastian came to her several times, and sent her extravagant gifts, trying to reconcile. That might have been the reason. Of course, Felipe—" Lady Lastra just shook her head. "Felipe swept in while she was still heartbroken and took advantage. Her relationship with him might well have distracted her from starting the divorce proceedings. Giada detested anything like paperwork."

"So probably more a matter of her putting off something she hated doing, rather than an attachment to Lord Barese? Got it." It more or less made sense, based on what I knew of Giada. I could see how a new relationship would distract her from breaking off an old one, at least temporarily.

I glanced at Henri and saw that he was drawing out an anti-sickness charm with considerable speed but probably needed another minute. I could buy him some time. And I had one more thing to ask. "How well did you know Felipe Iadanza?"

"Not all that well. I never had a good impression of him, and I only saw him when I saw Giada. He was…reactive, I think is the best word." Her lips pursed, and not in a good way. "He was normally in high spirits over something, good or bad. He could be incredibly charming when he put effort into it. Giada was certainly charmed by him in the beginning. She was always laughing or telling me some story about something he'd done. But as time went on, he put less effort into keeping her happy, his true colors coming out. She stopped smiling as much, started complaining more. I urged her several times to be shed of him. Nothing good comes from a man like that."

Henri finished off the charm, then with a cutting spell, separated the page from the notebook. Ever efficient, my boyfriend. "Do you have any idea of his family or acquaintances?"

She opened her mouth, paused, and then rethought her initial response. "Do you know, I think he did mention to me once that he was the son of a school teacher from Elsher. I have no idea if that was the truth or not. It was something Giada struggled with. Most of what Felipe said to her was either truth mixed with lies or outright lies. It was hard to believe anything he said."

Still, I made a note of the city, Elsher. No one else had mentioned that place; it bore investigating. Poor Niamh was going crazy trying to find Iadanza. It was going to become personal at this rate.

"Thank you." I gave her my best smile. "You've been so helpful."

"Have I really?"

"You've narrowed down possibilities for me, so yes. I hate investigating in the wrong direction. It eats up valuable time."

Henri handed me Phil so he could stand and cross to her. "Keep this charm next to you at all times until tomorrow morning. It will cleanse your system of the illness and bolster your immune system. You should be well by morning. If not, seek a doctor's advice."

"I will, thank you." She smiled up at him, the gesture a little sad.

Womanly intuition stirred. I think, all said, she wished Giada had been drawn more to men like Henri. The good, kind men who knew how to take care of the people around them. If Giada had a Henri in her life, she wouldn't have died. I would lay good money on that.

We said goodbyes, collected coats, and retreated back to our waiting taxi. As I settled into the seat, I said that thought aloud. "If Giada had a good person like you, I don't think she would have ended up dead."

Henri canted his head at me. "I'm not sure if you mean that as a compliment or an observation."

"A little of both. I don't know Sebastian Barese, of course, so I can't say one way or another about him. But I know he's not a *you*. You would never let your parents bully you and your wife to the point that separation was the only recourse."

Henri grunted sourly. "That's truly spoken. Nor would I continue to live with my mother after she'd driven my wife from the house."

"See? If Giada had married a man more like you, one that actually put her as the priority, I don't think she would have died. If I had shown signs of dizzy spells and paranoid episodes, you wouldn't have rested until we figured out what was going on. I'm telling you, if she'd just had one person properly in her corner, this woman would still be alive. I know her mother loved her, but I think she was also embarrassed by her daughter's decisions."

"It was kind of you to not point that out."

"Yeah, it would just be lye in an open wound right now. Even I'm not that mean." I shook my head, shifting cats aside enough that I could pull my pad out. I messaged Niamh now that I had something of a lead on Iadanza. *Hey, Iadanza might be from Elsher.*

Her response was quick. *Really? I'll check there.*

Any luck on what was missing in the drawer?

Staff said it was likely her diaries. I can't find any trace of them in the house.

Okay, they might be with husband. He took stuff out of Giada's bedroom. I'll follow up on that. You go to lawyer first, figure out what was in Giada's will. If there's time, go to

Elsher.

There was a pause before she responded. *Will do.*

Did you find any kind of medical log?

No, nothing like that.

Okay so the only copy really was with the doctor. Good to know.

Man, we *really* needed to find the lover. I had so many questions for him.

"Back to Ashbluff," Henri announced cheerfully. "I really want to give the medical records a thorough study."

"She was definitely being drugged, so if you can figure out some kind of pattern, maybe we can figure out who was doing it.

Henri glanced at me, caught my eyes. "You realize, unless it was a freak accident that caused her to fall over the garden wall, the odds of this being a murder is extremely high."

"Oh, it's a murder," I said grimly. "We just haven't found her murderer yet."

Sherard pinged me and I looked at my pad.

Need my help on anything?

He was a little bored, huh. Well, actually… *Yeah, can you portal me over to interview Lord Barese?*

Of course.

I'll be back in Ashbluff in about an hour. Meet me at the hotel.

Done.

I told Henri, "I'll take Sherard with me to go interview the husband. He'll portal us there and back, save us from being on a train half the day."

"A good thought. It might take a royal mage to get you a proper audience, for that matter." Henri pulled a face. "I can't imagine that Lord or Lady Barese will be easy to interview, as speaking to a policeman might be beneath them."

Oh joy. Those types, huh.

I'm really glad I have friends in such high places.

Report 17: Husband No Bueno

What does that mean?

Husband no good.

Ah. Well, we suspected that was the case.

Suspicion very much confirmed.

Sherard and I portaled right onto the front steps of a very grand house. It sat back from the city street, a curved driveway and manicured flower beds giving some separation. From my vantage point on the porch, I could only see pale brick, gold leafing on the windowsills, but it was enough to give the impression of extravagance. Even the holiday décor was mostly golden ribbons offset by greenery and elaborate bouquets. This was a house for show, most definitely.

Really glad I had Sherard with me right now. I seriously did not think I'd get through the front door without him.

I hoped Sebastian Barese was home. I'd called several times, trying to arrange an interview, only to catch no one but the butler, who was apparently not interested in passing along my messages. This avoidance only spelled out more suspicion, to my mind, because if Sebastian Barese really had been attached to his late wife, wouldn't he be eager to help with the investigation into her death? The man was invested enough to come and get some sentimental things out of her bedroom, after all. Surely talking to a policewoman wouldn't be that much of a deal?

It could just be the butler being snobby on behalf of his boss, but it was aggravating in the extreme. I wished that I could just call Barese directly. Ah, I longed for the days of personal cell phones.

With Clint in the crook of my elbow, I knocked firmly on the front door. I didn't have much of a wait before a man in very smart black and white livery opened it, looking down his nose at me in an obviously judging way.

Yes, I was in a suit, which most women wouldn't dream of doing in this culture. It was a nice suit, though, a dark blue that had been tailored just for me and it did not deserve the dirty look it was getting.

I tried to get a foot in the door, metaphorically speaking, before the guy just shut the door in my face. "Detective Jamie Edwards to speak with Sebastian Barese."

"Lord Barese is not receiving visitors at this time," he informed me haughtily.

Policemen were not allowed to throat punch people for being snobs. More's the pity. The temptation was there, though.

Sherard leaned in over my shoulder, his smile all teeth. "Royal Mage Sherard Seaton also requires to speak with Lord Barese."

The butler visibly paled. "O-of course, RM Seaton. This way, please."

We stepped through the doorway, him taking both our coats and trying to avoid my eyes. We were shown into what was obviously a receiving room for guests. Everything was white. Everything. Walls, ceiling, carpet, furniture. It gave me hives just walking in. How did anyone think something this sterile looked cool? Ugh, and I had to sit in here and act professional.

Sherard didn't even bat an eye. He took a chair, flipping his red coat back in a dramatic way as he sat down. I took a cue from him and chose the seat next to his, arranging Clint on my lap. I didn't trust him to not get distracted in this house. There were too many dangling, shiny things hanging off the furniture that would attract kitty attention. Tasha, I trusted to sit near my feet. Clint, I did not.

I shared a glance with Sherard, not sure what to make of all this. The butler hustled out, no doubt to give notice to his employer that we were here.

"Odds of me getting straight answers?"

Sherard tilted a hand back and forth like a scale tipping. "Fifty-fifty? I don't know Sebastian Barese well enough to guess. I think we've crossed paths at a party—that's about as far as we're acquainted."

"Ah. Got it. Well, I guess we'll see."

Like a dramatic whirlwind, a rather handsome man in his thirties twirled through the door. He was darkly handsome like a movie star, wearing a loose poet's shirt, fitted tan vest, and dark pants that flattered his figure. He had a hand clutched to his chest as he came straight to us, eyes already brimming with tears.

"My dear Detective, RM Seaton, I'm so pleased you came to me. I wanted to reach out, truly, but Giada's death has so devastated me, I've been at my wit's end. It's only today that I felt well enough to rise from the couch and properly dress."

Oh boy. Here we go. Was that Giada's type? The overly dramatic men? I tried to derail him before he could keep going on in this vein. Standing, I offered a hand. "Detective Jamie Edwards."

He clasped it but didn't shake, holding on instead. "Detective, you are very welcome here."

I was very proud of myself for not saying "You could not prove that by your butler," aloud. "Thank you. Please, sit, I have so many questions for you."

"I'm sure you do." He flopped onto the couch, sprawling like a puppet with all of its strings cut. "I have many for you as well. First, did my Giada suffer at all?"

I could answer this truthfully. "No, I don't believe she did. Her neck was broken in a clean snap. The coroner believes she was dead before she even hit the water. I'm sorry for your loss, Lord Barese. I can't imagine what this is like."

His tears were genuine, at least. I believed that, as it was an ugly sort of cry, and he had to look away. "We were at odds with each other, but I never wished her ill. I'd hoped to regain her affections."

"So I understand." I pulled out my notebook, balancing it on Clint's back so I could jot down notes. He purred at me, not at all bothered at being a lap desk. "Walk me through a few things. She moved out of your house six months ago.

How much contact did you have with her after she left?"

"I visited several times, at least until she took up with that odious twat, Iadanza. I couldn't stand seeing her with the man, so I didn't visit as often after that. I wrote to her weekly, sent flowers and gifts, but I'm not sure if she paid them any attention. I certainly never got a response."

"So you're not in a position to tell me what she was like the past, oh, three months?"

"No, I'm sorry to say I cannot. We essentially had no contact with each other; she never responded to me." Barese looked hurt by that. "I know that she and Mother are—were—at odds with each other. It's what drove her out of the house shortly after our honeymoon. But to dismiss me entirely because of it, that was too much."

I reserved comment. Took biting my tongue, though. "I understand after her death was confirmed that you came to the house and took a few things?"

"For sentimental reasons. I wanted something of hers to remember her by." He straightened only a little on the couch, mouth drawn down into a sad smile. "I have nothing of hers here. She left nothing behind when she moved out, you see."

"Ah. What did you take?"

"Some of her journals. The ones specifically from the time that we were courting and the first part of our marriage. The happy times."

Missing journals, confirmed. "Do you mind if I have those back? I need them for evidence purposes."

"Oh!" He looked truly surprised, snapping his fingers. "Detective, I'm so sorry, I didn't think of them in terms of evidence. Of course, you may have them if it will help you determine what happened to Giada. I'll fetch them. HANSON!"

By fetch, he meant someone would go get them for him. I felt like shaking my head.

Another liveried man I didn't recognize popped in and ducked into a quick bow. "My lord?"

"Giada's journals are on my bedside table," Barese

directed briskly. "Fetch all of them and bring them here immediately."

"Very good, my lord." Hanson turned on a heel and walked smartly out.

I called after Hanson, "Wear gloves! They're likely contaminated."

Hanson looked alarmed. "Excuse me?"

Sherard put a hand on my shoulder. "I'll go fetch them."

"Probably the safer option, yeah."

Barese looked just as alarmed. "Why do you say so?"

I ignored his question and asked one of my own. "Here's where we get to the next round of questions. Lord Barese, what do you know about jimsonweed?"

"I'm sorry?" he looked at me with such a blank expression I thought he was trying to impersonate a statue for a second.

"Also called devil's snare?" I sat, waiting. Come on, man, give me something.

Barese's mouth opened and closed several times, like a landed fish gasping for words. "What? Am I supposed to know something about it?"

He really did look clueless. "Alright, let me change questions. How did you feel about Felipe Iadanza?"

"Oh, that fumbling idiot. About as sharp as a marble, that one. I couldn't begin to see the appeal or why Giada chose his company over mine." Barese openly fumed, his fists clenching in his lap. "It was him, you know, that turned Giada from me. We'd had nothing but a lover's spat, but he found her at exactly the right time to slip in and seduce her."

"Lover's spat…that lasted two months? She'd moved out of your house and was on her own for two months before she met Iadanza."

Barese blinked at me as if I'd spoken some foreign language. "It was that long?"

I expected nothing from this man and I was still disappointed. Good grief, really? You didn't keep track of how long your wife was gone?

Giada, girl, I get why you left this sad sack. I'd met a

lot of pricks in my time, but Barese was a freaking cactus. Seriously.

"Her conflict with your mother was what drove her out of the house, or so I'm given to understand. Why not move with her?"

"Oh, I couldn't possibly leave Mother. She's so delicate in health, you know, and sometimes I'm the only one that can convince her to take her medicine. I told Giada that she needed to put more effort into charming my mother, but she just screamed at me and stormed out. Quite unreasonable, really." Barese blinked at me sadly, like a puppy that had been kicked and didn't understand why.

Yup. I see the problem. It wasn't Giada, either. This man was a walking red flag. "When Giada was still living with you, did she have any health concerns?"

"Er…no?"

Like, I'd love to trust that answer, but this was a man who hadn't even realized his wife had separated from him for two months before finding a new lover, so clearly his observation powers were right up there with amoebas. "Did she complain of any dizzy spells, or often take afternoon naps?"

"Not that I recall. Oh dear, was she ill?"

"She'd complained of such things before her death, yes. I'm trying to determine how far back this went. Was she seeing a physician in town?"

"Heavens no. She quite prided herself on her health and figure. It's what attracted me to her, initially."

Ladies and gentlemen, confirmation right here that it was lust that brought these two together. Not that I needed it. "I see."

Sherard strode back through the door, a cloth-wrapped bundle in one hand. "Diaries acquired."

There was that, at least.

Barese regarded the diaries with new suspicion. One could almost see the hamster in the wheel tentatively moving. He probably hadn't used his brain in a while, so no doubt it would take a minute to get it up to any kind of speed. "Why are her journals evidence?"

"I need an accounting of her days before her death. Frankly, my lord, I suspected you a little of her murder because you took them. If you'd destroyed them, we'd be having a very different conversation right now."

He didn't even look alarmed, just blank, like he couldn't contemplate why I would even think such a thing.

Giada, seriously, what *did* you see in this idiot? I've met brick walls with more intelligence.

Granted, Henri's spoiled me, but still.

I shook my head and went with the next question. "When you collected the diaries, where were they? Middle drawer of her desk, right?"

"That's where I took it from. That and the right-side drawer."

It was weird that he handled them and not suffered any kind of side effects like I had. Or had he? I probed that delicately. "Did you pick up the diaries with your bare hands?"

"I...no. No, I didn't. I'd wrapped the diaries up in a cloth to take them home, and while I intended to read them, I couldn't bring myself to do it. They've been sitting on my nightstand without being touched since her death."

"So at no point did you physically handle them? Did anyone?"

"I, ah, no. My man was wearing gloves when we went in and, as I said, I wrapped them in a cloth to carry home—as a protection to them. I don't think anyone touched them directly." His dramatic expression dropped and Barese looked at me seriously. "Detective, you're not acting as if Giada committed suicide or accidentally fell to her death. Do you think she was murdered, then?"

I matched his tone. "This is a murder investigation. I have no idea if someone intended for her to die or if they were trying to discredit her somehow, but it ended in her death one way or another. Lord Barese, I need a list of all who would wish her harm. Who can you think of?"

"I—I really don't know. Iadanza, perhaps?"

Hmm. Not helpful. "Truly, no one else comes to mind?"

"Giada wasn't the type to make enemies. Even my dear mother didn't hate her, although they didn't see eye to eye on many matters."

I'd take that with a pound of salt, thanks.

I had to go through the basics. "Lord Barese, just for the record, where were you the night of her death?"

"Abroad, in fact. I was visiting friends in Ciparis. I didn't hear of Giada's disappearance until a week later, upon our return."

"Can I have the name of the friend in question?"

"Certainly, it's Lady Dalris."

"Thanks." That matched with what I'd been told earlier. I'd reach out and confirm that later with the lady in question. "I'm going to leave my card with you, sir. If you can think of anyone, anyone at all who wished to either discredit or kill her, please call me."

"I certainly will, Detective." His jaw worked under strong emotion, eyes too bright with unshed tears. "This tears me apart, thinking about what happened to her. Do you believe it to be Iadanza?"

"Right now, I have no idea who it is," I answered frankly.

I didn't really have anything else to ask him. Not at this point. I stood, slinging a cat over my shoulder, and gave him a smile. "Thank you for your time. I'll likely be in touch again with you later. Make sure your butler understands to actually put you on the phone, if you would."

Barese gave me an odd look. "Did you call before?"

"Many times. He wouldn't let me speak to you."

"Oh. Probably Mother's orders. I've been so distraught, she's gotten protective of me. I'll straighten it out, Detective. Do keep me in the loop."

"I will. Thanks." I gave him a last smile and headed for the door.

Sherard beat me to it, shrugging his great coat back on, keeping a hand on the evidence. I was not sad to leave the house, that was for sure. I paused on the front porch to ask him, "Well? Contaminated?"

"Mixed news for you. Most of the books have traces of jimsonweed on the covers, but the last part of one diary has traces of jimsonweed on the pages."

I looked at the bundle with keen interest. "Just the last pages?"

"From the quick test I performed, yes. Henri and I will do a more thorough examination later."

"Okay." Now we were getting somewhere. I fully intended on reading those journals but definitely would handle them with kid gloves. And maybe a mask, just in case. "At least we got something from this interview. I swear, that man is a waste of the air he's breathing."

Sherard grunted in agreement, "Giada's taste in men was very questionable."

"I'll say. I fully believe he's torn up about her death, but he's also enjoying the drama of it all. He's about as reliable as a stump."

"Is he our killer?"

I shrugged, as I honestly didn't know. "If he is, he's a pretty stupid one to leave trace evidence right next to his bed. I'm not saying that takes him out of the running; murderers aren't known for their intelligence. He's about as intelligent as a water flea."

Sherard snorted in agreement. "So, still a suspect."

"Yeah. I have no way to link him to the crime except him taking evidence out of the house, and no real motive for him at this point, but he's definitely a suspect until I can prove otherwise. Let's head back."

Sherard offered me an arm, already readying a portal spell. "With pleasure."

Report 18: Data Should Be Helpful

The medical records didn't tell me much of anything I didn't already know. With Jamie and Sherard out interviewing Giada's husband, I had blissful silence to work in. I did appreciate that, even if I didn't find the answers I sought. Aside from the jimsonweed wreaking havoc on her, Giada Barese had been in the peak of health. She suffered no maladies, ate well and exercised regularly, and was otherwise fine. The jimsonweed episodes had taken a toll on her in the months leading up to her death, but that was to be expected since she didn't know the cause of the episodes.

It all matched with the coroner's report. I looked for the obvious reasons why someone might wish to kill her—was she pregnant? Any signs of abuse on her person? Nothing appeared in the records. It matched Weber's report.

I'd not really expected much to begin with. Both doctors would have alerted me if something had stood out. However, police work was often double-checking all the facts just to make sure nothing had been overlooked.

There was a clatter at the door of the room as Niamh and Foster came through. I turned in my chair to greet them.

"How did it go?"

"The lawyer was happy to cooperate," Foster reported as he joined me near the fire, shedding his coat. His ears flickered back and forth in a shivering movement. "It's beastly cold out there. I think a storm is blowing in; the wind cuts right to the bone. Anyway, he not only handed over Giada's will but was nice enough to break down the major points for us."

Niamh shed her coat as well, draping it over the back of a chair at the table before turning to me with a wicked gleam in her eyes. "It turns out, not all is as it appears. Everyone said Giada wasn't going to marry Iadanza, correct? That she had no interest in divorcing her husband?"

I perked up. "Was she?"

"She'd started the process for divorce," Niamh confirmed. "About three months before her death, in fact. The lawyer said he'd sent a notice of intent to Lord Barese but received no answer."

"How interesting. That's about the time she started being poisoned. No one else knew of this, though. They all wondered why she stayed married to him and urged her to either reconcile or divorce him." I rubbed at my chin, not sure what to make of this. "What else did you learn?"

"The will changed completely after she started divorce proceedings." Foster flopped into a chair, stretching his legs out to the fire with a happy sigh. "Her husband was cut out entirely—which makes sense—and she stipulated that Iadanza was not to receive anything from her. Not even a personal token."

I let out a low whistle. "She was very much done with him, it sounds like."

Niamh gave me a sour nod as she also found her own chair. "Giada changed her will twice. The first time, when she started the divorce proceedings. Iadanza was still in that will. The second time, three weeks ago, and that's when Iadanza was removed from the will."

"About the time that she suspected he was poisoning her?"

"The timeline matches up to that, yes. The lawyer

said she conferred with him about legally removing Iadanza from the property. He'd proven stubborn about leaving on his own, and she wanted a restraining order put on him to make sure he stayed off the property. It of course takes several days to process, but it was due to be served the day after her house party. His days with her were definitely numbered. Giada had also reworked it so that her estate was set to be sold and then equally divided between her siblings, with some of her personal effects to go to her mother."

"Interesting. Well, we wondered what motive anyone had to kill her. I do think we now have two possibilities."

"Iadanza and Barese," Niamh confirmed with a dark smile. "Both men were on the way out. Neither of them would have taken that well."

"Not at all," I agreed. "At the very least, being divorced from Giada would have embarrassed Barese socially. I've seen people kill over less. Good work, both of you. This case is finally starting to make some sense. Let's call this in to Jamie."

I had to shift Phil off my lap to reach the pad in my pocket. He moved to the rug in front of the hearth amenably. After almost two years of using the pad, it was automatic to draw my lover's name up and initiate a call to her.

Jamie answered with a cheerful, "*Hey, handsome.*"

"Hello, my dear," I answered with a smile. "We've news for you. Have you spoken with Lord Barese yet?"

"*Just left his house and we're about to portal back to Ashbluff, actually. What's up*?"

"Giada's lawyer was full of information. First, Giada had initiated divorce proceedings for Lord Barese three months prior to her death. A notice had been sent to him of the intent."

Jamie let out a low whistle. "*Well, well, well, that's interesting. Huh. He didn't breathe of a word of that to us. He was all torn up about her death and talking about how he wished they had reconciled.*"

"Do you think he was trying to hide this?"

"*Eh. Maybe, maybe not? His butler actually tried to block me from the interview entirely. When I told Lord Barese about that, he said it was likely on his mother's orders, as she's protective of him. It might well be he really doesn't know about this. Mommy might have blocked the information from getting to him.*"

"So he could well be ignorant of it. I see. Something to investigate further, in any case."

"*Oh yeah. That's motive right there. What else did the lawyer say?*"

"Iadanza was on his way out. Giada had every intention of legally removing him from her property after the house party. She also stipulated in her will that he was not to receive anything from her, not even a token."

Seaton's deeper voice joined in. "*Their relationship had disintegrated to that degree?*"

"Apparently so. The new will she made divided her estate between her siblings, with gifts for her mother. Neither of the men in her life were to receive anything from her."

"*Henri. You thinking what I'm thinking?*"

"The jimsonweed was either to discredit her state of mind, making the will invalid, or it was to drive her to death and madness before she could finalize her plans. My question is, who knew of her plans? How did they stumble onto it? Not even her closest friends or mother knew what she intended to do."

"*It's a really good question. I want to ask Lady Lastra. Let's revisit people and do follow-up interviews as well. Now that we know this, maybe we can catch someone in a lie, or they might be able to shed light on something. Can Foster and Niamh hear me?*"

"They can."

"Guys, hit the house guests again. Reinterview them and see if there's anything that pops out to you now that you know all this. Don't worry about going to Elsher, just call the station there and see if they know anything about him."

Niamh leaned forward and pitched her voice to carry. "We will."

"Cool, thanks. Henri, can you go through the will? I assume we have a copy of it?"

"We do, yes." I looked up and found Foster pulling it free of a file, handing it over to me. It was not slender—a good thirty pages at least.

"You can decipher legalese better than most of us. Read through it and see if there's anything else. Sherard and I are heading back in as I want to talk to Barese about the divorce papers before we return."

"I'll see you shortly, then."

"Yup. Love you, bye."

I returned the pad to my pocket, smiling at her words. It always tickled me when she ended a call in such a way.

I looked at the will in my hand. I'd mark anything that looked interesting, but most of this was standard language for all wills. It wouldn't get interesting until page three or so. In any case, it would take a good hour for me to read it. Jamie would probably return to Ashbluff before I finished it.

Maybe we could have dinner together. Sometimes, squeezing in personal time during a case took finesse. I would love a little time with her.

Smiling at the thought, I turned my mind to decoding the will in front of me.

You know, I felt like I was sneaking out for an affair going on this date.

Jamie's Additional Report: Goin' On a Daaaaaate

Why? We had to avoid Ms. King. She was lurking outside the hotel.

Can't someone accidentally drop her in an ocean with cement boots?

Don't put that in writing, you'll have no plausible deniability later.

Seaton, for magic's sake, don't encourage her.

Henri invited me out for a dinner date, which, really, we were both overdue for. He'd found a cute little restaurant that overlooked the sea at a picturesque angle. I had nothing fancy on me and so ended up in a suit, but he didn't seem to mind. The point wasn't to impress each other, just to spend time together.

The restaurant did a good job creating a cozy atmosphere. We were seated near the window, and I could feel the cold coming through the glass, but the fireplace behind us kept it at bay. The snap and crackle of the fire was a pleasant counterpoint to the band in the corner that played soothing, peaceful music.

It was such a perfect place for dinner, I couldn't help but ask Henri, "How did you even know about this place?"

"I asked Inspector Colombo," he admitted easily. "Married man that he is, I suspected he'd know."

"He certainly did. It's really such a lovely atmosphere here." I appreciated the chance to relax and set work aside—also to not have cats around to distract me. They were playing with Sherard. I wasn't sure who was babysitting who, to be honest, but appreciated not having furballs underfoot.

Henri reached across the table to take my hand in his, the grip loose but warm. I curled my fingers around his, just taking in this man I loved, who I knew loved me. It was a heady buzz, a feeling that lightened the heart. Especially when he looked at me like *that*.

"You're smiling," he murmured.

"Enjoying a quiet moment with you," I answered

honestly. "Sometimes that's freaking hard to manage, you have to admit."

"Far too hard to manage. Really, I often bless that we work together. Otherwise, I'd not manage to have time with you at all."

"Yeah, tell me about it. I hope it doesn't change in the future for that reason. Have you thought about that much?"

"Hmm, yes, I have. The more I think about it, the more comfortable I become with the idea. For all that Queen Regina's offer startled me in the beginning, I can now see why she made it."

I wasn't at all surprised but wasn't about to say so. I liked the expression he wore, as if he really had gotten comfortable with the idea. Henri was the type to mull things over, so this didn't surprise me much. "Are you confident about taking it, then?"

"I think there will be backlash," he answered, brow furrowing for a moment. "Historically speaking, the royal mages have always been magical powerhouses. More than one person will likely raise an objection to my appointment. That said, I feel I can prove my worth in time. I can't discount the challenge it represents, either."

I nodded, figuring that was a factor. Henri was an amazing magical examiner. He's thorough, detail-oriented, and a walking encyclopedia, so of course he'd be good in that field. It was something of a waste for him to be only that for his career. He had such a good head for innovation, it would be a shame for him not to use that ability. Of course he'd look at the position of being a royal mage as an intellectual challenge and be excited about it.

"I spoke to Seaton about this, and he's quite giddy over the possibility of having me as a colleague," Henri continued, his smile returning. The anticipation reflected in his eyes, shining. "I'm quite excited about working with him, too. Of course I'll be able to continue to work with you once you've become a kingsman, too, which is an extra bonus. While I do harbor some...misgivings about the future, I'm solid on my course. I want to take it."

"Good! I hoped you'd come around to that conclusion. I think you'll be brilliant at it. You realize your mother will flip when she hears about this."

Henri sighed. It was a sigh that came from the soul, as if he regretted a future conversation already. "I know. Trust me, I know. You realize that once she hears of this, she'll be even more determined to have us 'properly settled' before we change careers and all."

I shared his resignation completely. "I know. She's really, really keen on buying us a house."

"I really don't understand why."

"I think she looks at it as a way of pressuring us into making a more formal commitment. Why she thinks that would work with you, I don't know. You're not the type to rush anything."

His head canted as he looked at me, eyes thoughtful. "You don't seem in a rush to make a commitment either?"

"I'm honestly good as we are," I admitted easily. "I enjoy dating you. It's not that I don't look forward to what we'll be in the future, but I'm enjoying the now. I don't want to rush or speed through it."

Shrewdly, he guessed, "And we're both so busy on a day-to-day basis that adding one more changed dynamic isn't something you want right now."

"That too." We were just so good together, so compatible, that I felt we'd definitely get married in the future. I did look forward to that, but the idea of getting engaged while I was trying to put together a brand-new department gave me stressed-out hives. It was just way too much to do all at once. I'd rather tackle one thing at a time, thanks.

Maybe that was too logical of me? I don't know. If this was the me of three years ago, I probably would have done both. I wouldn't have hesitated. Changing planets, careers, friends, and adjusting to a new body all in the space of a year changes a person, though. I wasn't the type to do everything at once now, not if I could help it. I was kinder to myself than that.

I meant it when I said I didn't want to rush me and Henri. I didn't want to be so tired and stressed that I couldn't enjoy the engagement and wedding process. I had no complaints about our relationship right now. I knew he didn't, either, so I wasn't going to let people rush us because we didn't meet some arbitrary deadline.

Shaking my head, I offered, "Right now we have a good argument against the houses she's tried to show us. They're all in the country. No way we can afford to commute in, not with us working on palace grounds."

"I'll use that argument, too." Henri's grin was not nice. "I think we have a good distraction for now, though."

"What, you becoming a royal mage? Oh yeah, it's the king of distractions. Let's use the mileage while we have it."

"Do you intend to tell your parents the next time you speak to them?"

"Of course. I might even have an answer by then." I thought about it, how much time it would take to get royal approval for my proposal, and when I'd speak to family next, and waffled a hand back and forth. "Eh, maybe. I don't know how fast it'll take to get things in motion. Queen Regina was pretty adamant about me submitting a proposal, so I know she's keen on it. But she has other people who have to agree to this, too. I don't know how they'll all feel about it. Government doesn't normally work fast."

"Not at all." Henri shook his head with a thoughtful look. "I think you might have an informal answer by then, though. Dearest, I do have to ask, because I feel that eventually we'll need an answer to this. When we do reach the point of needing our own place, do you want a house?"

See? Henri was right in sync with me on this. "A house inside the city is going to be really expensive."

He gave me such a droll look that I laughed.

"Yes, I realize between the two of us, and your mother's very *enthusiastic* support, we'll probably be able to afford something nice. I think location is a bigger thing for me. What about you?"

"I admit I tire of living in an apartment. Having no sound muffling between me and my neighbors has worn thin over the years. I think I'd like a house."

I leaned in a little, as I hadn't expected that answer. "Really, a house? What kind? What's your style?"

Henri paused and I could see him mentally forming the answer before he gave it to me. It's something he did when he wanted to make sure he explained himself right the first time.

He answered, describing to me what he liked in a house, the warmth of the colors, the woodwork, how he disliked anything sterile looking as it reminded him of the lab at work. I soaked in the answer, tucking it away. I hadn't quite expected this answer, but once he gave it to me, it wasn't a surprise. It was so quintessentially Henri.

We sat over a very excellent dinner, and spoke of possibilities, and the future. We spoke in warm, unhurried tones, learning what the other wanted, what they needed. It painted a pretty picture, one I liked and hoped for.

With this sweet, supportive man at my side, I had no doubt it would happen.

Right. Now you're bragging.

Totally bragging. Hear my mad cackle.

MUWAHAHAHAHAHAHAHA

I love how a date with Henri makes you insufferable afterwards.

Report 19: Iadanza

The police in Elsher hadn't found any hint of Iadanza, but we couldn't just sit on a possible lead to his whereabouts. Niamh, Foster, and Sherard had portaled down stupid-early in the morning to take their own look around. If he really was from that area, maybe they could find someone that knew where he'd gone, pick up the trail that way.

Henri and I had decided to follow at a more reasonable hour, and were currently on the train to meet up with everyone. My brain was circling and shifting through facts, trying to come up with answers and failing when my pad rang. I answered it, hoping Niamh had something fun to share. I could use some kind of break in this case. Right now I had a lot of weird facts and nothing to draw conclusions from. "Niamh, tell me something good."

Her voice was full of victory. "*I've found Iadanza.*"

"Girl, you *rock*. Where?"

"*He was boarding a ship in Elsher when I caught up with him. I've got him under custody here, and the local station has been kind enough to give me jail space to keep him in. I'm holding him under suspicion of murder, is that alright?*"

"Perfectly fine, that's within our bounds. Do not lose that man."

"*Trust me, I don't want to track him down again.*"

I'd bet not.

"Niamh, ask Sherard if he'd be willing to come and snag us."

Sherard's voice answered clearly, "*I can, but where are you now?*"

"Still on the train, but we'll be at the station in five minutes."

"*I'll wait for you on the platform, then.*"

"Okay, thanks." I hung up and put the pad away.

We pulled into the station. From there, it was a flurry of movements as we quickly unloaded, eager to get down there. I didn't know how tough of a nut Iadanza would be to crack. Hopefully he was a blabbermouth. I loved those people. They saved me a lot of time and effort.

Once we alighted from the train in Elsher, I spied Sherard waiting for us on the platform. Bless that red coat of his, it made it so easy to find a him in a crowd. I waved to catch his attention, and he waved back, assuring me he'd seen us.

Henri and I were old hands at moving through a crowd and keeping three cats with us, so it didn't take us long to reach Sherard. Being the smart person he was, he stood off to the side, away from the crowd.

"Has he said anything?" were the first words out of my mouth once I got to him.

Sherard rolled his eyes heavenward. "Too much, really. The man oscillates between raging and crying. I've seen less dramatics on a theatrical stage. He either rails at the unfairness of Giada dying and leaving him in such a state of financial insecurity, or he's crying that she's left him and blabbers on about how she was the only woman he truly loved. Which I think is rather rich. When Niamh found him, he was seated with a widower, trying to charm her into hiring him as an escort for her trip abroad."

"Wow. What a douchebag."

Sherard's brows furrowed a bit. "Jerk?"

"Uh, that word didn't fully translate, huh? Yeah, jerk is a good equivalent. Does he seriously have no means of support except the women he preys off of?"

"Apparently not." Sherard shrugged. "At least, when we took his wallet and searched him, we found no bank card, no checks. Cash, yes. If he has his own income, it's not something he's carrying on him, which I find strange."

"I as well." Henri shook his head in disbelief. "I can see why no one had a kind word to say about him."

And this before we even interviewed the guy. Seriously, what did Giada see in this loser?

Sherard offered us both a hand, and once he had a good grip on us, he portaled us straight to the police station. Seriously, love portal spells. They saved so, so much time.

Elsher was a port town and it showed in the busy streets, and the strong scent of the sea wafting in with every breath. It was a little older, too, and I could see that the building housing the police station had been added onto recently. The mortar in the bricks was clean and fresh compared to the rest of the stone structure. To accommodate the larger population? Probably.

We stepped through the main door. Niamh sat at a desk chatting with another sergeant—who looked a bit tongue-tied around the kingsman beauty—but at our entrance, her head came up and she smiled.

"Oh good, you're here," she said, standing to greet us.

"Portal spells are my friend. Now, where is the idiot lover?"

"This way." Niamh turned to the desk she had just vacated and said, "Nice chatting with you, Detective. Thanks for your help."

He gave her a slightly infatuated smile. "No problem at all, Kingsman."

If Gerring saw this, he'd be green with jealousy. Should I tell him? The evil part of me wanted to tell him.

Niamh walked us through the open bullpen to the back, where jail cells lined the room on either side, iron bars solidly in place with pathetic wooden beds jutting out of the wall. The officer on duty waved us through, and we headed to the far back corner.

At my first look of Iadanza, I had to admit I wasn't impressed. He had Hollywood good looks, no doubt there. Thick, wavy dark hair, tanned skin, brilliant blue eyes set in a perfectly sculpted face. He also looked like an abandoned cat as he sat hunched over, his suit wrinkled, coat discarded on the bed next to him. Under the right circumstances, though, I could see why he would draw a woman's attention.

I used the key to unlock the door and step in. The grate of metal on metal brought Iadanza's head up. He looked confused as I stepped through, a cat in my arm, another poking her head out of my pocket. I usually did make an interesting sight, but it also disarmed people into talking to me, lowered their guard. I'd take the advantage.

"Felipe Iadanza? I'm Detective Jamie Edwards, Kingsman Consultant. I'm here because I need to speak to you about Giada Barese."

Iadanza's eyes immediately filled with tears. "You're with the other kingsmen, right? You don't really think I had something to do with my poor Giada's death? They said I'm being held here on suspicion of murder!"

Save the waterworks, please. I kept the thought off my face as I leaned against the wall, giving enough room for Henri to join me. He didn't choose to speak, though. Leaving this up to me, was he? I cast him a quick glance, but he was busy staring at Iadanza. Foster, Sherard, and Niamh chose to hold up the wall outside the cell, which made sense, as there was practically no space in here.

"Well, you sort of are," I said in an apologetic tone that was not at all sincere. "See, when Giada went missing, you really should have stayed with the house until she was found again. Not leave the same day."

"It's because I was being accused of doing something uncouth to her that I had to leave," Iadanza countered, hands clutched together in a plea. "Don't you understand how uncomfortable it was for me in that house? If not for having friends in the area, I wouldn't have had anywhere else to go!"

"Okay, so you went to stay with friends? Why not stay with them long enough to learn what happened with Giada?"

"I tried, but the lady of the house was high tempered and always angry with me. I couldn't stay. I loved Giada, I did, but I have to live, too!"

Ever meet someone and you want to buy them a taser for their bathtub? I was sure Ellie would make me one just for him once I explained the situation.

It took effort, but I swallowed back a few choice comments on that. "Tell you what, let's walk through what happened with Giada leading up to her death. I really just needed to talk to you more than anything. Okay?"

He readily nodded. "Yes, of course, anything to help. What answers do you need?"

I could tell from the way he reacted that he thought I'd let him go after he was done answering my questions. That probably wasn't going to happen. Would I enlighten him? No. "Right, so, let's start about three months before her death. Giada started having weird dreams and hallucinations. You saw those?"

"I saw them and told her the stress of having her heart going two directions was too much for her. It's what strained her to that point." Iadanza looked self-righteous saying this, straightening from his slouch. "If she'd properly divorced that cheating husband of hers and married me, her heart would have been more steady. She wouldn't have been plagued by dreams like that."

Uh-huh. "Is that what she told you, was that he cheated on her?"

"She'd confided it to me early on. Giada had no secrets from me."

I had to bite my tongue so hard over that one. So very hard. Teeth marks on my tongue kind of hard. "Okay, so you advised her to divorce him. Her symptoms got worse, though?"

"That's when she started seeing that useless doctor, even though I kept telling her a divorce would settle her mind. She wouldn't listen to me, though. I started sleeping in a separate bedroom from hers, as she often would be so restless at night, I couldn't sleep."

Ah. Hence why I found nothing of Iadanza, no trace

of a man in Giada's bedroom. "So, you started sleeping separately…when, exactly?"

"Hmm, I'd say it was a couple weeks before her disappearance at least. She was angry with me for doing it, but I really can't function without my beauty sleep. It wasn't like she was listening to me, either."

"When her symptoms grew worse, what then?"

He gave me a blank stare. "What do you mean they got worse?"

"She started having more severe episodes that sent her running around the house?" I had to ask this because he seriously looked like a blank chalkboard. He had no idea what I was talking about. "You weren't aware they'd gotten worse about three weeks before her death?"

"We were in a stupid argument," Iadanza explained, his eyes tearing up again on cue. "I went to visit friends for a few days at one point. We were fighting so much that she couldn't stand to look at me. Our time apart would help us both, I thought, but she didn't seem all that improved when I returned."

Ah, the days when she was testing to see if it was him poisoning her. Yeah, buddy, don't think that did anything to help your relationship. Not when she'd lost so much trust in you that she decided to test you. "I'm sure you were alarmed by that."

"Very much so. I didn't know how to help her when she wasn't listening to me."

When she refused to be controlled by you, you mean. "Did you read any of her diaries, try to figure out what she was thinking or feeling?"

He gave me another one of those blank looks. "Those silly scribbles she spent hours on? Deities, no, I'd be bored to tears if I even tried. Poetry is my thing, you see."

Poetry being useful in picking up girls. Yeah, got it. Still, the reaction was so unguarded that I honestly believed he had no idea the diaries were important or how they were linked to her death.

Discreetly, Henri pulled out a wand and muttered a spell, almost low enough I couldn't catch it. He grunted at the result before leaning into me and whispering in my ear, "There's no trace of jimsonweed anywhere on his person or in his aura. If he had contact with it, it was so mild that it's long dissipated."

I murmured back, "Is it possible to harvest this stuff and manipulate it without getting any on you?"

"Almost impossible, I would think."

Right. So, anyone aside from a magician would have traces of it, at least. Probably not a strong enough dose to feel the effects, but something Henri could at least pick up on.

Henri and I exchanged a look. I didn't think this guy was our killer, despite the fact he made such an amazing suspect. I had no evidence to link him to anything except for the fact he lived with Giada. Which was a rotten shame. I really liked him for this one. The complete lack of jimsonweed told us he didn't have a direct hand in it, but maybe he'd hired someone else to do it.

"I understand that your relationship with her had broken down to the point that she asked you to leave the house."

"She only said that in the heat of the moment, she didn't actually mean it!"

Lies. "She was in the process of a restraining order against you. I think she meant it. Now, how angry were you when you realized she really was going to throw you out with nothing?"

His face flushed an angry red. "Those are lies. She loved me. It was just an argument between us, we would have moved past it."

I met his eyes levelly. "She changed her will. I've seen it. Henri, what was the exact wording, do you remember?"

"Upon my death, Felipe Iadanza is to receive absolutely nothing from my estate, not even a token. He is not allowed upon the grounds under any circumstance," Henri recited in a bland tone.

Iadanza didn't look up, his angry gaze focused on the

floor.

"Oh, you knew, alright," I murmured. "You might not have known she'd gone through with putting it in writing, but you knew she was done with you. You didn't just leave that day because she was missing, did you? You left because you knew you had to get out while you could."

He looked miserable again, sinking in on himself. "I feared what would happen if I stayed. No one in that house liked me. Even with no evidence, they were ready to hang me for her disappearance. We didn't even know if she was dead or not and they were already casting blame on me!"

"Fair enough. Talk to me about her enemies. Who would want her dead?"

"No one, really. She'd already left that poisonous mother-in-law, and that was the only person she hated, so I can't understand why anyone would kill her."

"Hmm. Okay, switching questions. Where were you the night she disappeared? No one saw you after your last argument with her. They said you were shut up in your room until the next morning. I need an alibi for that night."

Iadanza smiled and it wasn't a nice expression. "I was consoling Mrs. Li Fonti."

I blinked. Blinked again. Say what, now? "Mrs. Li Fonti."

"She found out that night her husband was having an affair with the charming Ms. Collins. Really, they were hardly discreet about it, even I realized over dinner with the way they were not-so-subtly flirting. The man was quite stupid to do it right in front of his wife's nose. I found her crying in the garden after dinner and offered her a shoulder. We, ah, spent the night together. Talking."

Talking. Uh-huh. Well, that explained why Sophie Li Fonti didn't say anything about her husband's affair. Such a healthy marriage those two had. "I'll need to verify that with her, you understand, but okay. So you were with her…in your room or hers?"

"Mine."

I hated to say it, but if his alibi checked out, then he really wasn't our killer. Or if he did poison Giada, he wasn't the one that made sure she fell over the edge. I didn't have anything to prove he'd done this. That said, turning him free put a bad taste in my mouth.

Could I hold him on the grounds of being a douchebag? I'd be doing the female population at large a solid by keeping this guy behind bars.

A niggling thought abruptly surfaced. Wait a second, he had cash on him. If his sole means of support was Giada, where did the cash come from? Detti had supervised his packing, but what if he'd stashed away goods prior to that day and hawked enough valuables to give himself some traveling money. I could totally see him doing that.

To Iadanza, I gave a smile. "Thanks for speaking with me. I just need to clarify a few things with colleagues, okay? Hang tight."

He gave a charming, dazzling smile in return. No doubt sure he had gotten by with something—again—and would be free soon.

Not on my watch, dude.

I exited the cell, locking it behind me, and drew everyone back to the officer on watch before handing the key over.

Foster asked hopefully, "Is he the one?"

Henri shook his head. "No, there's no sign of jimsonweed anywhere on him."

"He also supposedly has an alibi with Mrs. Li Fonti. They spent the night together after she found her husband cheating." I rolled my eyes. "Because that's a healthy response. I'll need to verify it, but I believe he actually was with her."

Niamh let out a curse. "If that's true, it means I chased him down for nothing."

I tsked at her. "I wouldn't say for nothing. He's innocent of murder, but I'd bet he's not guiltless. Foster, you said he had cash on him." I arched a pointed eyebrow. "How much money are we talking about?"

"Too much," Foster said frankly. "Nearly four thousand crowns."

Henri let out a low whistle. "That is far too much for a man of no viable means to be carrying about. Oh dear, you don't think he..."

"Oh, I'd bet even money he did." I shook my head, not even surprised. "If he knew he was on the rocks with Giada, and she disappeared, and everyone in the house turned on him? Of course he'd grab some valuables and get out. What he stole is a good question, but I'm sure we can figure this out. Detti would be able to tell us what's missing. Niamh, Foster, can you follow up on that? Change the charge here to suspicion of theft. They can hold him for seventy-two hours on that, considering it's linked to a murder case."

Niamh gave me a firm nod. "We'll take care of it."

"Thanks bunches. You two have outdone yourselves tracking him down. I really wish he was the killer."

"Me too," Niamh muttered glumly. "Well, what next?"

"I want to call Mrs. Li Fonti first, verify his alibi. Just in case. Really, the only person everyone agrees who hated Giada was the mother-in-law and I really want to interview her. I want to go back to that house and see if I can sit on her for some answers. For now, though, just follow up on where he got the cash. I want to prosecute this guy for *something*. Turning him loose doesn't feel right."

Four faces said they totally agreed.

I blew out a breath. Not the lover, eh? Rotten shame, it meant I had to go back to the difficult suspects. Iadanza would have been easy to button up. The Bareses, not so much.

Alright, take two. Let's see if I can find some kind of evidence to make sense of this.

Report 20: An Inky Prognosis

Jamie, Seaton, and Niamh focused entirely on follow-up interviews. Well, Niamh was working through the stolen goods, tracking them down to make sure we could properly prosecute Iadanza to the full extent of the law. It left Foster and I to process the evidence, not that I minded. The weather outside had a distinct nip to it and I was quite happy to stay indoors on a day like this.

After getting back to Ashbluff, I borrowed lab space from the police precinct in order to more carefully examine the diaries. It was a small room, clearly used mostly for storage. Stacks of boxes lined the back wall, and there was barely anything more in here than a table, three chairs, and a window cracked open for some ventilation. Foster sat off to one side of the table, carefully reading through the diary from the beginning of her marriage, while I worked on the latest volume.

The traces of jimsonweed were intriguing. I used a diagnostic spell, wand held steady at the source, and started with a full scan of the book, recording its appearance and such for the record. The results detailed themselves on a clean sheet at my elbow, and I read them with acute interest. There was no evidence of magic anywhere in this, purely botany. When that spell finished, I started another diagnostic scan of its contents, recording the data onto a new sheet of paper to include in the evidence packet.

How interesting. The jimsonweed was not only in

the sand used to dry the ink, but also the ink itself. Now why was that the case? Had someone poisoned her pen?

"Foster," I said slowly, turning to look at him, only to pause in what I was saying. My colleague was sitting there with his ears doing this strange downwards flicker, his nose wrinkled up as if in acute embarrassment. "Foster?"

His head snapped up. "Uh, yes, Doctor?"

"Is something the matter?"

"Uh...um." He glanced back at the pages again. "Well, um, Countess Giada was very, uh, frank. Sir."

"Frank?" I didn't follow his meaning.

"That is to say, she had no qualms in detailing her...trysts."

Comprehension landed. "Oh. Oh my, is the content that explicit?"

"Leaves absolutely nothing to the imagination." Foster winced again.

I felt pity for him even as I swallowed a chuckle. Foster was inexperienced yet, but that would change in time. I was immune to the invasiveness at this point, as policemen often encountered people's personal lives in ways they really wished they didn't. I was sympathetic to his plight, however. "You can skip those scenes. It's not like it will tell us anything except who she might have had a rendezvous with."

"Or as Detective Edwards puts it, a randyvous?" he countered with a grin.

I laughed outright. "Did she say that? It sounds like a word she'd use. Yes, precisely so. Just mark down the name as someone of possible interest."

"I will, sir, but what's actually intriguing to me is the time this happened. This date was, I believe, about two months after Giada's marriage to Lord Barese."

"Now that is of interest. Lord Barese indicated the marriage was still in good shape at that point. It wasn't until a little later that their relationship soured."

Foster shook his head. "Not at all the truth, sir. Giada wrote some...I think it was two weeks prior to this, that she found him upstairs with the maid. She didn't confront him—I don't know if he realized she'd discovered him. It was a turning point for her, though, as she realized how capricious his nature was. She stopped being faithful to him at that point."

"Ah. So they both had affairs early on. It also explains why she didn't fight her mother-in-law to stay. There was nothing but broken vows between her and her husband."

Foster gave a nod. "Looks like it. What did you discover, sir?"

"The jimsonweed is in the ink itself. Also only on these last few pages. The timing of it makes it three months old, so the potency has waned, but still strong enough I don't suggest licking the page."

Foster held up a hand. "I'll pass on that offer, thanks just the same. It does lose its potency over time, then?"

"It does. Shelf-life of a plant is always thus. Which means, of course, that the dosage of the ink must have been refreshed." I tapped a thoughtful finger to the table. "My first thought is that someone must have poisoned her inkwell."

Foster's head canted as he stared blindly at the ceiling. "We never found it when we went looking. Just used, broken pens in the bottom drawer."

Shame, that, as I would dearly love to lay my hands on it. But perhaps the old pens could tell me something as well. I tested them one by one, noting down the particulars of each pen and recording them for the record. I hadn't found one poisoned yet, but I still had another five pens to go. What I did note, with interest, was that every single pen had been nibbled on. Giada's bad habit of chewing on the end of her pens was apparently pervasive.

"Doctor," Foster started, tone rising a bit with the question, "did you note the last date on the pages you were testing?"

"I did, yes. The last diary ended three months ago." I inclined my head to him, reading the intent of his question. "I, too, wonder where the most recent diary is. There was no other found in the desk. The murderer must have taken it, but I find it interesting that he knew precisely which volume to take."

"Could it be something is written in it that implicates her murderer?"

"We have no way of knowing. It could be the murderer took it just on the off chance it did."

"I really hope it isn't destroyed."

"As do I. Odds are it doesn't implicate her murderer since Giada had no idea what affected her so. Finding some clue inside those pages is a very slim possibility. Still, I'd like to prove that myself." I glanced down at the Felix curled in my lap. Phil looked entirely too comfortable, snoozing away the day without a care in the world.

I sometimes envied my Felix.

We went back to working on our individual tasks, on either side of the table, both of us working in companionable silence.

Foster once again broke it. "Doctor, I do wonder about the people who were exposed to Giada's letters and diaries. Wouldn't they be affected like Detective Edwards?"

"To a milder degree. If they didn't touch the ink itself, or licked it, then it would have been nothing more than a mild euphoria, as it were. Like an artificial happy spell, quickly passed."

"But Detective Edwards didn't directly touch or lick anything, so why was her reaction so strong?"

"She breathed in some of the dust."

"Really, just a breath did it?"

"As sensitive as she is, Jamie would have no immunity even to trace amounts." I tacked on thoughtfully, "And considering Giada's state on the night of her death, I have no doubt the jimsonweed had somehow been refreshed. It was extremely potent, after all."

"Good point. I'll be very careful what I touch."

I reached for the next pen. This one seemed more damaged than the others, the nib on it quite discolored and bent. A quick test determined it didn't have a trace of jimsonweed upon it. In fact, the ink was entirely dried inside of it, so it hadn't seen use in quite some time. Clearly not the pen we were looking for.

Foster frowned a little. "I do have to wonder if just writing with the ink and using the sand would really affect Giada that badly?"

I pointed to the pens lying on the table, now marked for evidence. "No, it wouldn't, but if you'll observe this one? It's clearly been nibbled on at the end. I will bet you Giada was the type to lick the tip of her pens, chew on ends, what have you. A bad habit, certainly, and one the killer knew of."

"And used to their advantage. Her murderer really must be a friend or relative." Foster shook his head. "So disturbing when the murderer is someone who knows the victim intimately."

"I heartily agree but it happens more often than not. I think it's time to call Jamie in and update her. She needs to ask more questions of where that pen came from and where it might have gone."

I was out of pens to test, so I picked up my pad and messaged my lover. Instead of writing back, she called. "*Hey, honey. What's up? Did you find anything?*"

"It's what we didn't find that's more telling. None of the pens were poisoned."

"*Oh-hooo, the plot thickens. So the jimsonweed is*

definitely in that missing pen set. Or was—it's likely long destroyed by now."

"I wish I could disagree, but you're likely right."

"I'm on my way to Lady Lastra's. I'll ask about the journal and pen set. If nothing else, she might be able to tell us where it came from originally. I'll also check back in with the staff, see if they know anything about it."

Since she liked interviews, I was more than content to leave her to them. "I'll leave that part to you, then. I'm relieved to have a firm answer on her method of murder, at least."

"Yeah. I'm also relieved to know I can tell a grieving mother her daughter absolutely didn't commit suicide. A tough pill to swallow, either way, but at least it's a cold comfort. Really, though, how did this pen get into her possession?"

"The question is even more complicated than that, my dear. The shelf life of jimsonweed is only two weeks or so before it starts losing potency. Whoever gifted this to her had a means of refreshing the dosage on a regular basis without Giada questioning it."

There was a digestive pause. *"You didn't tell me about the shelf life. That makes this even more tricky. You're telling me someone filled up her ink on a constant basis and she didn't question it even once?"*

"Correct. Someone who knew she liked to nibble on her pens, no less."

"Someone who knew her at least semi-well, then. Wow, okay. I have a lot of questions to ask. Find me something good, love. We're up a creek with no paddle if we can't lay hands on physical evidence."

"I know. Trust me, we'll search until we've exhausted all possibilities. I think we'll head out to the mansion, use it as a nexus for a refined seeking spell. Perhaps searching for the ink will produce different results."

"Sounds good, keep me updated. I'll call you if I find something on my end." A kissing sound, and the

connection ended.

I put the pad away only to find Foster smiling at me, a mixture between wistfulness and indulgence. I wasn't sure why I was on the receiving end of this look, but it made me shift a little in my seat, a heat touching my cheeks. "What?"

"It's just really nice," Foster explained, smile growing. "I like seeing the two of you interact. It's sweet, and also sets relationship goals for me, if that makes sense. I'd like to find someone I have that much trust and rapport with."

"That takes time." I reflected back on our relationship, now two years in, and shook my head in nostalgia. "We were good friends for the first year and a half. I think some people rush the courting process and then the relationship suffers because of it. I have no such desire to do that."

Foster's whiskers twitched in a chuckle. "I understand your mother keeps trying to rush you, though. Detective Edwards mentioned something about her trying to buy the two of you a house?"

"Yes, I refuse to be rushed," I deadpanned back. "Now, let's see if we can find our missing murder weapon, shall we?"

Report 21: Searching

Fortunately, the trip to Lady Lastra's and back was brief. I was able to get the answer I needed and then reversed immediately back to Ashbluff. It was a crazy trip, but thankfully I arrived with the rest of the team to the hotel in three hours, hoping that Henri had found an answer in the past hour since we'd last spoken. I, at least, had some very interesting facts for him. Facts that might well blow this case wide open, assuming I could get the pieces to slot together right and prove my suspicions. Niamh rendezvoused with us there, as she'd hit the limits of what she could do in town, and had her own findings to report.

"Henri!" I called as I went through the door.

"In here, dearest!"

His voice had come from the right side, the parlor. I made a beeline in that direction, people and cats on my heels.

Someone had started a fire in the grate, as it was too cold to just sit there. It also told me clearly that they'd finished their search and were waiting on us. Henri, Foster, and Phil were all huddled in chairs in front of the hearth, wrapped up tightly in their jackets, so that fire hadn't been going for long.

"Did you find it?" I asked eagerly.

"No pen or diary," Foster replied. "And Doctor Davenforth did several seeking spells."

"It's nowhere in this town, at least," Henri confirmed with a grimace. "That's about the range of my search."

"Rats. I was hoping the killer had just chucked them somewhere nearby, since they're basically poisonous."

Since Henri's chair was one of those wide chair-and-a-half pieces, I plopped in next to him, snuggling for warmth. The taxi had not been warm, to put it mildly. I immediately had a lap full of cats, heat-seekers that they were.

Sherard and Niamh also settled on the nearby couch, but with an air of anticipation, as if they were ready to pop right up again. I rather shared the feeling, but then, we'd discovered fun things.

Henri could read that off my face, as he sat up a little straighter, eyes glued to mine. "You've found something."

"Oh boy did we ever." I held up a finger. "In fact, Detti held the answer. This just proves that people really don't know what they know. The pen and ink set Giada used was a gift from her mother-in-law."

"The plot thickens," Henri murmured, dark eyes growing a little round. "Really, a gift from a woman she disliked?"

"It was apparently a very nice set, the last gift exchanged before Giada moved out permanently. Now, fun fact: new ink arrived from the Barese household every two weeks like clockwork. Sivi the maid would fill her inkwell with it when it arrived, as apparently Giada went through ink like it was on sale, so they were just in the habit of topping it off."

Henri got so excited he almost vibrated in place. "That matches perfectly with the pattern of her episodes. Also, it makes sense—the shelf life of the jimsonweed is roughly two to three weeks."

"Which mother-in-law apparently knows." Foster looked around at us, face scrunched up in slight confusion. "Why? Why would she do this to Giada? If this had continued much further, Giada might well have been deemed mad—wouldn't that be more embarrassing?"

"The notice of divorce went to the Barese house," Niamh said slowly, clearly thinking aloud. "But Lord Barese didn't know anything about it, right?"

"He had absolutely no clue. He was shocked by the news, so much so that he was at a loss for words for a full minute. Considering what I had to go through to get into the house, odds are Mummy dearest intercepted it. She seems to be firmly in control of her son."

"If she knew Giada planned to divorce her son, would she have poisoned Giada to get rid of her?" Niamh frowned some more.

"Quite possibly, but to what purpose?" Sherard had his thinking face on, staring blindly into the flames. "The initial episodes Giada suffered were disturbing, but mild. She would hallucinate or have vivid dreams, but she wasn't crazy. Her medical records detail this. I think in the beginning, Lady Barese was trying to prove her daughter-in-law unsound of mind. They weren't even married a year when Giada moved out, so if she could prove something was wrong with Giada, then she could have the marriage declared null. No smirch upon her son that way. It was only when she didn't net immediate results that she would have been thrown into panic. Her plan wasn't working. So the next dose of ink would have been much stronger, something that would affect Giada so badly it would be stunningly obvious."

I felt like Sherard had hit the nail on the head. The timing for the latest ink delivery matched that theory, as it had come in mere days before Giada's death. "I still don't know if this was intended to be murder. It might have been solely to discredit Giada enough to annul the marriage."

Henri made a face. "There's too many unknowns here. We've only got theory right now."

"How did they even know the process to make jimsonweed?" That part still bugged me. "I asked Barese about it, and I would swear to you, he genuinely had no clue what it was. This isn't common knowledge, apparently, so where did the know-how come from?"

"It's probably an academic question until we can locate our murderer." Henri shrugged. "We can ask them then. Let's focus on the vehicle it was delivered in for now. We can only prove that the ink and pen set came from their household. We need to see if we can find it."

"I suggest moving to Gallio." Sherard tapped a finger to his mouth, looking like he was up to something. "I can do another seeking spell there, see if anything turns up. I doubt the pen is still there, but we might find some other trace of her machinations."

"I'm up for it. Besides, you'd be surprised at what people will do to conceal evidence. Sometimes, they think burying it in their own backyard is the best idea." I stood, taking cats with me.

Henri stood as well, maneuvering Phil into one of his front pockets. "I helped solve a case, once, where the master of the house had killed someone and then thrown the knife into the rubbish bin. One of his servants discovered it the next day while throwing out the rubbish. She fished it back out and kept it, not realizing the significance."

Sherard threw a fire-suppressing spell on the hearth, putting the fire out so we could safely leave. "I doubt our luck would run that good on this case."

Niamh grumbled, "I think we're about due for some luck, although I doubt just finding the pen in her household will prove it, either. This is a powerful countess. We'll need more than one shred of evidence to prove it was her."

There was truth.

The taxi could hold all of us at a squeeze. We just had to love each other very much for the fifteen minutes it took to get to the train station. Unfortunately, it was early evening, so we wouldn't have much light and time to work some magic once we got to Gallio.

Reminded, I asked Niamh, "How is the stolen goods thing going?"

"Detti was able to tell me what's missing, so I have a list. I contacted three pawn shops here in town, but he was smart enough to only sell one thing to one of them. I'll need to go into Elsher and check the pawn shops there. I can at least prove he stole and sold one piece of jewelry, though."

"Enough to hold him, then. Good. Thanks, Niamh, I know I kind of threw that into your lap."

Niamh's smile was not nice. "Trust me, keeping him behind bars is my pleasure."

"Preach." I settled onto the bench seat and messaged Regina, wanting to update her on matters. Also, I felt it wise she was fully aware of what I was doing just in case I had to call in the big guns. Niamh was right in that Lady Barese was not a lightweight. She might well have enough power and pull to get away with murder.

I could tell by Regina's responses that she was upset. She promised that she fully had my back if I had to put cuffs on Lady Barese and drag her out of her own home, but also warned me to make sure I had enough evidence proving it was her.

I took the warning to heart.

Our queen was also kind enough that she called in a search warrant for me to the local judge in Gallio, fast-tracking that, so all I had to do was meet the judge at his house to collect it. Poor Judge Crady looked shell-shocked he had a queen calling him and demanding a search warrant for a powerful former countess, but the man pulled through. He had every i dotted, t crossed, and was relieved I had a royal mage in tow.

As we left the judge's house, I leaned into Sherard's side and confided, "I realize you only came onto the case because I was trippin' and Henri panicked, but you're really proving useful."

"I live to serve," he deadpanned back at me, then winked.

Seriously, I had the best friends. "Can I ask you to do one more favor?"

"Of course."

"Here's the thing—we don't have enough people. If I'm going to make arrests and collect evidence here, which I hope to heaven I can do, then the five of us are not enough. I need like, four more. Can you pop back over and grab any kingsmen on hand and portal them back here?"

"For you, I'm sure there's at least four people willing to drop everything and run over here," Sherard drawled with a wink. "Meet you at the house?"

"Yeah."

The judge lived a block down from the Barese house.

I gestured down the street. "We'll walk the distance, that should buy you some time."

"Back in a moment, then." He was gone in a poof, like he'd been beamed up to the mother ship.

I really, really wanted to crack *Star Trek* jokes with him but no one's seen even the original series. It had to happen soon. My one-liners were begging to be used.

Niamh leaned over my shoulder to ask hopefully, "You really think we can make arrests today?"

"If we can find any kind of evidence, I'm not above arresting both mother and son on suspicion of murder and then working out the details in an interrogation room. But yes, I hope we find lots of evidence."

We all kind of had our fingers crossed as we walked the distance.

Our timing was such that we were on the steps leading up to the front door when Sherard portaled right into the driveway. He had four in kingsmen red—Gibs I'd expected (my brother would have volunteered without even being fully read into the situation), as was Marshall. I was happy to see Evans and Lewis too. They were my buddies and going on a search party with them was always a good time.

Marshall greeted us with a laconic salute, drawling, "We better not be after magically melting grimoires this time."

Heh. Come to think of it, that was the last time I'd pulled him in, when we were dealing with a grimoire hoarder. "No melting grimoires."

Henri pitched in drolly, "How about poison?"

Gibs sighed, sounding like a mountain deity vexed with mortals. "You're having too much fun. I need you to dial it back a notch."

I'd laugh, but it was too close to home, so I kind of groaned as well. "Tell me about it. Anyway, touch absolutely nothing with your bare hands and don't sniff anything. Especially don't sniff anything."

Gibs' eyes sharpened on mine. "There's a story there."

"Is there ever. I'll fill you in later. Right now, we have a lot to do, and we need to pair off to do it. I'll partner you up with someone who knows what's going on so we can fill you in as we go. Marshall, with Niamh. Lewis, with Foster. Gibs, you're with me. Evans, can I ask you to be evidence keeper? We don't have our usual lock boxes with us."

Evans gave a nod. "Sure."

"Great. Try to pick a front room so you can keep an eye on the door, too. King has been relentlessly stalking us, and I have a feeling she's going to show up and try to barge her way in."

Gibs' brows arched. "Why do you expect her to show up?"

"Because I don't want her to." I made a face. One of these days, I'd figure out how King managed to always find my investigation team. Despite us portaling places, she could still find us. It was uncanny, not to mention annoying. "Alright, follow me in."

Henri held up a hand, pausing me. "Wait. Let's at least do the seeking spell first, so we know where to start."

"That's fair. Go for it." I had no problem cooling my heels for a second while they worked their magic. No pun intended.

They were searching specifically for the pen set, I knew, but they were also searching for the tainted ink itself, in case any of it was still around. Even trace amounts would help right now. Diary, too, of course, although I didn't hold out any hope for that. Any sane person would have burned that thing immediately. I kept one ear on them even as I kept an eagle eye on that door. Any second someone would realize we were lurking out here and demand to know what our business was.

Sherard started cackling. "I have a lead on the pen."

I whipped around, nearly tripping over my own feet. "You do not!"

His face was lit up with evil glee. "I really do. Shall we go straight for it?"

"Absolutely, yes." I was confused on why the pen was still

in the house, weeks after Giada's death, but most killers were admittedly not as smart as they thought themselves to be. I wasn't looking the gift horse in the mouth right now.

Henri gave a grunt. "Not a firm sense of the diary, but I have a tentative trace to...its remnants? I think she burned it somewhere."

"I certainly would have," Foster remarked. "Detective, I'll follow Doctor Davenforth if you want to follow RM Seaton."

"That's a good plan, let's do it."

Henri tilted his head to look at Niamh, who stood behind him. "If you could, take the Felixes with you and Marshall and scour the area. The jimsonweed came from somewhere, and I'd like to know if this was readily at hand or if we need to find the source."

Niamh gave a nod. "Done."

I looked down at Clint and Tasha, both in my arms. "You've got the scent in your noses? Good, just make sure not to get into the weeds themselves. I don't need *you* tripping."

Tasha's nose wrinkled up. "No problem."

"Don't want," Clint agreed with the same expression. "You were scary."

"Heh. I bet I was, at that. It's no fun coming down from that high, either."

Henri's hand landed on my shoulder, squeezing reassuringly. "Don't worry, my dear. The bulb of the plant itself produces the hallucinations, and it has to go through a process to become digestible. Unless they bite or lick the bulb directly, they won't be in danger."

"I feel better hearing that, thanks."

He gave another squeeze before letting go.

I heard Marshall mutter in question, "Jimsonweed?"

Niamh, in a low tone, started rapidly explaining. I left her to it.

I faced the door to the opulent manor house and braced myself mentally for battle. I had no doubt that dragging Lady Barese out of this house would involve a lot of yelling. From her son, if no one else. He leant towards the dramatic, after all. It wasn't going to be pleasant. Still, I was determined to see it through properly.

With my shoulders set, I marched up the steps and knocked loudly on the front door. The same snooty-faced butler from before opened the door and gave me another look down his nose—until I displayed the search warrant for him.

"I have a warrant to search this house and detain my suspect," I informed him. "Move."

He stared at the paper in shock for a full five seconds. "You can't do this!"

"My good sir." Sherard's smile was all teeth, like a shark smelling blood in the water. "The queen herself called in for this search warrant. I assure you, we can. Jamie, Gibson, this way."

I followed, his wand acting like a compass as he led us along the main floor and into the back, past the opulent rooms for show, and into the staff's area. The butler protested, following us, getting louder with every step.

I finally had enough and turned, getting right in his face. "I will charge you with interference in an investigation and put you in jail for the night if you'd prefer."

He stopped abruptly, pale, and didn't dare move a toe after that.

Better. I hightailed it after Sherard, catching up quickly. I was very curious where that pen was, and I had to serve as a witness of where we found it.

I was pulling on gloves as we moved, Gibson was too, and it was much safety precaution as preserving evidence right now.

Maids and footmen alike startled as we walked through the house, staring after us as we passed and whispering to each other. Sherard confidently went through the kitchen and then further, into a hallway of what was probably the staff's rooms.

"YOU CAN'T DO THIS!"

Ah, rats. The noisy one had found us. I turned sharply, annoyance flaring. Lord Barese was in mismatching clothes, nothing quite buttoned or fastened right, like he'd been yanked out of something and had to throw clothes back on. He looked wild with panic, and almost ran over three people on his way to us.

"Lord Barese, I have a warrant to search this property—" I started, trying to stay professional.

"You can't just come in here and throw allegations about!" he insisted, as petulant as any child told they couldn't have dessert. "My mother is close friends with a judge, he'll have that overturned!"

"The *queen* signed off on this warrant," I informed him flatly.

That stopped him, and he stood with jaw gaping. "Wh-wha?"

About as quick as landed fish, this one.

Gibs put a hand on my shoulder and said, "I'll deal with him, you find that pen set."

"Thanks, Gibs." Nothing could get past him. I turned and quickened my pace, catching up with Sherard, who was further ahead of me. He hadn't let the commotion stop him, intent on following the thread of the spell.

Sherard stopped dead, almost at the end of the hallway at a plain, closed door. "In here."

I ignored the argument between Barese and Gibson, which was loud, and turned to address a group of young women in maid's outfits clustered together at the end of the hallway. "Whose room is this?"

A hand tentatively went up by a pretty cream-colored weredog. "Uh, mine?"

"You're not in trouble," I assured her with a smile, waving her in closer. "But we need to get in. You've picked up something that's evidence for a case."

She scurried forward, ears flicking back and forth in agitation. "I have? Are you sure?"

I pointed to the man standing patiently at my side. "RM

Seaton is doing the seeking spell. Trust me, I'm sure. Just let us in and answer my questions, please."

Her hand shook as she opened the door, immediately snatching herself back as if she didn't want any part of whatever was in there.

The room wasn't large—maybe ten feet by twelve feet, barely enough room for a double bed, dresser, washstand, and a desk. The desk held a collection of books, letters—and a very elaborate bronze pen set. Bingo.

Sherard let his wand drop, inclining his head toward it. "There it is. I better test it to see how dangerous it is before you bag and tag it."

"Please and thank you." I turned to the maid. "What's your name?"

"Ginevra," she answered, bewilderment in her eyes. "The pen set is what you're looking for?"

I had no doubt she was innocent in all this. She wouldn't have dared use it if she really knew what part this thing had played in a person's murder. "It is, yes. How did you come to have it?"

"Oh, well, m'lady threw it out some weeks ago. It was a strange business to begin with. I watched her wash it out herself, and then she marched it out to the rubbish heap and threw it out. Throwing out such a fine piece didn't make sense to me. I fetched it out again, washed it myself, and didn't see the harm in keeping it if she had no interest in it."

Even with it being washed twice, I doubted that every trace of the ink had been taken out. The interior of a pen was a hard thing to wash, after all. Still, I had an eagle eye on my friend as he ran the pen set through the tests.

A satisfied expression grew over his face. "It's there. Diluted—no doubt from the washings—but there. We can link it to the drug. My dear child, you are a lucky woman that this didn't affect you. What have you written with this pen?"

"Oh, um, a few letters?" She pointed to the ones on the desk. "I haven't had a chance to post them yet."

I slipped on a glove before picking them up. "I need to

confiscate these, I'm afraid. You'll need to write them again. These things are poisonous—literally."

"Poison…?" she repeated blankly.

"You'll figure out the story soon enough." Sherard carefully maneuvered the pen set into an evidence bag.

Murder weapon acquired. We could at least link the pen set to Lady Barese. It wasn't quite enough evidence to lock her into this murder entirely, though. We needed one more thing—two if we could somehow pull it off. I didn't want this woman to skate out of this because we hadn't presented enough evidence in court. I'd drop this off with Evans, let him sit on it.

Henri, Niamh, I hope the two of you have something. Otherwise, we might not get Giada the justice she deserves.

Report 22: Evidence

My seeking spell led me straight to the back side of the house, specifically the latrine pit in the very back of the property. Even with charms back here, it smelled...less than pleasant, shall we say. Have I smelled worse, working as a policeman? Unfortunately so. It didn't deter me. I did make sure to keep Phil on my shoulder, however, as I didn't want him to pick up any of this stench. I also resigned myself to throwing these gloves out after using them here, as there would be no way to remove the stench later.

"Why here?" Foster asked in bewilderment. "Surely someone wouldn't burn something in the latrine pit."

"No, but the ashes would have been swept up and deposited here as a matter of course," I replied with grim satisfaction. Ashes were always swept from the grate and deposited here to help with the smell. I was not surprised to find the remains of a diary here.

What I could pull from those ashes, though, that was the tricky question.

I dropped the seeking spell and refocused my energy. Criminals often liked to burn things. To them, it was the easiest and most effective method of destroying evidence. Granted, it worked a good majority of the time—ashes look like ashes, so no one questions it much. Most trace evidence would be completely destroyed as well, so the method works in their favor. That said, we magical examiners had learned a trick or two about putting something burned back together.

I had no way of knowing what, if anything, remained of that diary. The only way to know was to call on its remnants and try to assemble the pieces together. I was an old hand at this, having done it many, many times in my career. "Bring what is lost back to being. Restore from the ashes and form once more."

From the latrine pit, flaky, black pieces of paper flew up into the air, accompanied by what seemed to be the remains of something blocky and leather-clad. The cover of the diary took shape first, the hardened cover forming with pockmarks, the edges jagged as parts of it couldn't maintain integrity. This spell wasn't perfect. It couldn't restore something that was utterly destroyed. I aimed for what pieces hadn't been completely consumed by fire.

Next, the pages—what remained of them—fit and slotted back together, trying to once again adhere to the cover. It was imperfect, of course, most of the pages long gone, only six or seven partially-filled pages restored inside the cover. I eyed the dark, sooty sections and hoped there was enough there to prove without a shadow of a doubt it was Giada's diary.

It took several minutes to assemble, with Foster, Lewis, and me holding our breaths the whole time, but eventually the spell eased and ended itself, not able to pull anything else from this area. I gingerly took the diary from where it stayed suspended mid-air before the spell could end completely.

With the tip of a finger, I flipped gingerly through the pages, trying to discern what I had managed to restore. It was enough for me to verify that it was Giada's handwriting, and one page had a date showing four weeks ago.

I had the right diary.

Blowing out a breath, I gave Foster and Lewis a nod. "Alright, we have firm evidence that the Bareses are involved in this somehow. Let's see if we can find any trace of where this was burned. The more we can tie to either mother or son, the better."

"How, though, sir?" Lewis questioned. "You already did a seeking spell that led you here."

"I used a restoration spell for this, which has a very limited range. If I can get it in proximity of where it was burned, we might well be able to pick up trace elements from the area."

Foster looked at me steadily, a wicked grin teasing up the corners of his mouth, revealing sharp canine teeth. "You want to march into their bedrooms and test their hearths, don't you?"

"Lady Barese's first. My hunch is on her."

"Oh, I'm with you on this, sir. Let's test the theory."

It was gratifying Foster was on the same page as I.

We went into the house via the kitchen door, with me gingerly holding the diary away from myself as we moved. It still smelled, of course; my spell did nothing about the stench the pages had been lying in, but I couldn't clean it. I didn't dare. It would remove whatever trace evidence still left behind, for one. For another, a cleaning spell would be far too stringent and might well damage the pages even further.

I could not wait to put this in an evidence bag, though, and have pity on my poor nose.

The kitchen staff hovered around the table, clearly gossiping when we entered, but I paid no mind to what they were saying. I looked to the most senior of the lot, a werebadger with greying fur, and inquired of her, "Where is Lady Barese's bedroom?"

"Oh, she won't want you in there," the maid assured me hurriedly.

"I assure you, I could not give two shakes what her opinion is. Lead me to it."

She didn't want to, that was clear, but Lewis and Foster's red kingsmen uniform was a declaration of authority like none other. She didn't dare cross them, either. With a hesitant nod, she turned on her heel and led us out, up the back servants' stairs, cramped as they were, and onto the second floor. The bedroom in question was conveniently right at hand, the corner room that had the best view of the garden. Its door was closed, but I didn't let that deter me, just walked in with Foster at my heels. Phil darted ahead, then screeched to a stop, his hackles rising and his nose sniffing the air.

"Henri!" he reported in an alarmed voice. "Bad sniffy in here!"

I swore, dove for him, and scooped him off the ground. "How thick is it?"

He put a paw against my chest, bracing himself as he sniffed harder. His head swiveled toward the fireplace in the far wall. "There. Old smelling."

That was precisely where I'd expected the diary to have been burned. It had been stupid to burn the pages here, considering the potency of the jimsonweed ink, but that was neither here nor there at the moment.

I turned, handing Phil to Foster. "Hold him. I don't want him walking on the floor here in case some of the ink was spilled."

Foster took Phil, cradling him with both hands as I turned once again towards the fireplace.

I once again weaved the restoration spell, carefully teasing the ashes in the grate back together again and coaxing them to return to the diary still in my hand. Ashes swirled in the grate, mostly coming from the back corners, coalescing into the open diary splayed on my palm. There wasn't much, barely enough to fill a teacup, but the remnants whirled and slotted in with the pages, some of them forming trace amounts of new pages I hadn't had before. Even as little as it was, it was enough to verify that the diary had been burned here.

That was truly all I needed.

The spell's white light faded from the diary as it finished, nothing else left to work with. I once more studied the pages, easily deciphering Giada's elongated, swirling handwriting. The newest addition had a date at the top, right before her death. I let out a sigh of relief.

"Did it work?" Foster asked eagerly.

"Yes, fortunately. Foster, I need an evidence bag."

"Absolutely, sir. Phil, up on my shoulder. Good."

He handed me the containment bag out of my black bag, and I took it before sliding the diary in. The containment bag would keep it together and protect it until I could properly deal with it at the station.

I regained my feet as I heard a clatter at the door.

Jamie entered with a smile, looking both worried and victorious. "Found the pen. The maid had it, said Lady Barese had thrown it out and she retrieved it. How goes it here?"

"The diary was burned, but I was able to piece part of it back together." I indicated the bag in my hand. "I fear it might not be the conclusive evidence we'd hoped it to be. After all, Lord Barese openly admitted to taking several diaries. Any good lawyer could argue that this was one of the ones he took and burned in a fit of pique. Our only counter is that it was burned here, in Lady Barese's hearth."

Jamie grimaced. "I admit that's crossed my mind more than once."

Foster looked between us with dismay. "But that means we need more evidence if we're to prove it was Lady Barese, right? Will we be able to make an arrest?"

"I think we could arrest her," Seaton opined, frowning darkly at the floor. "I just fear it wouldn't hold. Another piece of evidence to firmly lock her in as the culprit is necessary."

Jamie gestured to the room at large. "Foster, Lewis, search this room. Let's see if anything else comes up.

When you're done with this room, go to Lord Barese's."

"Their studies too?" Foster asked.

"Yes, anywhere they might stash something. Anything, I do stress anything, that looks odd to you, just bag it and take it to Evans."

"On it," Lewis assured her.

Jamie led the way back out of the room, talking as she went. "Gibs is sitting on Lord Barese right now because the useless idiot is doing nothing but screaming about injustice. I've got to keep him contained and out of the search until I have more to hold him with. Henri, which would you rather tackle, in-house search or outside?"

I did appreciate she gave me the choice, but I grimaced down at my ruined gloves, knowing they gave me no option. "I best do outside. These are not up to handling anything in the house."

"Fair enough."

I collected Phil from Foster before leaving, freeing up his hands with a murmured thanks. Phil chose to perch on my shoulder, as usual, which I didn't mind. At the top of the stairs, our pads all lit up with an alert. I pulled mine free of my pocket, pausing in place to answer Niamh's call. "What have you found, Niamh?"

"*Jimsonweed, and a lot of it. Clint*! *If you fall in there, I will never hear the end of it. Get off. I'm serious, off. There's a whole section of weeds here along the back of the garden wall, where the rubbish bins are stacked.*"

"My darling cat," Jamie drawled, "If you fall into something, I will not rescue you. Kindly return to Niamh before she has a heart attack."

"*He's complaining that he never falls, but he's back with me. Thanks, Detective.*"

"First of all, that's a blatant lie. I've watched him fall straight onto his side. As surefooted as he is, even he has his moments." Jamie shook her head. "Bag some of that, Niamh."

"*Marshall already is. We'll run it to Evans before I continue looking around. There's a lot of sheds along this back wall, I'm hoping that one of them has a distillery or something that we can link to the poison.*"

"From your lips to the gods' ears," Jamie intoned, expression heartfelt. "Go for it." She hung up, replacing the pad in her pocket with a thoughtful frown. "This is good news for us. We can prove jimsonweed is readily available at this house."

"It's a common weed found everywhere, though; that's not conclusive evidence either," I protested.

Jamie opened her mouth to respond, then closed it. I could see some spark of inspiration cross her face, watched it bloom into a full idea. "Henri. Did I ever tell you that plants have DNA?"

I blinked at her. "As in, like mammal species do?"

"Right. Did I tell you that?"

"No," I answered slowly, the same spark of an idea transmitting from her to me. I understood in a flash what she meant. "The remnants of the jimsonweed from Giada's pen...can we use it to track the parent plant it came from?"

"Sure. I mean, the DNA will match, as it will come from the same family of plants." Her voice rose in excitement, eyes locked on me. "Can you do it? I mean, is there a spell that will work for that?"

I didn't answer her, my eyes snapping to Seaton. "Get as many trace elements as you can. I'll rework the Blood-Hunting spell."

His smile was full of a satisfied victory. In a second, the royal mage spirited himself away, gone with an almost audible snap of magic.

"Ah, so this can be done." Jamie grinned with satisfaction. "You know, Henri, I think I'll join you in the backyard."

I hurried back down the steps, heading for the front door once more. As I went down, I saw a smartly dressed man standing with both the butler and Lord Barese, all of them looking upset. I didn't even have to guess that this must be the family solicitor. Gibson had moved to stand with them, as a guard to prevent them from going further in.

Jamie put a hand on my arm, leaning in a little to say in a low tone, "I'll handle them, go work your magic."

I gave her a nod of agreement before turning sideways and sliding past them, going through the open door.

"Greetings, gentlemen," Jamie said smartly, drawing their attention to her.

"Detective Edwards, just why are you in my house?" Lord Barese demanded of her, his hands wildly swinging about his head in distress. "You keep claiming you're finding evidence of Giada's death, like you're accusing me of having something to do with my own wife's demise! It is beyond discourteous!"

"So's murder. Sir."

I snorted at the answer, amused once more at my lover's frankness. Jamie was not the type to be influenced by another's status, and I loved her for it.

I headed for the kitchen door, the faster route into the backyard. It was chilly out outside, enough to turn my breath white, and I encouraged Phil into a pocket—partially for warmth, partially because I needed both hands free. I didn't want him anywhere near those jimsonweed plants.

I reached the corner of the house shortly after that, Marshall standing guard over a patch of the jimsonweed and giving an evil eye to anyone who came in too close, encouraging them to give the area a wide berth.

Pulling free one of my smaller notebooks, I flipped to a clean page, working out the logistics of how to change the spell so that it followed plant DNA. It didn't take much re-wording, as I already had to do this once, changing the Blood-Hunting spell to follow saliva. Because I understood this spell so well, I knew precisely what to change to alter its intent and search parameters. There, that should do it.

Seaton was back in a pop of sound, startling all of us into jumping a little. In his hand was a glass bowl, held carefully in front of him, with a tablespoon's worth of black dust. I looked at it with satisfaction. More than enough to go on.

"Good, I think I have this spell worked out."

Seaton leaned over my shoulder and read it through, giving a grunt. "Yes, that should work. Will you do the honors or shall I?"

"I best do it, considering I'm officially on this case and you're not."

"Heh. True. I do forget that from time to time."

I enacted the spell without hurry. "Parent to child, connect through your essence. What is, to what it has become, recall your source."

In immediate response—since I was standing directly near them—the plants clustered at the base of the brick wall glowed, my wand snapping in their direction, a thin green line connecting the two. It couldn't be any clearer than that. "We have our answer. I need to very carefully collect what is here for evidence purposes. Seaton, hand me that bowl."

Marshall looked between us, eyebrows arching. "Does that mean we have enough evidence to prove she did it?"

"I'm not sure if it's enough," I answered frankly. "We know the pen set was from her. We know the ink refills came from her. We know she had jimsonweed here that matches what was in Giada's house. The diary was burned in her own bedroom hearth. But it can be argued her son had access to all the same things, which is what concerns me. We might need a confession to lock this case in."

Seaton shook his head. "She might still manage to wriggle free somehow, but I think if we properly read our good queen in on the situation, she'll make sure justice is served. Where is Jamie, anyway?"

"Inside dealing with Lord Barese and his lawyer," I answered.

"Ah. I'd best go in and make it clear what's going on out here."

"Go, do that. I'll manage things here and join you in a moment."

Seaton gave a nod before collecting Clint and Tasha, hauling them along with him. Smart to get both out of the way. Clint couldn't help but balance on any tall thing he could find, and the garden walls were proving too much of a temptation.

Marshall pointed after the royal mage, brow confused. "Since when does Jamie need backup?"

I snorted. "He's overprotective. Alright, where's Niamh?"

"She's tracking something. She said she's got a link between the plants here and a shed further down." Marshall paused, nose wrinkling. "She tried to explain it, but she rather quickly lost me in the details."

If a tracker said that something was linked, then something was linked. I gestured for him to follow. "Let's see what she's found."

Report 23: Well, That's One Way to Get a Confession

Do you know what's worse than lawyers?

Reporters.

I was in the middle of arguing with the Bareses' lawyer when none other than Ms. King arrived on scene, purple hat and all. Her timing, as usual, could not have been more atrocious. I wanted to swear. I didn't, because she'd probably try to quote me.

She marched right through the front door like she owned the place, her cameraman following her and snapping off shots wildly—or as fast as he could with still needing to change out the film—and she barely gave any of us a chance to notice her before she was shooting off questions.

Gibs, bless him, moved like lightning to check her, meaning she didn't get more than a foot inside the house. He kept his arm in a block, pushing her physically back, not that she didn't try to squirm around him somehow.

"Move," she snapped at him.

"King, you don't have the authority to be in here," Gibs snapped back. "Leave, now."

She ignored him, looking around his body to address me, "Detective, are you here to make an arrest?"

"Yours, if you don't get out of this house," I told her bluntly.

King wasn't fazed. Sadly, she was probably used to worse being said to her. "Was it Lord Barese who killed Lady Giada Barese?"

For once, the lawyer was on my side. "Any word along those lines is slander, and if you dare to even suggest that about either of my clients in your article, I will have you up on claims of libel before you can blink."

Go, lawyer, go!

What was the world coming to? I was cheering on the man I'd just spent the better part of fifteen minutes arguing with. The enemy of my enemy was my friend? I guess.

"And who are you?" King challenged him. "The Bareses' lawyer, am I right? Why do they need a lawyer if Detective Edwards isn't here to arrest someone?"

Ugh, someone, make her stop. I was tapped out at this point. I had no more energy to give, certainly no more patience.

I got in her face, dropping my voice to a dangerously low growl. "King. I have not verified, one way or another, who killed Giada Barese. I *can* prove, though, that you're interfering in an investigation right at this moment and I am all too happy to throw you into jail over it. I have no patience left, lady. Stop pushing it."

Her expression was righteous, like I'd given her ammunition. "The people have the right to the truth, Detective!"

"Well, they can't have it when I don't know what the truth is right now, can they? You've got three seconds to get out of here before I stop being nice."

Of course she ignored that too. "Lord Barese, did you kill your wife because she had an affair on you?"

Lord Barese, like an actor on cue, wailed and crumpled to the ground. Really, he even cried on cue, it was real talent.

It was also the last straw for me. I caught Gibs' eye and we both agreed—time for King to stop pushing us around. Gibs caught the woman by the shoulders, spun her around, and with a practiced move, slapped a cuff on one wrist. "Ms. King, you're under arrest for interfering in an active investigation. Not to mention trespassing."

"I'm not trespassing, I'm doing my job!"

"Trespassing in front of multiple officers, no less." Gibs was smiling from ear to ear, not at all bothered by her attempts to wriggle free. He had the cuff on her second wrist like the pro he was. "Mr. Cameraman, if you give me that camera nicely, I'll let you walk out of here."

The cameraman seemed to think this was a good deal. He promptly handed it over and then hightailed it back down the steps. Wanted nothing to do with this, eh? I couldn't blame him.

King yelled obscenities after him for deserting her, but I ignored those. "Evans, can you come sit on her?"

Evans proved he was a friend when he came promptly, even though he didn't look happy to haul the screaming woman away.

Lord Barese was still on the ground crying, because that's basically all he's good for, but I could ignore him. I leaned into Gibs' side and offered, "If you can find a phone and ask the local station if they'll come pick up King? I don't want to deal with her while we're in the middle of this."

"Sure." Gibson looked around, spotted a phone alcove further down, next to the stairs, and headed for it.

Right. One down, one to go. I blew out a breath, turning back to the lawyer. He was back to staring at me mutinously, not willing to give an inch.

I went with the big guns. Mostly because I was tired of this crap. "Sir. I have a warrant, ordered by *Queen Regina herself*, giving me recourse to search this property and seize any and all evidence pertaining to Giada's death. That warrant includes making an arrest if I find I have the grounds to do so. No matter what connections you have, what precedence you want to throw at me, you cannot top that."

He opened his mouth, thought better of it, and shut it again with a snap.

"Stay out of my way so I can get this done. Be on standby, because I assure you, if I have my way? An arrest is happening today." I marched off before he could get another word out.

Everyone was in the back yard, I knew that, so I headed there again. I wanted to organize a thorough search of the house. There was likely other evidence here, something I could use to prove which of the Bareses had done it; I just hadn't asked the right questions yet. Foster and Lewis weren't enough manpower to search the whole house, I really had to pull someone else in to help them. They'd be here all year if they tried to search a house this gargantuan by themselves.

My pad lit up with an alert. I pulled it free of my pocket, answering Niamh's call. "What have you found, Niamh?"

"*There's a shed here along the back of the garden wall, where the rubbish bins are stacked. It's got a rough kind of chemist's worktable with a burner, crucible, and a saucepan. It's been cleaned off, but even so the Felixes were able to pick up the smell strongly. I tracked it from the jimsonweed plants near the garden wall to here.*"

"So we can prove jimsonweed was distilled here. Any sign of who was using it last?"

"*Tasha's tracking the last person in the shed with me now. We're heading into the house via the kitchen.*"

Of course they were already on top of this. "I'll meet you there."

I rounded the corner of the house, only to bump into Sherard.

He looked me over, asking, "Lawyer?"

"Fuming. King burst in, she's in cuffs and Evans is sitting on her. Niamh's tracking the last person that was in the poison-making shed."

"There's a poison-making shed?" he asked in interest.

"Along the back wall, she and the cats found it." I was already moving, trusting him to keep up.

"Jamie, slow, slow," he complained. "The rest of us don't have super speed."

Oops. I normally matched pace with whoever was walking with me, but sometimes I forgot, usually in moments like this when I was excited. I'd walked Henri's poor legs off more than once in the past.

We made it to the kitchen door and inside, my ears following Niamh's voice.

"—sit, now, and wait. Don't bother protesting, I know

you were the last person in that shed."

Oh, she'd found whoever it was already. I rounded the corner into the dining room and found Niamh facing off with the butler.

What was this, *Clue*? The butler, in the shed, with the poison? No way. Not unless he had some weird, whacked sense of loyalty. I slowed and looked him over. He didn't look surprised, more resigned—a stodgy sort of resignation that pulled the corners of his mouth down, setting his shoulders back in a rigid way. Like a soldier facing court martial, that was the image he presented.

I looked him over and sighed, then pointed to a chair. "Sit. What's your name?"

"Reames." He looked me dead in the eye, voice flat, with absolutely no intonation. "I poisoned Lady Giada. She'd embarrassed my master. I wanted to get rid of her for him so that he could remarry, happily this time."

"Wow, I have to tell you, that has to be the easiest confession I've ever been handed. I didn't even get a question out." I squared off with him, eyes searching his face. There was truth there...but also evasion. He was holding my eyes too steadily. People didn't really do that, it was uncomfortable to just look at each other without wanting to look away for a second. He was making an effort to sell me on this idea.

Loyal, yes. This man was loyal to a fault. I didn't think the loyalty would go both ways. The Bareses were too self-indulgent to care for people like him. Would I convince him of it? Probably not.

I tested his knowledge instead. "How did you poison her?"

"With jimsonweed."

"Collected from where?"

"The back wall of this property. I distilled it in the shed."

"How did you know the process?"

"I served in the army, once. I was stationed in Ciparis for a time. We were introduced to it there. It's not difficult to do. Just extract the juice from the bulb, let it simmer for a while, then mix it with something else as a vehicle to ingest it."

He really did know about it. This could be the source of the information. Did I think he was the driving force behind Giada's death? No, but he was clearly an accessory. "How did you give it to Giada?"

"Her sanding powder, at first. It proved to be too mild of a vehicle, so I doctored her ink too."

"How did the pen set and the diary end up here, in this house?"

"When Master Sebastian went in to collect her diaries from her bedroom, I was the one who went with him. He didn't question what I took, he wasn't paying any attention to it. I was able to sneak in the ink set without him realizing."

No question, then, on who had done the dirty work. You're saying Lord Barese wasn't the one behind this?"

"Correct."

"Who ordered you to do it?"

"No one, I acted on my own."

I smiled at him a little sadly. "That's the first lie you've told me. Niamh, cuff him. We'll take him to the station and book him. Gibs and Evans are holding King, so just take him there so he can be taken to the station along with her."

She gave a nod, already pulling handcuffs from her belt.

I turned and walked away, going back up the stairs. Sherard was right on my heels, leaning in to ask in a low tone, "Where are you going?"

"There has got to be something else in this house that proves either mother or son did it," I responded in the same low tone. "We need to search this house thoroughly. I'm starting at the top and working my way down."

I went for the stairs, only to realize that Lord Barese had moved at some point. I deviated to the parlor, sticking my head around the doorframe. "Evans? Where is—" I cut myself off when I realized that Barese was flat on his back on a couch, a cloth over his face. Uh?

Evans was standing guard over King—wise precaution, she would run if she could—but turned his head to give me a look that spoke volumes. "Barese fainted. The staff carried him over here to rest."

"He...fainted," I repeated, waiting for the punchline. "From what?"

"Apparently, having his house searched and being accused of murder was too much for his frail heart." Evans rolled his eyes expressively.

Oh for the love of... I sighed. "Yeah, okay, I'm not touching that. We're going upstairs to search, let me know if he wakes up."

"Sure thing."

Shaking my head, I retreated back to the staircase. Halfway up the stairs, I heard Foster calling for me from the main floor and poked my head over the balcony.

"Up here. What?"

His head craned around until he spotted me. "Oh good, there you are. Come back down. I searched Lady Barese's desk and found some interesting things."

I liked his expression, one of wicked glee, because it promised he'd found fun things. I immediately turned and hustled back downstairs, enough pep in my step that Sherard was scrambling once again to keep up with me.

The study was one of pristine white with soft wood tones. I felt unnerved just stepping inside, like I was in the plush version of a hospital room. The only thing different was the furniture, with the desk, armchairs, and a settee all arranged in front of a fireplace. Not a single bookshelf was in this room, no traces of a book anywhere to be found. Lady Barese was apparently not a reader.

Foster stood next to the desk, two piles of paper on the top. He waved to them like a magician revealing his final trick, a wide grin on his face. Lewis was still going through a filing cabinet in the corner, although he had stacked a few things on top, which meant I had something else to look through. Foster's pile first.

I looked them over, the one on the left first, and felt the same wild glee grow over my face. The left was the divorce declaration, dated three months ago, and it looked rough as if someone had crumpled it angrily before smoothing it back out. Ha! It had come here, and intercepted by Mummy dearest, as suspected.

The paper on the right was a letter, and at first I didn't understand what I was looking at. Then I really paid attention to the sender and my jaw dropped. "She intended to send Giada to a sanitarium?"

"Giada was set to go in this very month, a week after her death," Foster confirmed, pointing to a date further down. "The room was paid for and everything. It absolutely proves that she was poisoning Giada and trying to discredit her state of mind. She intended to send Giada away to this place and get her out of mind."

"Oh, good show, Foster!" I gave him a high five. "I'd kiss you if it didn't make Henri jealous."

"No, please don't, they'd never find my body." He grinned back, fully pleased with himself, as he should be.

I laughed, mostly out of relief and happiness. Finally, finally, concrete evidence to prove which one of them had done it. "Alright, let's bag and tag these—"

"What," an icy voice demanded from the doorway, "is the meaning of this?"

I had just been about to say that we needed to lay hands on Lady Barese, and low and behold, speak of the devil herself. I put the letter down, then turned, already mentally braced for an argument.

She looked like she'd come from some party, dressed to the nines with a hat on her silver hair, white gloves still on her hands, and the coldest expression to ever grace a person fixed on her face. She looked like a wannabe Snow Queen. She was so pale herself, the light grey or white dress she wore made her like a walking monochrome scale.

I stepped forward, showing my badge as I moved, as this was definitely the time to adhere strictly to protocol. Especially with her lawyer hovering right behind her. "I'm Detective Jamie Edwards. I'm here to arrest you for the murder of Giada Barese."

It was like she didn't hear me. Her eyes blinked, showing she wasn't a statue, and then she spoke in that same icy disdain once more. "What gives you the right to come into my house and go through my personal things? I will not tolerate this behavior."

Uh, lady? Did you not hear me? "Lady Barese, I have found conclusive evidence that you played a direct part in Lady Giada Barese's death. I need you to come with me down to the station."

She turned her head, speaking to the lawyer behind her. "Reginald, I want these people out of my house."

The lawyer looked back at her with a poleaxed expression, really not sure how to obey that order. He could hardly lay hands on us and throw us out, after all. I'd lock him up too if even tried.

I reached into a pocket and pulled out the warrant. "Lady Barese, I have a warrant here signed not only by a judge, but by Queen Regina's hand, authorizing me to be here. Listen, okay, I'm not saying this again. I'm arresting you for the murder of Lady Giada Barese."

She didn't. She just stared at me like I wasn't speaking any human language she could decipher. "Why are you not leaving?"

It was like she really couldn't understand why I didn't automatically obey her. Wow, the arrogance. Where it came from, I didn't know. Not even Regina acted like this.

You know what, nothing I said was going to impact her. I might as well save my breath. I gave Sherard a look, a silent heads-up, and he gave me a tiny dip of the head in acknowledgement. He had my back if this went sideways. What an elderly woman using a cane could do to me, well, she probably couldn't do much. I didn't put anything past her, though.

I waded in, taking out cuffs as I moved.

The lawyer immediately protested. "Detective, the cuffs are entirely unnecessary!"

"I'd normally agree," I answered without looking at him, "but if nothing else, the cuffs might ram it home for her that she's not above the law. Lady Meryl Barese, you have the right to remain silent—"

Lady Barese flinched backwards, eyes wide with outrage. "You will not dare—"

I dared, lady. Her failing reflexes were no match for my speed or strength. She couldn't even begin to put up a fight. I had both cuffs on her in a second flat, then maintained my grip on her wrist, just in case she decided to use the cane to hit me. She looked plenty mad to do it. I kept reading her rights to her in a bland tone, even as she completely ignored me.

"Unhand me at once!" she snapped, uselessly tugging.

I ignored her, turning to the others. "Guys, pack this up. Foster, if you'll grab the paperwork, I want to take that with me. Lewis, continue searching the house in case there's something else I've missed. I'll leave Marshall and Evans here to help you. Sherard, will you stay and help direct?"

Sherard waved me on. "We've got it, don't worry."

The lawyer once again tried to intervene. "Detective, you can't arrest a peer of this realm for murder!"

I met him eye for eye. "I just did."

I feel like Foster was the man of the hour this time.

I certainly feel that way.

Report 24: The Real Culprit

I left Sherard, Marshall, Evans, and Lewis at the house to keep searching. We weren't quite done there, and I trusted them to look for fun things.

It took some coordination getting everyone over to the local station, who were nice enough to not only put people into cells for me, but to offer up two interrogation rooms. I had to take two taxis to manage it, but it was a short trip, thankfully. The silence in the taxi was lethal. Lady Barese wasn't the type to rant and rave. Her death glares, though, they could slice a person to ribbons.

We had to do due process, which meant interrogating her, so I marched her into a small interrogation room with Henri at my side.

I'd been training my two ducklings on interrogation techniques and I figured I might as well let them actually work this time. I sent them off with the butler into one room, hoping they might get him to crack and give something away. He'd been working under Lady Barese's orders—I knew it, everyone else did as well. The problem was proving it. He was up for accessory to murder regardless, but the length of his sentence might change depending on what he said in confession.

Gibs leaned in and murmured to me, "I'm going with them, in case they need a hand."

It was a bit much to send them in solo when they'd never done it before. I gave him a grateful nod and shooed him on. That left only Henri and three cats with me, but I was pretty sure I was tougher than a spoiled aristocrat.

I marched her into the interrogation room, her and her lawyer, and sat them down in the hard, wooden chairs. Lady Barese looked a lot like the grouchy mother from the *Pride and Prejudice* movie, the one with Kiera Knightly.

Henri and I took the seats across from her, the cats settling as they wished.

"You've gone through considerable trouble to bring me here, Detective," she said with a voice dripping ice. "I do hope you're prepared for the consequences."

"I do hope you're prepared for yours," I returned in a level tone.

The lawyer at Lady Barese's side cleared his throat. "Detective, there's no need for such harsh words."

I ignored him. He was a smarmy bootlicker, anyway; I could tell from the way he treated the countess like she walked on water. It was safe to ignore him. "Let's go over the facts, shall we? First, the pen."

Henri had all the evidence in a bag at his feet. He laid out the pen—now tagged and secured in a containment box so we didn't handle it directly—on the table.

"I have many witnesses who say you gave this to Giada as a gift. I also have many witnesses who say you supplied her with fresh ink every two weeks so she could continue to use it. Not a shipment from the stationery store, which would make the most sense—you, personally. Why is that, Lady Barese?"

She stared at me stonily, mouth clamped together.

"Next, the ink itself. The magical examiner at my side tested that ink and found it heavily laced with a hallucinogenic drug called jimsonweed. It's a common weed, but we have proven that the drug came from plants bordering your back garden wall. We even found the set up in the shed used to make it into the drug."

"You can't possibly prove such a thing!" the lawyer scoffed, the mouth under that truly ridiculous moustache lifted in a sneer.

My eyes cut to him. "The man at my side is a candidate

to become the next royal mage. Do not doubt his magic."

The lawyer's eyes flew to Henri, jaw dropping.

Henri just smiled a little secretive smile and didn't say a word.

My lover did have a twisted sense of humor sometimes. It's why we got along well.

I cleared my throat and moved on. "Next, we have retrieved portions of Giada's diary burned in Lady Barese's bedroom hearth. Those pages revealed jimsonweed-laced ink, and it is the very diary that detailed the days leading up to her death. You understand that looks like you were destroying damning evidence?"

Still, not a word. She refused to even look at me, her eyes fixed on some point over my shoulder.

Henri pulled out the next piece of damning evidence, laying it flat on the table for all to see. I leaned in a little, one hand flat on the table's scarred surface. "Lady Barese. Do explain to me why you had reserved a room in a sanitorium for Lady Giada? Why we found a letter confirming the reservation in your desk? For that matter, why was your son's divorce decree—something he knew nothing about—in your desk?"

She stared at the letter and decree as if it might burst into flame at any second.

The lawyer didn't know how to answer this either. His eyes were on his client's face, waiting for some cue so he knew how to jump.

The silence in the room would make ghosts in a graveyard uncomfortable. I didn't interrupt it, though. Sometimes, the best technique was to let silence play out.

Finally, she cracked open that stubborn mouth and spoke. "Giada's mind was unhinged. I did that for my son's sake."

"Absolutely no one knew Giada was suffering from hallucinations," I returned mildly. "She only confided in one person: her doctor. Not even her mother knew of them. So, do tell me how you came to know about them?"

Silence again. She was back to staring at that spot on the

wall.

I had enough evidence on her that I could charge her for this. Still, I'd feel better if we had a confession.

I sat back as if I had all the time in the world. I kinda did. I could keep her in here for up to six hours before procedure dictated I had to take a break until the next day. Did I want to be in here for six hours with her? Hard pass. Still, I was willing to do it if that's what it took.

So I sat back, crossed my legs, and encouraged Clint to come up for pets. He did so with a happy purr before turning to glare at the countess as if ready to rend her to shreds.

Such a good kitty.

"Lady Barese, here's my theory. Tell me if I'm wrong." I stroked Clint's back idly as I spoke. "I think you hated Giada. You didn't like her, didn't feel like she was worthy of your son. That's why you drove her out of the house. You were fine with her being gone—out of sight, out of mind—and letting your son go back to his life before he married. Your opinion changed when you saw her take up with a new lover—someone who might replace your son in the will. And then when you found out she had filed for divorce…" I let the insinuation hang.

A visible tic developed at the corner of her mouth. She was glaring at the wall now, and it was a wonder the poor stone didn't confess to every sin it had committed.

Henri leaned into my side and said, sotto voce, "Divorce would have been entirely shameful for their family, wouldn't it?"

"Oh, absolutely," I agreed, playing along. "Giada didn't see it that way. She was just getting rid of a husband who liked to have affairs."

Lady Barese slammed a hand against the table, making all of us flinch. Her expression was like a mother storm, filled with energy and anger. "My son did no such thing! She was the one flaunting other men in his face!"

"Your son had an affair with one of the maids less than two months after their marriage," I corrected. "Giada's diary details how she discovered it. It was that, plus your hatred of her, that drove her to return to her own house."

Her jaw worked but she had no words for me. Hadn't known that, huh? Did she really think her son the innocent party in all of this? Was this naivety or was she the type of mother where her son could do no wrong?

My bet was the latter.

"You think your son deserved better than her, didn't you?"

"She was a divorced woman," Lady Barese spat, the words venomous. "She was ruined in society's eyes, not that I could convince my son of that. He just had to have her. They were barely married two months before I saw her take up with another man!"

"Yeah, she didn't see any need to hold to vows your son had already broken." I didn't agree with that, mind you, but I had this lovely button I'd been handed. I had to push it, just to see what else I could get out of her.

"My son was faithful!"

"I heard he keeps a mistress in town." I really had no evidence of that, but sometimes guesses got great reactions.

"He's supporting the arts, she's not a mistress!"

Bingo. So he'd slept with more than the maid, unsurprisingly.

"Oh, so you do know about her. Now, what do you think Giada made of this woman, that your son supported, and visited on a regular basis? In her shoes, would you have just shrugged and looked the other way?"

Lady Barese scoffed, head snapping to the side so she no longer had to look at me. "My son is entirely innocent in this whole affair. That's the only thing you've been smart about. It was Giada who was the stupid one. With her affairs and her tantrums, it was no wonder someone murdered her in the end. She was a loose woman with loose morals."

"You hated her, huh?"

"I detested her. She was better off dead."

Her lawyer hissed at her before trying to hastily cover

it up. "She doesn't mean that to the point of actually killing Lady Giada, of course."

I ignored him. We both did.

"It must have enraged you to hear your son talk about reconciliation." Henri spoke mildly, in an almost sympathetic way. "You'd worked so hard to drive her out of his life, to prove what she really was, but he still wanted her."

"It was just spite, that was all. He couldn't stand to see her with another man. My son has always been possessive." Her jaw worked under angry emotion, looking ready to stab someone. "I knew that if I could just discredit her a little more—"

With a snap, she realized what she'd almost said and closed her mouth on the rest of the sentence.

Rats, almost had her. "Yes? Almost discredit her how?"

Nothing.

Henri tried his hand at poking her. "Discredit her as crazy, I believe you were going to say? You did believe she was crazy enough to pass a sanitarium's standards of health. After all, you booked a room for her."

I twisted the handle of the knife a little further, trying to get her to say something else. "You surely didn't think that just because she walked away from your cheating son."

"It was my son who was madly in love with her!" Lady Barese snapped, slamming both hands against the table hard enough to make it jump. "She couldn't care less! She moved out so quickly, leaving him desolate, and I couldn't stand to see him like that! She *deserved* what she got."

"Deserved it? Deserved it enough that you made sure she got her comeuppance?"

The lawyer put a hand on her wrist, trying to settle her. It kind of worked, although she threw his hand off, too angry to be calmed.

I almost had her. Almost. "You decided to capitalize on the gift you gave her, a token you'd given to keep up appearances. If you could make her a little mad, then you could say to all and sundry that's why the marriage had failed. Giada wasn't sane. You could have the marriage annulled without her consent, as she'd no longer be considered sound of mind, and life would go back as it was. When the divorce decree arrived, that's when you started shipping her poisonous ink."

Still nothing, eh? It's alright, I knew what to say next to get her to react.

"Giada would have processed the divorce faster, I think, except her health was giving her trouble. The weird hallucinations and trips she randomly had took a toll on her. Still, she was very determined to get rid of the men in her life who supposedly loved her but had no problem hooking up with other women."

"That's speculation, Detective!" the lawyer snapped.

"Eh, not so much. Giada was very detailed in her diaries." I let that sit for a beat before reinforcing it with, "*Very* detailed. There's not much she didn't record."

"Still, you have no cause—"

I held up a hand to forestall him. "What Giada would or wouldn't have done is not important, I agree. What is important is what happened next. After that initial filing for divorce, a follow-up was sent, a demand for motion of agreement. You were running out of time. You only had sixty days before that motion was automatically passed and it was publicly filed in the courts that your son was a divorcee."

Back to stony silence, although she had both hands curled into fists in her lap as if mentally strangling me.

Try me, lady. I'm both stronger and meaner than you.

I leaned in a little, voice flat as I recounted, "You knew then that you had to do something to stop her. Your plan of embarrassing her, of locking her away in an insane asylum, wasn't working. She was made of stronger stuff than you'd bargained for. You had to up the dose in the ink, hoping to make it so obvious that she could no longer fake being well in front of other people."

"My question is this." Henri tapped a finger to the letter on the table. "The date on this letter suggests you intended for her to go in this very month. Were you following your original plan? Or had you decided that her death would suit you better?"

The lawyer squawked, "That's conjecture!"

"So it is," I agreed, all relaxed as if this was an academic question I really wanted an answer to. "We don't know which it is, hence why we're asking. Lady Barese, set the record straight for us. Did you only intend to drive Giada mad? Or did you kill her?"

"My client doesn't have to answer that!"

"Your client will, in fact, have to answer that. In front of a jury, if nowhere else."

There was a clatter at the door and I turned, not sure who would want to interrupt me during an interrogation. It abruptly opened without a knock or apology.

Queen Regina swept inside, head held high and eyes snapping with fire. Right at her elbow was Sherard, escorting her through. Held in her hand was Khan, looking ready to go full tiger at any second. He had his mean face on. Even in miniature size, it was a little scary, not going to lie.

We all scrambled to our feet, bowing to her, which she barely acknowledged. Why on god's green earth—oh. Come to think of it, I had messaged her on the way into the station to let her know I had our suspect in hand, and what evidence we had on her. I was trying to make sure that if we came across trouble later holding the countess, I had her backing to make sure the woman stayed in jail.

I did not anticipate that she'd want to confront Lady Barese herself.

Sherard gave me a little wave over her shoulder and mouthed, *Sorry*!

I gave him a nod of *it's okay* in return. If the queen demanded he portal her here, there wasn't much he could say to that except yes ma'am.

Regina came around to stand at my side, staring at Lady Barese as if she were something that had been scraped off a boot heel.

"I have been informed of all the evidence found at your

house," she said without preamble. Lady Barese had trouble meeting her eyes. "Two pieces of evidence, I understand, were within your very desk. I have no doubt of your guilt, Lady Barese. What I want to know is your intent. Did you intend to kill Giada?"

Lady Barese's face rippled as if she were suppressing some strong emotion. Still, she kept her head up as she looked at the queen. "That woman's death is entirely on her own head."

Regina was steaming mad. She stepped in further and breathed, "If you so altered her mind that she could not even safeguard herself, then it is *you* who is responsible for her death. There is no other answer. No peer of my realm is above the law, as you will soon discover. I will make sure they prepare a special cell just for you."

Lady Barese was already pale as porcelain. At that announcement, she turned grey, as if she'd already put one foot into a grave.

Regina, however, wasn't done. "The nobility of my country are caretakers of its people. I think sometimes you forget that. That you would fall to such a base level, to murder another soul, speaks too much to your arrogance. I do not have the power alone to punish you as I wish to. I will put it forth, however, to strip you of your title, and recommend it to the strongest degree. You will go to prison a common citizen, if I have my say about it."

Whatever held Lady Barese still up failed her, and she sank into her chair like a marionette with its strings cut. She seriously looked on the verge of fainting.

I thought Regina's punishment a nice touch. After all, this woman had killed to protect her family's reputation and status. Removing it was just desserts in my mind.

Regina stepped back, then turned to me. "Jamie, Henri, with me."

I followed her out of the room, curious where this was going. She'd more or less just finished my interrogation; there wasn't much I could say to top that.

With us all out in the hallway, the door shut behind us,

she turned to face us with tears in her eyes.

"I knew when I asked this of you that you'd find Giada's killer. This might well be manslaughter in Lady Barese's mind, but to mine, it's murder. She didn't care if Giada lived or died so long as her own desires were met."

"I have to agree." I shrugged a little. "Even now, she's not showing much remorse. I'll process this as murder."

"Thank you. I'm sorry for barging in, I just couldn't sit still knowing what had happened." Regina lifted a shaking hand to her forehead, beyond upset. "To think Giada was killed just to save face is...appalling. I will make sure her family is helped through this time of grief as much as I can."

I gave a nod, agreeing with her. It would hit the family hard when they learned of this. I didn't envy them trying to cope with the loss of Giada, especially over such a stupid reason.

"Was Lord Barese involved in this?"

"We've not found any evidence to suggest it. I think his mother did this all on her own. She was shielding him from even knowing about the divorce decree. Frankly, I don't think he has it in him to murder anyone. Just the accusation of it made him faint. He was on a couch, out cold, when we left."

Regina snorted. "I won't have to find someone to replace his seat, at least. I'm glad Giada wasn't married to her own murderer, although I suppose that's cold comfort. Did Lady Barese act alone?"

"No, her butler helped her. He's claiming he did it all on his own, but of course, we know better. He was acting as her hands."

"Ah. Of course she wouldn't do the dirty work herself. You're confident it was only those two?"

"Pretty sure. We're still searching the house to see if anything else turns up, but I think Lady Barese was playing this pretty close to the chest."

"I certainly would, in her shoes. Good work, as usual." Regina pulled herself together enough to give Henri a small smile. "I understand that you have once again created a new spell? You never cease to amaze me, Doctor Davenforth. I hope that I'll get a positive answer to my proposal after you've finished here."

Henri looked at her, head canted a little, and completely surprised me when he answered, "I think I will, at that."

We'd talked of this—I knew he was interested in accepting her offer, but he did make me proud in that moment. He was confident now in his answer, no longer baffled by the offer.

Queen Regina lit up with a smile. "Excellent. I look forward to your return, then."

Sherard stepped in closer to Regina and said, "We really must get you back, Your Majesty."

"Yes, I know."

She did look as if she'd dressed in the dark. She'd probably come out of a sound sleep with this news, and snuck out here in the witching hours in order to finish this.

I couldn't let her leave without offering some comfort. This woman had just found out her friend was murdered. It was hard to go back out in public with a smile on her face after that. I stepped in closer too and murmured, "Girls' Night this weekend, okay? You can get drunk and cry on my shoulder."

Regina's smile was genuine as she nodded, eyes still too bright. "Sounds perfect. I'll be there. Thank you so much, Jamie."

"My pleasure. Go on. I'll throw the wicked witch into a jail cell. I promise not to be gentle about it."

Regina closed in for a quick hug before releasing me and letting Sherard whisk her away.

I turned to my better half and asked archly, "You realize she's going to tell absolutely everyone you said that, right?"

"We can discuss it later, my dear. At length, along with *your* proposal. Right now, I want to process Lady Barese and her butler so we can finally be done with this case."

"Yeah, I hear you there." Although I hoped he realized that if he didn't call home soon, and his mother heard about this through the grapevine, she'd skin him. He'd better call home sooner rather than later.

He was right, though. We had a murderer to deal with and I, for one, was very much looking forward to going home.

Final Report: Celebrations Abound

The party was in full swing at the Davenforths'. I'd lost track of Henri five seconds inside the door, as everyone wanted a word with the man of the hour. Henri was not the type to enjoy this sort of attention. I figured I'd have to rescue him in about an hour and give him a quiet corner for fifteen minutes. For now, though, he was the center of attention.

Henri, as of three hours ago, was officially a royal mage. His appointment had taken all of about two weeks to process, mostly the finer paperwork of salary, oaths, and him disengaging from the police force to take up this new career. It had been a whirlwind of activity, needless to say. Henri had looked both overwhelmed and determined throughout the process.

I moved through the drawing room, noting that the furniture had been rearranged to give lots of floor space to the guests, and meandered over to the buffet table laden with finger foods. Between rushing this morning to the swearing-in ceremony, and rushing to get ready for the party here, I hadn't had much more than a light breakfast. There was a rumbly in my tumbly, as Pooh would say.

Rupert had the same thought, as evidenced by the plate in his hand. As I joined him in line, he turned to look at me, a wide smile on his face.

"There you are. I haven't seen you since the ceremony this morning."

"We're all basically running around like headless chickens," I pointed out dryly. "It was a miracle I kept track of Henri, to be honest."

"Yes, I can imagine. I'm still surprised at the speed with which this appointment happened. I didn't think something like this could happen in just two weeks."

"Really, the offer was made more like three weeks ago? It was given to him right as we took on the Giada Barese case."

"Ahh, I hadn't heard that part." Rupert looked slightly enlightened.

"I think it normally would have taken longer. There's this whole peer-review process a mage normally goes through." I paused for a moment to look over my food choices. It all looked delightful, but I couldn't put one of everything on my plate. Not enough room either on plate or in belly for that. Okay, skip the finger sandwiches for now, then. "In this case, though, the review wasn't necessary. Every royal mage has worked with Henri at least once, so they know what he's capable of. With a queen and three royal mages all saying they want Henri, no one was willing to argue the point."

"I think he'll be brilliant at it. I know he only partially agreed to it because of your own career change. I wanted to ask how that's progressing? Do you have an update yet?"

"Queen Regina gave me one this morning." We maneuvered closer to the fireplace, where there was a clear spot at a small table. It was the better place to chat and eat. "Everyone liked my proposal. I've gotten a lot of questions. They want me to revise parts of it, which is fine. I'll work on it tomorrow. Basically, though, it's unofficially passed. They're revising this year's budget to include the new department. It's the finances I have to adjust in the proposal, basically."

Rupert blinked eyes at me that looked in danger of falling out of his head. "Again, so easily?"

"Mine's been in the works longer than Henri's." I shrugged, amused at his surprise. "Really, when I first came to this planet and explained what my job had been on Earth, I'd gotten a lot of questions from both kingsmen and Queen Regina. The interest was always there. I think they were giving me enough time to get my feet under me, enough experience in this culture to figure out how to adapt the FBI to here. This has been years in the making. Now that I'm willing to do it, no one's giving me the chance for second thoughts."

"So when will it officially be signed off on?"

"Probably at the end of the month. Which means I have tomorrow to make changes."

Rupert was quick to do the math. "That means your new department will start in just a few weeks, though! Are you ready for that?"

"Uh...to be honest, not at all. I'm still arguing the point with Gregson, as he's not happy to lose both me and Henri all in one fell swoop. Not to mention I'm still pulling people aside and asking if they're up for a career change—without an official offer in hand, which makes for an interesting conversation, let me tell you."

He snorted, eyes twinkling with amusement. "I can imagine. Has anyone said no?"

"Fortunately, no. I've been asking friends first, though, so I didn't expect to get a refusal. Really, for all that I have experience in this, it's going to be a lot of me learning as we go. I figured starting with friends would be the easier route. That way they can compensate for the mistakes."

"Wise of you." Rupert leaned in and lowered his tone to something more confidential. "I've dissuaded my wife from house shopping for you for the time being. I've convinced her that trying to rearrange your lives while you're in the middle of such a large career change is uncharitable, if nothing else."

I clinked my glass with his. "You're my favorite."

He chuckled, toasting me in return. "I thought you might appreciate my intervention in this case."

"I truly do. Speaking of..." I caught sight of my better half across the room, surrounded on all sides and holding his Felix familiar like a shield. I recognized the signs all too well. "I might need to rescue Henri. He's looking a little peopled out right now."

Rupert turned and spied Henri. "Ah. Yes, so he is. Go, we'll catch up more later. I have reports on your strawberry emporium that you need to look over, too, when you have a moment."

Was that in between me breathing? I didn't know when I'd find the time otherwise. "Sure."

I abandoned my plate and beelined for Henri. I could hear a live band playing in the ballroom off the drawing room; I could use the excuse of a dance to gracefully extract him.

Henri spied me coming and lit up in relief. It wasn't subtle. "My dear, didn't I promise you a dance?"

Great minds. They do think alike. "You certainly did."

"Excuse me, please." Henri headed straight for me, passing Phil off to his sister as he moved, which both were happy about. He took my hand with more force than grace, almost dragging me into the ballroom.

I didn't protest, just kept up as he swung me into position, falling into the beat of the music without hesitation. I flowed with him, following his lead. Henri looked strained around his eyes, a sure sign that he'd had enough people. "You're done in, aren't you?"

"I told my mother I didn't want a party," he grumbled at me. More like a whine, really.

"She was far too excited to listen to that. But hey, we're an hour in, and I have a quiet spot for you to hide in for thirty minutes while you get your wind back."

Henri's eyes sparkled with love. "Have I told you lately that I love you?"

"You could stand to mention it more often." I laughed. So easy, this man. "I think you'll last the night. How does it feel to officially be a royal mage now?"

"Strangely...different. I didn't expect that. I feel like I've taken on more responsibility, the weight of it upon my shoulders. Not an uncomfortable feeling, I don't mean to suggest that. It's just something I have to adjust to."

"Well, that's not a surprise. You do have more responsibilities now."

"It's also strange to realize that I won't have to get up

tomorrow to go to the station. Instead, I'll be headed to my new office at the palace. I know it's temporary, they're basically just letting me use a spare kingsmen's office for now, but I foresee I'll be there a few months at least until they can get me more permanently situated." Henri paused and added thoughtfully, "What will I put in that office?"

"Oh, I'm sure you'll collect things." He'd had quite the collection of things in his lab at the police station. It had taken the better part of three days to pack it up and shift things out. Granted, his new office was bigger, but I had no doubt it would be filled with books and weird things soon enough.

When the song came to an end, we politely clapped, but Henri was not at all inclined to return to the drawing room. He looked at me hopefully. "Where's that hiding spot you mentioned?"

"Follow me," I instructed, a wicked grin on my face. "I know the secret path."

"How you know this is also a question."

"I have interesting friends."

"Somehow, that doesn't surprise me. Even if this is my parents' house and I should know it better than you do."

"Should. We'll see if you know this spot or not."

His hand in mine, he followed me with explicit trust as I led him out of the ballroom. Hopefully, we made a clean escape before someone realized we were ditching the party for a while. It felt a little like two kids off on a grand adventure, and I had to fight the urge to snicker as we speed-walked away.

There was absolutely no rule that said you had to be responsible adults all the time.

Is that where you two disappeared off to? You realize everyone was looking for you at one point.

We had important recharging to do.

If you found a napping spot and didn't invite me, I'll be quite cross with both of you.

Next time. If there is a next time.

You really got a nap? Some friends you are.

Jamie's Notes to Herself:

Guys, pray for me. I have to somehow come up with a name for the new department. In two weeks. I can't name anything to save my life. Do you think I'd be in trouble if I called it the Avengers?

Oh, and did I mention I have to design a new uniform for this department? Me, who's definitely artistically challenged when it comes to fashion? I need to call in support on this, I just haven't figured out who to beg yet.

I have got to re-work my inventions list. Again. I managed to sneak in two kitchen items, because I'm tired of living without them. If I can just get technology to catch up enough to make a microwave, I'll be set. Oh, and a dishwasher.

We now have prototypes for:

- Answering machines
- Velcro (it was like the zipper thing all over again, with people just latching and unlatching things like it was the best time ever)
- Headset (Ellie really, really likes the idea of being hands free)
- Toaster
- Blender
- Movie projector—not that I've had a chance to play with it more than once.

Days of the Week

Earth – Draiocht

Sunday – Gods Day
Monday – Gather Day
Tuesday – Brew Day
Wednesday – Bind Day
Thursday – Hex Day
Friday – Scribe Day
Saturday – Rest Day

Months

Earth – Draiocht

January – Old Moon
February – Snow Moon
March – Crow Moon
April – Seed Moon
May – Hare Moon
June – Rose Moon
July – Hay Moon
August – Corn Moon
September – Harvest Moon
October – Hunter's Moon
November – Frost Moon
December – Blue Moon

Werespecies: werehorses, wereowls, weremules, werefoxes, weredogs, werebadger, weremouse, werewolves, werebeavers, wereelephants, werebears, wereweasels, wererabbits

Thanks for reading *Death Over the Garden Wall*! There were a lot of challenges with this getting this book out, so thank you for your patience, and I hope it was worth the wait. I look forward to the next Case Files and their new job roles. It'll be fun to have everyone together all the time. Until then! Also be on the lookout for news about my new steampunk series! Think reverse Tomb Raider/Indiana Jones.

Shape shifting dragons, mages, and time travel your jam? What about Chinese-based mythological creatures? Star-crossed lovers? If so, enter the world of the Tomes and start reading *Tomes Apprentice* HERE.

Who do you call when there's a curse? A sorcerer? A mage? A witch? What if all of those people have failed to remove it?

Well, call for an Artifactor, of course.

Check out *The Child Prince* HERE

Other books by Honor Raconteur
Published by Raconteur House
♫ Available in Audiobook! ♫

THE ADVENT MAGE CYCLE Jaunten ♫ Magus ♫ Advent ♫ Balancer ♫ ADVENT MAGE NOVELS Advent Mage Compendium The Dragon's Mage ♫ The Lost Mage♫ WARLORDS (ADVENT MAGE) Warlords Rising Warlords Ascending Warlords Reigning THE ARTIFACTOR SERIES The Child Prince ♫ The Dreamer's Curse ♫ The Scofflaw Magician♫ The Canard Case♫ The Fae Artifactor ♫ THE CASE FILES OF HENRI DAVENFORTH Magic and the Shinigami Detective♫ Charms and Death and Explosions (oh my)♫ Magic Outside the Box Three Charms for Murder Grimoires and Where to Find Them Death Over the Garden Wall	DEEPWOODS SAGA Deepwoods♫ Blackstone Fallen Ward Origins Crossroads Jioni FAMILIAR AND THE MAGE The Human Familiar The Void Mage Remnants Echoes GÆLDORCRÆFT FORCES Call to Quarters IMAGINEERS Imagineer Excantation KINGMAKERS Arrows of Change ♫ Arrows of Promise Arrows of Revolution KINGSLAYER Kingslayer ♫ Sovran at War ♫ SINGLE TITLES Special Forces 01 Midnight Quest THE TOMES OF KALERIA Tomes Apprentice♫ First of Tomes♫ Master of Tomes

File X: Author

Dear Reader,

Your reviews are very important. Reviews directly impact sales and book visibility, and the more reviews we have, the more sales we see. The more sales there are, the longer I get to keep writing the books you love full time. The best possible support you can provide is to give an honest review, even if it's just clicking those stars to rate the book!

Thank you for all your support! See you in the next world.

~Honor

Honor Raconteur is a sucker for a good fantasy. Despite reading it for decades now, she's never grown tired of the magical world. She likely never will. In between writing books, she trains and plays with her dogs, eats far too much chocolate, and attempts insane things like aerial dance.

If you'd like to join her newsletter to be notified when books are released, and get behind the scenes about upcoming books, you can click here: NEWSLETTER or email directly to honorraconteur.news@raconteurhouse.com and you'll be added to the mailing list. If you'd like to interact with Honor more directly, you can socialize with her on various sites. Each platform offers something different and fun!

Printed in Great Britain
by Amazon